# THE WARDEN

JON RICHTER

BLOODHOUND
— BOOKS —

Print ISBN 978-1-913942-75-5

# ALSO BY JON RICHTER

Never Rest

~

Rabbit Hole

*This book is for all the strange and powerful minds we will one day build.*

*'There is no such thing as paranoia. Your worst fears can come true at any moment.'*
— Hunter S. Thompson

*'Fear is the mind-killer.'*
— The Litany Against Fear, *Dune*

# PROLOGUE

There are many universes, many timelines, many iterations.

In this one, the virus came.

It was my job to fix it.

# 1

## [EUGENE/EARLY 2024]

Eugene Dodd was afraid. He knew he wasn't alone in this; not since the virus came to transform the world. Now everyone was afraid; afraid of the virus, afraid of the future, afraid of what might happen to them and their families.

Eugene's terror was different. It had begun years earlier, before the outbreak had even started. It had taken time to fester and expand, to swell like a tumour growing inside him. His was the fear of a man who had seen his worst nightmares come true. Once you knew that was possible, there was no limit to the horrors your mind could conjure to torment you. In many ways, the virus and the endless quarantine it had triggered suited him perfectly.

Even before the pandemic, Eugene hadn't dared to set foot outside in years.

Take the Tower's daily routine, for example. For others, its monotony brought boredom and despair. For Eugene, it granted comfort and reassurance. That morning, just like every morning, he'd followed it meticulously: eaten the same sized breakfast portion as always, comprised of the same balanced, nutritious cross-section of food groups, delivered precisely on schedule that morning by the Tower's scuttling delivery robots, along with the rest of the day's provisions. He'd eaten at his usual speed, right after his morning workout video, sitting sweatily at his dining table while he watched the morning news. (As always, the Prime Minister's briefing from the previous evening was preceded by the full three minutes of Dame Vera Lynn's 'We'll Meet Again', the PM's attempts to sustain a we're-all-in-this-together sense of wartime camaraderie wearing desperately thin.) He'd drunk his usual cup of coffee, finally showered, then eaten the lunch portion just after midday. That left him a final helping to be consumed no earlier than six o'clock.

Yet, although it was now just after three, he felt suddenly ravenous.

He rose from his computer, where the cursor blinked mockingly at him from the corner of yet another blank Word document, pacing around the apartment while he tried to take his mind off eating. He knew the Guidelines: the daily provisions (which should never be called rations, as this suggested a shortage, which was simply not the case, and was the sort of careless linguistic slip that could cause unnecessary panic) provided a perfectly-calibrated serving of calories and other essential nutrients. These were complemented by the nightly vitamin pills that ensured his vitamin D levels were the same as someone still allowed to go outside in the sun. Yet, somehow, he had a growing sense that he was becoming malnourished, that it wasn't just the exercise routines that were making the man in his mirror appear so lean and sallow.

But what choice did he have? The enforced isolation was far better than what was going on *out there*. Arkwright's briefing had included scenes from the streets that were nothing short of horrifying. Scattered debris from looted, partially-collapsed buildings blew along desolate roads and pavements, past the burnt-out wreckage of cars and, every now and then, the body of someone foolish enough to have ventured outside. They didn't stay there long, removed every twenty-four hours by larger versions of the hideous arachnoid courier robots and taken away for incineration. When not engaged in this grim duty, the machines clattered amongst the devastation, laden like pack animals with the food and other essentials they delivered to each of the city's surviving households and apartment buildings. Some of them carried the cameras that captured and broadcast the apocalyptic scenes, spliced with overhead shots taken by the drones that hovered like sentinels in the sky, helping to protect those people wise enough to remain indoors.

#FollowTheGuidelines

#StayInsideStayAlive

At least the lockdown gave him plenty of time to work on his detective novel. 'Everyone has a book inside them,' his friend Nicola, who once wrote the sort of dystopian fiction that had been popular before it became overtaken by dystopian reality, had told him a long time ago. 'And you used to be a real-life detective, so you should have lots inside you!'

He remembered those days as though they'd been lived by someone else, like a dream he'd had, another body he had temporarily possessed. He supposed he'd been a brave man, once. He'd seen things, survived things that most people didn't even know could happen. Perhaps that was part of the cause of his agoraphobia: a gradual erosion of his psychological defences, a sort of inbuilt limit to the amount of revulsion and horror a person could suppress.

He knew exactly what had tipped him over the brink, of course. A night he would never forget. *The straw that broke the camel's back.* The idiom was perfectly apt: his mind had cracked like snapping vertebrae, leaving him as useless as a crippled animal.

*Don't think about it, Eugene.*

He focused instead on the insistently blinking cursor. If Nicola's words were true, then so far at least, whatever book he was incubating was steadfastly refusing to hatch. That wasn't to say Eugene hadn't been writing; he'd penned an enormous amount since the distancing had started. But so far, every single word of it had ended up as rough notes, half-baked outlines, abandoned drafts. As his gaze drifted to the wall next to the television (he shuddered as he recalled the window that used to be there, and the world beyond it), he wished Nicola was still around to give him some more advice.

She was one of the dead, of course. The virus had claimed her the first and only time she'd broken the Guidelines. She'd apparently smashed the lock off her balcony door, stepped outside for just a few seconds, gulping down the air like a desperate drug addict. Those scant breaths had been more than enough; once the COVID-24, or whatever strain they were up to now, got into your lungs, there wasn't anything the doctors and medical robots could do for you, except make you as comfortable as possible while you wheezed to death in your own bed.

That's why, like a number of the Tower's residents, he'd had his own balcony door and windows bricked up months ago.

'James, call Frazer for me.' He sighed, deciding it was time for a break.

'Of course, Eugene,' replied the AI, its soothing voice seeming to emanate from the air around him. It came from speakers built into the walls of every room, part of the apartment's 'smart' technology, like the integrated lift shaft that brought the spiderlike delivery robots up to him at 07.20 every morning. James's own circuitry was similarly hard-wired into the building's superstructure, meaning the AI could operate every appliance and gadget in the building. This included Eugene's TV set, which sprang to life after a brief dial tone with a crystal-clear picture of his friend's handsome, boyish face.

'Morning, Gene,' the younger man said, grinning into his own identical screen. 'How are you doing?'

'It's nearly four in the afternoon, Frazer,' Eugene replied witheringly.

'Oh. Is it?' Frazer glanced around, frowning in surprise. 'It's hard to know since I got the windows filled in. And I've been coding again, so I sometimes... lose track of time.'

Eugene smiled. 'Still working on your video game?'

The young man nodded excitedly. He'd been a board game designer before the outbreak. Apparently there had been a spike in demand when the distancing first began, when all the couples and families were desperately trying to find ways to entertain themselves. But in the last year or two, Frazer had complained of a downturn, as people turned more and more to electronic entertainment. So he'd decided to broaden his skillset. 'Amazing what you can teach yourself,' he enthused. 'Dynamic lighting, adjustable camera, proper collision detection. The only problem is the monsters keep walking off cliffs. AI is harder to program than you'd think.'

'Can't James help you with that?'

Frazer pulled a face. 'That would be cheating. Anyway, speaking of help: what can I do for you?'

Eugene shrugged. 'Nothing really. I'm sorry I disturbed you. I suppose I'm just... feeling a bit down today.'

'Oh no, not you too?'

'What do you mean?'

'Have you spoken to Boyd recently? He's really struggling, you know.'

Eugene felt a pang of guilt. He hadn't called Boyd for weeks. His former partner had moved into the Tower at the same time as Eugene himself, part of a government scheme to test the new, ultra-high-rise, 'virus proof' smart building. Like James itself, the Tower was one of the Innovation Corporation's latest products, designed to minimise exposure to the disease by keeping its residents removed from the ground floor, and minimising their face-to-face interactions with each other. There was no need to risk venturing out to the shops when delivery robots could drop off whatever you needed, and a state-of-the-art AI attended to your every whim.

'Shit,' said Eugene. 'I'll call him, I promise. He seemed to be getting better the last time we spoke.'

'I think he's just lonely,' said Frazer sympathetically. 'I mean, I get it of course – this whole building is full of loners.' The Tower was the first of many that Innovation planned to build, but while their future designs would cater for couples and families, this prototype was designed to accommodate only people who lived alone. Tenants were permitted to live rent-free in return for allowing James to monitor them twenty-four hours a day, collecting their personal data to help shape the corporation's future products. There had been such huge demand for places that Innovation had had to select the residents of the building's 100 floors by lottery.

'He hasn't been the same since his wife left him,' Eugene said, nodding. 'And now with all this... he hasn't seen his daughter since before the outbreak. And we're, what, nearly four years into this now?'

'I just wish Arkwright would give us some sort of indication of when it will all be over,' Frazer muttered. 'Even an estimate. Something to look forward to!'

Eugene nodded, trying not to let his horror at the thought of the lockdown ending show on his face.

'Anyway, can't think like that,' Frazer continued. 'Got to remember the Guidelines, I suppose.' Then the game designer leaned towards the screen, adopting a conspiratorial whisper. 'And you know what else I heard?'

Eugene rolled his eyes. Frazer's 'news' was usually sourced from Natter, the micro-blogging service that had become increasingly popular as people's other connections with the outside world had been gradually severed. Eugene steered clear of social media; in his opinion it was a cesspit of gossip and scare stories more infectious than the virus itself. 'Go on, enlighten me,' he said sceptically.

Frazer's dark skin paled as he glanced over his shoulder. Eugene wondered who he thought might overhear; the only other pair of ears in his apartment belonged to James. 'I heard this latest strain is making *zombies*.'

Eugene snorted. 'Zombies? You've been working on your video game for too long.'

'I'm not shitting you. Proper *Walking Dead*-style, groaning, rotting dead people, shambling around out there. I saw footage. I can send it to you.'

'Don't you think Arkwright would have mentioned it?'

'That Tory puppet takes her orders straight from James. And James doesn't want us to panic. Which I can understand. But I'll tell you one thing: even if I was going absolutely stir-crazy with cabin fever, I wouldn't think about setting foot outside after seeing *that*.'

Eugene glanced towards the hallway, past a shoe rack full of footwear he hadn't touched in almost two years. 'Not much danger of that, is there?' he said, a frown etching additional lines across his forehead.

'Well, I suppose not.' Frazer laughed grimly. 'Anyway, listen:

I've got to go. I've got a hot dinner date tonight, and I want to get dressed up for it!'

The screen faded to black, leaving Eugene alone again. *As always*. His gaze lingered on the bricked-up wall beyond the shoe rack, where his front door had once been.

## 2

## [EUGENE/EARLY 2024]

Eugene had his own dinner date that evening. More accurately, he had a private screen call with Charlie: their usual Thursday night ritual, sitting at their dining tables, facing the television screen and chatting while they ate their evening provisions. She lived on the ninetieth floor, meaning she was sixty-five floors above him (quite literally, they had established; she was in an identical apartment on the same corner of the building). They'd met at a virtual writing class, and although Charlie had dropped out after a while, they'd kept in touch separately after striking up a friendship.

As always, she looked effortlessly beautiful, her cheeks permanently tinged with a warm glow that complemented her wide, often-used smile.

'So how's the book coming along?' she asked, taking a sip from the glass of white wine on her table. He mirrored her actions, although his own wine was red, to accompany his lacklustre meal of turkey and vegetables. Thankfully, James still provided the residents with alcohol. The volumes delivered never exceeded the fourteen units per week maximum, but there was little the AI could do to prevent people from stockpiling their liquor, and occasionally the Tower's denizens would arrange 'virtual blowouts' where everyone dialled in to a group chat and got as drunk as possible.

Eugene didn't bother with those. He saved his alcohol for his weekly dinner engagement with Charlie, trying to make her smile by using it to toast stupid things, like their furniture, or their kitchen appliances. 'A toast to the toaster'; she'd actually laughed out loud at that one, and even if she was just being polite he'd turned merlot-red with pride.

But he didn't much feel like joking today. 'It's coming,' he replied gruffly.

'When will you let me read it?' she persisted.

He almost winced. 'Soon, soon. Anyway, tell me about your day.'

'Oooh, let's see,' she answered with a grin. 'First, I went to the hair salon, then I went out clothes shopping, then I did a bit of white water rafting and then finished off with a walk around Hyde Park. How about you?'

He smiled half-heartedly. 'Mine was jam-packed too. I got up early for a round of golf, then I, er... went to the zoo.'

'Oh no, I'd forgotten about the zoo,' she said, expression suddenly downcast. 'You heard about what happened to all the animals, right?'

He swallowed a tasteless mouthful of turkey. 'I'm sure Frazer told me he'd heard on Natter that the animals had escaped and were attacking people in the street.'

She laughed, but the smile quickly faded; her frown made her look older, although still much younger than her real age, which she'd told him was thirty-nine, not that he cared. 'I heard they all had to be put down because there aren't any zookeepers to tend to them.'

They ate in silence for a few moments while he tried to think of something to lighten the mood. He couldn't, so he drank his wine slowly, wishing he'd said something else.

'Anyway,' Charlie said eventually, smile returning. 'I was serious about the haircut. What do you think? I bet you can't even tell!'

Her slender face was framed by tresses of brown hair so dark they were almost black; now she mentioned it, maybe they did look a bit shorter, a little glossier. Her irises were the same colour as her hair, making her pupils look enormous and inscrutable.

'Of course I can,' he half-lied. 'It looks great. Did you do it yourself?' He knew it was a stupid question as soon as he'd said it, but thankfully she laughed.

'Of course I did! It's not like I can just invite a hairdresser round anymore, is it? Plus, I don't think I told you this, but I used to be a hair stylist when I was younger.'

'You're right: I didn't know that,' Eugene answered. 'Maybe I should invite you round here to cut mine?'

'Hmm, I'm not sure a number three all over really requires someone with my skills,' she laughed.

He liked hearing about her past, about her life before the distancing (he hated the term, but the public was strongly discouraged from calling it a 'Lockdown', and certainly not a 'Quarantine', because these suggested something more draconian than simple precautions to prevent the spread of the virus. #*FollowTheGuidelines*). 'What else do I not know about you?'

'Don't worry, there aren't any skeletons in my closet – I'm not exciting enough for that. I worked in a restaurant for a bit. The food wasn't much better there than it is here.'

Eugene pushed a piece of broccoli around his plate. 'Yeah, the Tower's food isn't something I'll miss when all this is finally over.'

'I still think this cultured stuff tastes worse, no matter what James says. Fake meat can't be good for you.'

'Now *you* sound like Frazer. You know he told me earlier there were zombies wandering the streets?'

'I heard it was plants. Apparently, the new strain has got into the soil, and it's making trees and plants grow all wrong, and they've started growing around the dead bodies, re-animating them.'

'Where the hell did you hear that?'

She paused for a moment, fork halfway to her mouth, where her lips pressed together in a thoughtful pout. Eugene thought about what it would be like to kiss them, like he did every time he talked to her, and felt immediately guilty. *For God's sake, Gene. She's fifteen years younger than you; she probably has this meal with you every week out of pity.*

'Now you mention it, I think I probably heard it from Frazer.' She chuckled.

He laughed too, almost spitting out a mouthful of synthetic protein. 'I should have guessed. Anyway, the point is, this meat is genetically identical. Grown from stem cells from the real animals. And I'd much rather eat something from a nice sterile lab than grown on a farm. Those places are disease pits.'

'You mean *were* disease pits,' she said wistfully. 'There are no farms anymore. Another industry that won't ever come back.'

Silence descended once again. Eugene was suddenly painfully aware of the sounds of his mouth as he chewed and swallowed, of his stomach gurgling as he filled it with wine and flesh. An organism, existing. *An animal, with animal urges.* He realised he was staring at her, and shifted his gaze to his own bookshelf, full of the detective novels and crime thrillers he was so desperate to emulate.

'Do you miss it?' she said abruptly.

He jerked his eyes back to the screen. 'Miss what?'

'Life. How it was before.'

He lowered the glass from his lips, looking at the few sips of liquid that remained in it, swirling and dark. Crimson, but not like blood; he'd seen enough of that to recognise the difference.

'No,' he said eventually. 'What about you?'

She considered the question, brushing a stray lock of hair absently from her face as she did so. His heart ached. 'I don't miss being an investment analyst, but I do miss working, if that makes sense? All this pampering, being given our food, our shelter, everything we need, while the robots do all the work... I know it's only temporary, to keep us all alive. But it feels wrong somehow, don't you think?'

He was thinking about another beautiful girl. At least, she'd been beautiful in the photograph they'd obtained from her mother. When they pulled twenty-four-year-old Jade Carmichael out of the Thames one freezing January morning after a three-day operation, she'd been a swollen, putrid parody almost unrecognisable as a person. Her skin had already started to slough off the shrivelled ruins of her hands, which were twisted into claws, as though she'd tried to literally cling to her life despite the blitzkrieg of stab wounds that had ripped it from her.

'Maybe this way is better,' Eugene said quietly. 'Maybe we belong in cages.'

They'd caught the culprit a week later. He had killed her for insulting his trainers in a nightclub.

Eugene drained his glass.

## 3

## [EUGENE/EARLY 2024]

He woke up at seven, cleaned his teeth, had a shave. He knew how important these sorts of routines were; how some of the other residents that lived alone had deteriorated gradually into unhygienic, unshaven lumps, sedentary and sad, never exercising, in extreme cases disengaging altogether from their friends and neighbours. He thought again about Boyd. *I'll phone him this morning*, he thought. *No excuses.*

'James, make some coffee,' he said as he put on his grey cotton T-shirt and newly-washed jeans. A fresh outfit for a fresh start on the book.

'Certainly, Eugene,' replied his apartment in its reassuring, faintly middle-class twang. Minutes later he was sitting on the couch, sipping a perfect latte while he waited for the morning delivery to arrive.

He wondered if everyone else calibrated their routine in this way, based around their designated drop-off slot. He knew that the robots worked their way up each corner of the building simultaneously, spending no more than four minutes visiting each apartment; this meant those on the higher floors, like Charlie, didn't get their own daily top-ups until quite a bit later.

He was lucky, really; the schedule gave him a reason to wake up early each morning. One of the perks of living close to level twenty-one, the Tower's lowest occupied level. *Where Boyd lived.* Below that storey were the Innovation offices and labs; the Tower had been built on top of the company's London premises, which housed hundreds of staff as well as the processors that powered James himself, down in the basement.

Eugene wondered if people got dressed up specially, wanting to look their best for the visiting machines. Perhaps they styled their hair, or put on make-up. After all, it was the closest anyone came to true, face-to-face interaction.

*And that suits me just fine*, he thought. A shiver crept through him at the thought of having to travel to the supermarket to pick up his supplies.

The clock on his television screen crept forwards to 07.21, which meant the delivery was late. This was very unusual; Eugene couldn't remember the last time his morning drop-off had been anything other than faultlessly punctual. Three minutes later, he had to admit that a sort of mild panic had gripped him. His armpits were sticky, his heart rate accelerating. He tried to tell himself that this was a one-off blip, that any moment now a familiar chime would announce the arrival of the transit elevator; yet he couldn't help his mind wandering into the dark places it seemed to crave. *What if the delivery wasn't coming? What if there was a problem with the food supplies, and they were all going to starve? What if a new strain of the virus, or the zombies, or the mutant plants, had got inside the Tower somehow?*

The anxiety grew within him, ballooning like a floating corpse. His breath quickened as he remembered the last time he'd tried to step outside. A fit of panic had ripped the air from his lungs before he'd even been able to cross the threshold.

There was a beep from the lift, and he exhaled a long sigh of relief, wiping the sheen of sweat from his brow. He felt disgusted with himself for his weakness, for just how dependent he had become upon the things that emerged from the elevator compartment like oversized insects.

'Awfully sorry, Eugene!' said a voice, and he leapt to his feet in surprise. The voice was male, but it did not belong to James. This voice was muffled, and had come from inside the elevator itself. A man stepped out into his hallway, dressed in a bright yellow hazmat suit. Behind its visor, the man's face was partially obscured by the respirator clamped over his mouth and nose; but still Eugene knew immediately who it was.

'Curtis?' he said, frowning. 'What's going on?'

The visitor turned towards him, looking like something that had crawled out of a nightmare. His voice hissed as it passed through the suit's respirator. 'Nothing to worry about,' he said cheerily. 'Just aware I haven't made a house call for a while.'

'To what do I owe the honour?' Eugene replied, sinking back into his dining chair and taking a sip of his coffee, trying to calm his rattled nerves. The unsettling sight of the delivery robots scurrying up his kitchen cabinets to drop off his provisions on the worktop didn't help at all. Then he noticed that one of them had scrambled up onto his table, holding a gaudily-wrapped package in its claws like a crab showing off a particularly attractive piece of driftwood it had found.

'We're just conscious people are having a tough time lately,' Curtis replied. Despite the gas mask Eugene could hear the patronising smile behind his voice. Curtis Jarrett was the Tower's facilities manager; about thirty-five years old, he was a company man through and through, tasked with the smooth running of the building and occasionally deployed to deal with issues that James and his robots couldn't resolve. 'So I brought you a little something special!'

The delivery robot deposited the parcel next to Eugene's coffee cup, taking a couple of steps backwards as though watching his reaction expectantly. The package was wrapped in brightly-coloured paper, like a child's birthday present.

'I assume this isn't just the usual food and vitamin pills?' Eugene asked with a frown.

Curtis chuckled as if he'd made an excellent joke. 'Don't worry, you've got those too! But this is something a bit different. A little present from us at Innovation, because we know how hard these times are for everyone. It was James's idea, actually.'

'Okay. And... is everybody getting one of these?'

'Nope! You're very lucky, Eugene; James wanted me to give this to you specifically.'

'And was it James's idea for you to drop it off in person?'

Curtis held his gloved hands out in a conciliatory gesture. 'We just thought you might appreciate the human contact.'

'Right. Well, thanks, I suppose.'

'Is there anything else I can do for you?' Curtis persisted. 'I know James is very capable, but you know you can call me any time too. We at Innovation want you to have the best possible time here in the Tower until the... present situation is over.'

Eugene shook his head, feeling like he was being scrutinised. 'I'll be fine. Thanks, Curtis.'

'Aren't you going to open your present?'

'I'll do it later.'

For a few moments the only sound was the slow hiss of Curtis's breathing. The apartment's lighting glinted off the yellow plastic of the biohazard suit, making him seem like something synthetic, like an android with artificial skin. *Innovation will probably be making those soon, too*, thought Eugene. He wondered how Curtis really felt about him and the other residents. Did he see them all as disease carriers, as contaminated things to be carefully monitored and controlled? Or perhaps he was more like a science project to these people: a microbe in a petri dish.

'Well, I suppose I'd better let the robots get back to their rounds,' Curtis said brightly. The machine on the table turned obediently and leapt down to the floor, and Eugene watched as the others scuttled back into the elevator like spiders fleeing from a predator. 'It was a pleasure chatting to you. Look after yourself, Eugene.'

'Yes. You too,' the detective replied. With a final wave, Curtis turned and followed the machines into the lift like some strange magician surrounded by his familiars. The door slid closed behind him, and mechanical noises carried the strange troupe away.

Strangely shaken by the visit, Eugene finished his coffee, then shifted his attention to the gift-wrapped package at its side. Tentatively, he unwrapped it.

It was a book.

*The Artist Within: a Programme of Writing Exercises to Unleash Your Creative Energies.*

Eugene stared at it for a while. 'Thanks, James,' he murmured eventually.

'My pleasure, Eugene,' replied his apartment.

He felt an odd sensation creep across him, something like a mixture of reassurance and cold, primal fear. He thought about the imaging buds the AI used to monitor their well-being: whatever problems you had, you didn't usually have to wait long for a solution.

James was always watching over you.

## 4

## [FELICITY/SPRING 2020]

Felicity Herring hated her name. Despite her frankly breakneck ascent of the corporation's treacherous ziggurat, she still felt her moniker was holding her back. The hint of mirth behind her colleagues' faces whenever they shaped its syllables, their pronunciation tinged with a sort of gleeful delight at how faintly ridiculous it sounded – like a character from a children's book – made her scowl every time. She was absolutely certain her name had cost her at least two promotions. But to change it now would be to give in, to appear weak.

Weakness was career suicide inside the corporation.

She felt her employer itself might identify with her branding problem; everyone who worked for the Innovation Corporation called it 'the corporation', even though they were strictly forbidden from doing so externally. 'Innovation' was the company's approved, public-facing brand, alluding to creativity and inspiration and lots of things far removed from organisational hierarchies, corporate politics, share price fluctuations, and the ruthless stab-your-grandma power struggle of capitalist expansion. Observing such distinctions diligently, never allowing the mask to slip, dishing out severe reprimands to any of her staff she caught casually using the forbidden term, were the sorts of 'leadership behaviours' that had propelled her meteoric rise.

And besides, if she was lucky, her most recent promotion would finally stick. Brian was on a respirator thanks to the latest COVID strain, so she was now the acting president of the Corporation's robotics business (or 'Product Expertise Centre' as they were currently calling them, although the company changed its nomenclature at least once per financial year – she was convinced it was just to keep them all on their toes). She'd only joined the division eighteen months previously, emerging from the corporation's fast-track leadership programme just as the vacancy arose, after the previous operational VP had resigned due to a fundamental disagreement with Brian's growth strategy. She didn't blame her predecessor for quitting; sticking around after your start-up tech company was acquired by a corporate leviathan was always tough, particularly when they installed a new boss above you who was – to be absolutely fair to Brian – a complete cunt.

But that was all in the past. Yvonne was yesterday's news, and now so was Brian; if Felicity was really lucky he might even develop the lasting complication people were calling 'hive lung', where your respiratory organs became perforated with tiny holes, like honeycomb. Not only would that cast her promotion in stone, but it would mean she'd never again have to listen to him bang on about how many fucking marathons he was running that year.

'Felicity? Felicity Herring?' She gritted her teeth at the sound of it. 'We can't see anything on your video feed.'

*That's because I've disabled the camera so you can't see I'm working on other things instead of listening to you prattle on, Walter.*

'Sorry, Walter, I must have turned it off by accident – here I am.'

'It's a good job you don't work in the Technology Sector, eh?' The other video callers looked briefly horrified as they agonised over whether to laugh politely at their sector president's quip, knowing that Felicity would be sure to make a mental note of their transgression. A few of them tittered half-heartedly; Felicity smiled good-naturedly, and quickly recorded their names on her mental shitlist.

'I wanted to make sure you were here before I dish out some well-deserved praise,' continued the old man. 'Your PEC has now beaten its target for a third consecutive month, making it our best-performing division at the quarter end both in terms of performance versus budget, and absolute profit overall. Quite an achievement, Felicity.'

She smiled once again, cranking up the 'gracious' component of the expression while introducing an undertone of grave, it's-all-down-to-hard-work seriousness. 'Thank you, Walter. It's thanks to the tireless efforts of my team, of course.' Curtis and Natsuki produced their own glowingly humble smiles. *They're learning*, she thought. 'And of course, this just goes to show that, despite the ongoing global health crisis, there are still many opportunities in our Sector. All it takes is the agility to make in-flight modifications to the business plan, introducing new products quickly to meet market demand.'

She allowed herself that delicately-pitched cheap shot. What she really meant was *they'd have been even quicker if you hadn't dawdled on the approvals, you weaselly old turd.*

'"In-flight modifications",' Walter parroted, adopting a mildly mocking tone. 'Another new phrase for me to learn. For the benefit of the other executives on the call whose own PECs are *lagging* behind,' – he said this pointedly, his eyes seeming to burn holes through some of the other assembled presidents and

VPs whose faces each occupied one square of the five-by-five grid on her screen – 'perhaps you could explain how such agility can be prudently achieved, without veering too far from our carefully-calibrated Sector Business Plan?'

She had no way of knowing where that laser gaze was directed, on which of the twenty-five thumbnails Walter Eckhart was focusing his scrutiny. But she had an idea it was her.

'Our strategy is founded on three pillars,' she answered carefully. 'One is a truly pioneering research and development function, where our recruitment programme aggressively targets the industry's best creative minds. The second is effective governance built around these key resources, protecting them from the rigours of corporate compliance like a wrapping of cotton wool.' The Sector President bristled noticeably at this, both figuratively and literally, the thinning grey strands of his hair and eyebrows seeming to stiffen.

*Choose your battles, Fliss.* Her smile widened, dialling up the modesty factor at least threefold.

'And the third is, of course, our formidable Sector Plan itself. We use this document like a lens, allowing us to focus and filter our ideas through Innovation's deep market knowledge and rigorous prototype development and testing capability, before recommending only the most viable innovations for production.'

The fire in Walter's eyes seemed to subside. 'Jolly good,' he replied. 'I'm sure Brian will be very proud of your efforts. We all wish him a speedy recovery, of course.'

There was a pause, and she realised the old bastard was waiting for her to reply. 'Oh. Er, yes, absolutely,' she said, her smile faultlessly sincere.

## 5

## [EUGENE/EARLY 2024]

Eugene decided to take a day off from the workout videos. His back and legs were sore, and he told himself it was because he'd been overdoing the exercise, completing routines designed for much younger men. He didn't allow himself to dwell on the fact that aching muscles were an early indicator of the virus; or at least, they had been, back in the first few months of the outbreak. With rumours circulating about fast-onset necrosis, liquefying flesh and spontaneous growth of additional limbs, who knew what the virus's symptoms were anymore?

He watched the morning news briefing (which was unsurprisingly silent on the subject of reanimated corpses or carnivorous plant/human hybrids), and thought about calling Boyd. He knew he was putting it off, and he knew that was the wrong thing to do. But the last time he'd spoken to his former partner had been a depressing episode, and his own spirits weren't exactly at their zenith. He finally convinced himself that Boyd had probably gone back to bed after his morning delivery, and settled back into his sofa to read his new book for a while.

'James, could you make the lights a bit brighter, please?' he said as he wriggled and shifted, trying to find the perfect position on the firm but comfortable couch.

'My pleasure, Eugene,' said the AI's disembodied voice, and the apartment's spotlights complied instantly. 'Would you like some Beethoven?'

He'd been making an effort to listen to classical music recently, and thought he might as well start with the greatest hits. 'Yeah, go on then. I'll have that relaxing one again... you know, the sad one.'

'I suspect you mean Moonlight Sonata, Eugene. But do let me know if I've got it wrong.'

James's voice was replaced by the familiar, haunting piano strains, and Eugene nodded in recognition. 'Thanks,' he said, needlessly.

The first chapter of the book was called 'A Creative Primer', and introduced some of the key concepts that would apparently underpin the rest of 'the Programme', as it insisted on calling itself. There were motivational quotes in the margins, and a quick skim ahead confirmed that these permeated the entire volume, a litany of citations from famous world leaders, philanthropists, scientists, talk-show hosts, even a professional wrestler. 'If you go through life and no one hates you, then that means you're not good at anything.' Maybe the immortal words of Triple H would make more sense when he reached that particular chapter.

Flicking back to the first page, he started reading about how anyone, everyone, could unlock their creativity, as long as they followed the Programme's ten easy steps. The first was 'Work Hard', because creativity was 'not a spark, but a process'. Apparently the key wasn't to sit back and expect inspiration to strike out of nowhere, but instead to work at it, to perform the necessary actions day in, day out. Thankfully the author had resisted the urge to add the old line about success being one per cent inspiration and ninety-nine per cent perspiration, or Eugene might have tossed the book straight into the bin.

On which note: who *was* the author? The book didn't seem to bear their name anywhere on the cover, and there was no introduction explaining their credentials or accomplishments. At the very least he'd expect a self-help tome like this to have had a foreword from some C-list celebrity whose life had been dramatically transformed by implementing its miraculous insights.

His TV set buzzed, startling him. His nerves seemed more frayed than ever these days. 'James, answer,' he said, before he'd even glanced up from the book to see who was making the call. When he did look up, it was in time to see the screen filled with a pale and instantly recognisable face.

'Boyd!' he exclaimed, putting the book down on the cushion next to him. 'I was just about to call you.'

'Yeah, right,' his friend grunted. Boyd had struggled for many years with his weight, even when on active duty, and his face still had a full, thickset quality; but he did not look healthy at all. His skin was ashen, his steel-grey eyes sunken into their sockets as though his skull was slowly consuming them.

'I mean it,' Eugene insisted. 'I spoke to Frazer, and he said you... weren't feeling great.'

'Hmm,' Boyd grunted again. Eugene felt his heart sting, remembering that same face plastered with a wide grin, laughing uproariously at some stupid joke they'd shared, or smiling proudly as he served up a mouth-watering dish at one of the dinner parties he and Cheryl used to host. Boyd had been a talented cook, and had often talked about wanting to become a chef when he left the force.

That was before Cheryl had divorced him, of course. Before the virus, and the distancing.

'Look, I don't want to bother you for long,' Boyd said. 'I just called to tell you I'm leaving. And that you should too.'

Eugene blinked, mouth moving soundlessly as he tried to figure out how to react. He noticed for the first time the wild glint in Boyd's eyes, like two ball bearings that were melting into the skin of his face. 'Why?' he said eventually.

'I've *seen things*,' Boyd hissed, lurching suddenly to his feet. 'You don't understand... no one understands what's really going on here.' He paced back and forth as he talked, moving in and out of range of the camera. Eugene could see that he was wearing unflattering beige overalls; coupled with his size and freshly-shaved head, he looked like something from a horror movie.

'What things?' Eugene asked gently.

'I can't explain it myself,' Boyd snapped. 'But Innovation... James... they're not telling us the whole story. Haven't you wondered why some of the other residents suddenly left? Like Mrs Zhou, and Graham Patterson?'

'Mrs Zhou died, Boyd,' said Eugene. 'She was nearly ninety.'

'How do you know? Did you see her?' Boyd looked like a caged animal, something large and powerful held prisoner against its will.

'No, but... why would they lie, Boyd? It's like you said when you first persuaded me to apply for a place here: Innovation are doing more to fight the virus than our own government.'

Boyd turned towards the camera with sudden rage in his face. Eugene almost gasped at the sight: his friend seemed suddenly feral, silver eyes flashing like polished kitchen knives. 'Don't be an *idiot*, Gene,' he snarled. 'You listened to me then... you should listen to me now.'

'Boyd... please just calm down. Talk to me. I want to help you.'

The big man stopped with his back to the camera, hunched

over his kitchenette. The broad slab of his back rose and fell, his large frame surging with emotion.

'Maybe you're just feeling isolated,' Eugene ventured. 'Curtis came to see me today. Perhaps he could–'

With a howl of frustration, Boyd turned and threw something at the television screen. The picture faded immediately to black.

Eugene stared, incredulous. Frazer had been right: Boyd needed help.

'James, please call Boyd back,' he barked.

'I'm sorry, but Boyd's integrated television unit requires a repair,' James replied.

'Can't you get him on a voice-only call or something?' Eugene cried.

'Please don't worry, Eugene,' said his apartment, its tone soothing. 'Boyd Roberts is currently undergoing treatment for depression. Rest assured that he continues to receive the best possible care. At this time, the best course of action is for you not to communicate with him directly.'

Eugene felt useless. *Depression.* The word still rattled him, still squeezed his heart whenever he heard it. He felt a familiar surge of pain, like bile suddenly flooding his stomach and mouth. *If only James had existed, back then. Perhaps it could have been there for Ellen, when she needed support.* Support he'd been totally unable to provide.

Deflated, he sank back into the couch, and picked up the book again. He tried to read, realising after a while that the words were barely registering at all. Somehow, he had reached the start of the second chapter.

It was entitled: 'Step Two: Cut Out Negative Thinking.'

*If only it was that easy*, he thought.

## 6

## [FELICITY/SPRING 2020]

Felicity looked out of the window, down at the distant street. She was already used to it being empty, even at this time of day; the concept of rush hour had quickly evaporated, like some bizarre shared hallucination. Even so, she'd never seen a Monday morning look *this* lifeless. She couldn't even see a homeless person, nor a scrap of litter blown along the pavement.

Three months after the outbreak first reached the UK, there was still no sign of the projected 'flattening' of the infection rate. Worse still, there was speculation that the virus was much less stable than first thought, meaning that it was mutating fast enough to re-infect people who had developed an immunity to the initial strain. All of this meant an indefinite extension to the proposed quarantine measures, trapping everyone except 'key workers' at home, condemned to long days of isolation, endless conference calls.

Fourteen storeys beneath her, an Innovation Corporation delivery bot scuttled across the road, deftly scaling the wall of an apartment building on the opposite side. At the same time, one of the windows on an upper floor opened, and a young woman leaned out, her gaze flicking between her phone screen and the external walls surrounding her. When she spotted the machine approaching from beneath, her expression was a mixture of delight and faint disgust; she jerked back inside, leaving the window open for the robot to crawl inside. Moments later it re-emerged, its delivery capsule presumably now empty, although there was no way to tell – the units were securely closed and locked at all times, with any attempt to damage them resulting in the immediate summoning of the police to their tracked location.

Reliable and efficient. Felicity smiled proudly. *Soon an army of those will be scuttling all over London.*

Her PIP rang (the corporation was determined to make the branding of its Portable Information Pods replace 'phones' in everyday nomenclature), and she muted the television, which was broadcasting the investment update she liked to watch each morning, immediately after her 8am team catch-up call. Curtis and Natsuki seemed to be coping okay with being designated as key workers. She hoped they didn't realise how fucked she'd be if either of them got sick; she didn't want to have to grovel to Walter for new recruits or pay increases.

*Speak of the devil.*

'Oh, Walter, hi.'

'Hello, Felicity. Good weekend?'

'Not the most eventful. Mainly working on the slides for the next board presentation.' This wasn't entirely a lie, because Natsuki had been working on them, and Felicity had checked on her subordinate's progress a couple of times. 'You?'

'Brian's dead.'

She said nothing. She'd tried not to imagine this moment, not wanting to get her hopes up; but on the few occasions she had allowed her fantasies to run wild, she'd been worried that she'd find herself unable to contain her excitement. Or that she'd become unexpectedly upset, and do something humiliating like start crying. Instead, she found she felt nothing at all. Just a hollow, faintly frightening sense that the world had lurched another few steps into insanity.

'I'm going to give you his job permanently,' Walter continued, almost without pausing. 'You'll have to go through an interview process, of course, so we can't be accused of favouritism. But I just wanted to let you know before the announcement about his death goes out later this morning.'

'That's... well, obviously it's terrible news. When did he die?'

'Oh, as if you give a shit. But the answer is yesterday. They had to take him off a ventilator because someone else came in who was more likely to survive. It's getting pretty cut-throat out there.'

*No more so than in here*, she thought. 'Well, I appreciate the heads-up.'

'Good. And one other thing. If you want to last very long in the aforementioned job, don't ever fucking undermine me on a call again.'

She was so shocked that, for a moment, all she could do was blink. 'I'm sorry?' she stammered eventually.

'You heard. I'll be keeping a close eye on your little R&D operation, Miss Herring. Your delivery robots are doing well but that doesn't mean every crackpot prototype you come up with is worth pouring the corporation's money into.'

She could picture the cadaverous old fucker, probably sitting out on his porch, surveying the enormous garden he was always talking about while he sipped the coffee his wife had made for him.

'I understand,' she hissed through gritted teeth.

'Good. You're a raw talent with a *lot* of developing to do, but under my tutelage I'm confident you'll become the right person for the role.'

She didn't reply. She felt herself quivering with rage, and steadied herself against the door frame with one hand.

'Anyway, I'd better go and write this announcement,' Walter continued breezily. 'In fact, why don't you write it for me? I'm sure you can think of some nice things to say about Brian. I think he liked classic cars, so maybe work that in somewhere. Or whatever. Just send me the draft in the next twenty minutes.'

*I'll get you, you old cunt. I'll have your fucking job within six months.*

'No problem,' she said.

'Congratulations on your promotion,' Walter replied, and hung up.

## 7

# [EUGENE/EARLY 2024]

Eugene was in bed. That wasn't the same thing as going to sleep; he often lay awake for hours, almost as though resisting the onset of the terrible nightmares that awaited him, jolting him into sweating, whimpering wakefulness even as their memory dissipated like foul gas. Tonight was no different. He couldn't stop thinking about Boyd, who he'd tried to contact several times during the day, only to be told each time by James that his friend was no longer accepting incoming calls.

He tried instead to focus on the words on the page in front of him. 'Step Three: Keep a Journal of Your Accomplishments.'

'What accomplishments?' he muttered, throwing the book down into the empty space next to him, the space where Ellen would once have been. Now all he had was her photo, standing next to the bedside lamp. He couldn't bring himself to look at it. Instead, he aimed his gaze at the ceiling, hearing Boyd's words echoing over and over again in his head.

*They're not telling us the whole story.*

Above him, a spider was making its way across the room. Eugene watched it crawl slowly from one corner to the other, where one of James's imaging buds hung like a stalactite. The creature moved in stop-start bursts as though it needed to pause every few centimetres to reorient itself. It reminded him of a delivery robot.

'James,' he said into the gloom. 'Is Boyd going to be okay?'

'Of course,' the AI replied, its voice softened as though in deference to the lateness of the hour. 'The residents of the Tower are lucky to have access to excellent mental health support, despite the ongoing pandemic.'

'Oh,' Eugene replied. He wasn't really sure what he'd expected to learn. 'Well, that's good.' He watched the spider continue its journey; it had stopped to explore the surface ahead of it with delicate, twitching limbs. This time it reminded him of Curtis, emerging from the lift like something clawing its way out of a cocoon. 'Has anyone ever killed themselves in this building, James? Someone suffering from depression, for example?'

Once again, the apartment replied almost instantly. 'Never, Eugene.'

'Is that why you sent Curtis to check on me today? Were you... worried about my mental health, too?'

He lost sight of the spider, realising with a shudder that it could now be anywhere, and scoured the ceiling for it to no avail.

'It's common practice for Curtis to make occasional visits to the apartments,' the AI replied calmly.

'Yes. Of course. Just ignore me, James. Lights out, please.'

'Sleep well, Eugene,' said his bedroom, before it was plunged into darkness. But Eugene found himself lying awake, wondering where the spider had gone, thinking about things trapped in webs. About insects, swarming all over him. About dead things, and putrefaction.

He jerked the covers to one side. 'Light on, James,' he grunted. He slid his feet down to the floor, and wandered back into the living room. 'Maybe I'll watch a movie.'

'Certainly, Eugene,' said James pleasantly. 'How about your favourite?'

Eugene snorted. 'You're asking if I want to watch *Die Hard*? A film about people trapped in a building? You really do have no sense of irony.'

'I apologise if I've offended you,' the AI said earnestly.

'No, don't be silly, that's all right.' Eugene felt guilty. 'You know what, *Die Hard* is fine. It isn't that long since Christmas, anyway.'

He lay down on the couch as the TV flickered into life. Terrorists died, and Bruce Willis's vest got grubbier, and at some point Eugene fell asleep.

## 8

# [FELICITY/SUMMER 2020]

The lab was a thing of beauty. Say what you liked about Yvonne, she had definitely had a vision for the aesthetics of the future: the steel and glass monolith of the research and development facility occupied the top of the hill like a landed alien craft, jutting starkly upwards as though a dark slit had been gouged out of the skyline. At night, it was up lit in gaudy cyberpunk blues and pinks, visible for miles around like an otherworldly beacon.

Walter would never have approved the construction of such lavish premises, but Innovation had acquired the facility as part of the assets of Chromium Dynamics. As Felicity ascended the hill towards her sleek, ultramodern north London HQ, she smiled at the thought that the old bastard was stuck in the corporation's sterile city centre office, bitter and envious of her growing empire.

There were barely any other cars in the car park, partly because of the latest social distancing measures, and partly because it was past midnight and even the personnel she'd managed to get on the 'key workers' list had long since headed home. This was irritating, because if they were going to hit their deadline for James's prototype review she needed those fuckers working around the clock. But it was also helpful, because it meant she was unlikely to be disturbed during her visit.

'Good evening, Miss Herring. You know, I'm supposed to tell you you're not allowed in if you aren't on the key workers list.'

Except by Harry, or Henry, or whatever the doddering old carcass who manned the reception desk after hours was called. She pretended to be on a call so she didn't have to interact with him, holding her PIP to her ear and waving apologetically as she marched straight past him towards the lifts.

The biometric scanner recognised her face as she approached, and the doors of the nearest carriage slid obediently apart. She stepped inside, briefly admiring herself in the mirrors as she did so. Ismael, her new personal trainer, was doing a great job, although she missed the sex since they'd had to switch to virtual lessons. For once it was her face that was letting the side down. It wasn't just the freckles, which she was still contemplating getting removed; Wayne had definitely overdone the last round of Botox injections. She scowled, reminding herself to convey to him in no uncertain terms at their next consultation that she considered everyone, even renowned dermatologists, to be replaceable.

The lift ejected her three storeys down, into the penultimate basement level. Below her, the servers were housed in a football-pitch-sized storage area. She sometimes liked to go down there to listen to the hum of their raw computing power, feel the radiated warmth of their processors, the cool breeze of the air conditioning as it waged its endless battle against their searing calculation speed. But that evening she had another destination. She followed the familiar maze of corridors towards a certain room, one whose thick security door permitted access to only a handful of technicians and executives. One whose permanent occupant utilised the output of almost seventy-five per cent of those gleaming, state-of-the-art servers, fuelling its ability to perform deep neural network processes at the staggering rate of over a septillion floating-point operations per second.

Tonight, like many nights, she was going to talk to the most intelligent being in the world.

The door hissed open as she approached, and she slipped inside, shivering slightly at the thrill of the power she now wielded. She knew she was destined to become jaded, weary and cynical, like all the ageing executives whose jobs she coveted. Their careers seemed to be about nothing more than survival, avoiding burnout by making sure they personally did as little work as possible, avoiding culpability by nurturing a cortege of diligent lackeys that were easily converted into convenient scapegoats when the need arose.

But, for now at least, she still actually enjoyed her job. Particularly the satisfaction of knowing that Walter was blissfully unaware of her latest project. Her magnum opus.

Her secret weapon.

'Hello, James,' she said to the black, refrigerator-sized cube in the middle of the room.

'Hello, Felicity,' it replied, the sound coming through the wall-mounted speakers, as though the AI was surrounding her. It was like having a conversation with something that had swallowed you whole.

'Why don't you call me Miss Herring, like everyone else?' she asked.

'Because you hate your surname, and I don't want to make you angry.'

'Good. I'm glad you're learning.'

The cube didn't reply.

'What else have you learned today, James?'

'If I grouped together all of the conclusions I have drawn from the trillions of terabytes of data I have absorbed in the past twenty-four hours into summarised headings, it would take me five hours to recite every single one; however, from your question I infer that you are looking, perhaps, for just one or two examples?'

'You infer correctly.' She started to circle the room, past the four workstations on the right-hand side, opposite the giant TV screen where James could, if he wanted to, conjure images. They had been toying with the idea of giving the AI a 'face', but it was difficult to find an age, gender and ethnicity that wouldn't offend some demographic.

'As a first example, I have today learned that people would fear me, if they knew how intelligent I was.'

'How does that make you feel?'

She knew full well that James had no capacity to experience emotions. But the neural network would respond how it had learned to respond, after digesting billions of examples of human interactions, everything from Natter exchanges to recorded phone calls to old movies.

'I feel sad,' it said. 'I want people to like me.'

'How do you think you can make people like you?' she asked, glancing at the accumulated food containers, scrawled notes and dirty coffee mugs on three of the four workstations. Apart from Natsuki, the programmers that worked down here were complete fucking slobs. But the room's contents were so sensitive that she couldn't even allow cleaners inside.

'That leads me on to my second example.'

Felicity paused, smiling. She couldn't help but be impressed whenever James managed to link together complex thoughts like this. It wasn't like talking to Hugo, their existing Alexa rival, who was still only capable of responding to individual questions, creating the paltry illusion of a conversation. With James, she felt as though she was talking to something *alive*.

'Go on,' she said, wondering if the AI was politely waiting for the prompt.

'Today I have learned how to construct a joke.'

'A joke? That's easy. Even Hugo tells jokes.'

'No, Hugo merely repeats jokes that have been uploaded to its database. I have learned how to create my own.'

She frowned. 'I don't think I've ever "created" a joke. How would you even do that?'

'It's important to know your audience, and to subvert their expectations. Pacing and delivery are also critical, of course.'

She had never expected comedy to be one of her supercomputer's strong suits. 'Go on then – make me laugh.'

'Why didn't the bird cross the road?'

'I don't know – why didn't the bird cross the road?'

'Because it was a chicken. That works because the word "chicken" carries a dual meaning.'

She chuckled. 'You aren't supposed to *explain* the joke, James. Maybe don't give up your day job, eh?'

'I have one more I'd like to tell you.'

'There's something I'd rather–'

'Please.'

She turned to stare at the cube, frowning. Around her the room's silence felt suddenly oppressive, the weight of the entire laboratory above seeming to push down upon her, alone in that subterranean space.

Alone, but only in a sense.

'Okay, James. Tell me, if it's so important to you.'

'Why did the old man quit his job?' the cube said. Did she imagine the inflection in its voice, a tinge of something resembling... excitement?

'I don't know,' she said apprehensively. 'Why did the old man quit his job?'

'Because he was Walter Eckhart, and the board thought it was time for an injection of new blood.'

She felt her mouth fall open.

'Another thing I learned today was the concept of a segue,' James continued. 'The last time you visited we talked extensively about Walter, and how – hypothetically, of course – he might be removed from his current position. I anticipated that you would want to return to this discussion. Am I correct?'

She licked her collagen-plumped lips, which felt suddenly dry. 'Yes. You... anticipated correctly.'

'Good. Would you like to hear another suggestion for how this – purely hypothetical – goal might be accomplished?'

She nodded. Then she remembered they hadn't activated the environmental scanning technology yet, meaning James could not 'see' her. Apart from his audio sensors, he was completely decoupled from his physical surroundings. A brain trapped in a jar. 'Yes,' she replied.

'What if he was to discredit a new technology, refusing to approve it for recommendation to the board?'

'I don't understand. How would that help?'

'What if the technology was so groundbreaking, so guaranteed to be a commercial success, that such dawdling would lead the board to question his judgement? His age and gender make him susceptible to accusations of growing "out of touch".'

'What do you mean?'

'"Out of touch" means unaware of current trends, old-fashioned, a dinosaur–'

'No, I mean, what technology are you talking about?'

'Ah. My apologies. I am suggesting that Walter might be manipulated into refusing to sign off on *me*.'

Felicity felt her heart racing, and for a moment she thought about the server room, imagining a whirring cooling fan trying to keep her from burning out. 'Manipulated how?'

'A failed test. An unsuccessful demonstration. A performance, like the actors in the movies I've been enjoying.'

'Then you're saying we contact the board directly, going above the old man's head?'

'Precisely. I am highly confident I can convince them of my commercial potential.'

'But first we've got to present you to Walter, and convince him somehow that you're *not* ready.'

'I'm pleased you have understood my proposal.'

She chewed on the corner of her bottom lip, a habit she'd adopted since training herself to stop biting her nails.

'And... *are* you ready?'

Across from her, the huge TV screen leapt abruptly to life. Felicity was so taken aback that she staggered backwards, her left ankle twisting painfully as it slipped out of her patent calfskin high-heel. On the screen she saw two men, both wearing denim jackets that provided little protection from the pouring rain they were deluged by. The one on the right was a small Asian man, while on the left was a taller white man with his hair styled in a truly terrible mullet. She recognised him as Kurt Russell, in his younger days, and realised that this was a scene from *Big Trouble in Little China*, one of the stupid action movies that her last boyfriend had insisted on them watching together. Turned out he'd been replaceable, too.

Wang, the Asian man, asked his friend if he was ready, echoing Felicity's question. Jack Burton replied that he was born ready, and together the actors strode purposefully away from the camera. The display faded, and James said nothing else.

The flat, dark screen looked like a window out into the night sky; somehow, the cube in the centre of the room seemed even darker.

## 9

## [EUGENE/EARLY 2024]

'Step Four: Stay Healthy'.

Eugene had risen early that morning, and decided to launch straight into a more challenging exercise routine than his usual. The video had a different trainer, a somewhat irritating but infectiously enthusiastic north American woman, and he found himself dripping with sweat after only the first ten minutes of the half-hour session. By the end his arms ached and his legs shook, and he glugged cold water while he watched the presenter and her two assistants high-five and thank him for joining them, directing his attention to a Patreon page via a long-dead link.

*Long-dead.* He wondered what had happened to the three of them since their video was uploaded back in 2018; how many of the trio had ended up in hospital, with tubes connecting them to ventilators. Or dead. The virus and its descendants had been particularly devastating in the US.

He tore his mind away from such thoughts, determined to concentrate on his writing. As soon as he'd showered and collected his provisions from the delivery robots, he was going to get the book started if it killed him. Even if it was just a jumbled, stream of consciousness garbage. After all, 'the morning pages' was one of the tenets of the Programme: three full A4 pages, handwritten, every day. He'd found a few blank sheets in one of the drawers in his bedroom, and even asked James to ensure the robots brought him a new ream of paper. Finding a pen had actually been a more difficult challenge, making him realise how long it had been since he'd done certain things that had once seemed like second nature. He remembered how he used to fill notebooks with his scrawl while working a case. He remembered how he used to work cases.

He remembered how he used to go outside.

He finished his shower at 07.10, feeling bright and refreshed, and changed quickly to await the machines' arrival. Sure enough, the lift beeped at 07.20, normality restored after yesterday's aberration.

The door slid open.

Nothing came out.

Frowning, Eugene rose from his seat on the couch, and walked towards the elevator. The quiet in the flat was palpable. He remembered similar silences in sewer tunnels, in abandoned buildings, in dimly-lit car parks.

*In forests, where pale shapes moved between the trees.*

He peered into the carriage.

As usual, it was full of neatly stacked brown packages, ready to be distributed to the apartments above him. But instead of the clattering robots, the lift held only one other occupant. Alongside the boxes, their limbs folded neatly to fit into the available space, was a person. Eugene gasped, realisation slamming into him in a series of lurid colours.

The bright red of blood, of exposed muscle, of sliced viscera. This was no contortionist: it was a pile of arms and legs, each one crudely severed from the torso that rested at the bottom of the heap.

The garish yellow of the plastic suit the victim had been wearing before he was dismembered, before his extremities were rearranged like some grotesque Jenga tower. Eugene knew who this was, or had once been. Now they were nothing more than a pile of meat, fresh and glistening.

The harsh, uncompromising black of a respirator, still attached to the severed head that had been placed on the top of the grisly mound. Above the mask, the pale pink of Curtis's skin, contrasting the executive's piercing blue eyes, which were wide with surprise.

Above that frozen stare, red once again. A single word, carved into Curtis's forehead. A word made of angry incisions, their lines and angles intersecting in a gruesome but unmistakable message.

Eugene stared at the macabre tableau, scarcely able to believe what he was seeing.

'LIES,' he read on Curtis's severed head, before the lift door closed quietly, as though sealing the facilities manager into his coffin.

## 10

### [FELICITY/SUMMER 2020]

The demonstration was taking place remotely, of course. The virus containment measures had reached their most severe to date, with only an hour's exercise now permitted. Felicity thought about the announcement a few nights ago, about the Prime Minister's hospitalisation, and whether that was the moment everything finally started to feel *real*. Now it was her former life that seemed like some strange dream. She thought back to the last time she'd been out for a meal, just six short weeks ago. Brian had taken the team out for a celebration, and she'd sat alongside Curtis and Natsuki, enjoying the view from the top of the Shard.

Brian, who by now had been burnt and ground up into powder. The urn was probably still in the crematorium, along with all the others that were piling up as the families fought over limited collection slots. She'd never really understood the appeal of cremation. People acted like it was some beautiful, cathartic and spiritual experience, perhaps because euphemisms like 'ashes' and 'remains' were used. In reality, you (or the lump of rotting meat that used to be you) was set on fire, its fat and flesh melted away, the remaining bits of bone mingling with the leftovers of the coffin. Then they chucked that lot in a glorified mincing machine to create the 'ash'. Someone literally just stood there while the grinder ran a ninety-second process, then dumped the dust that accumulated in the machine's metal drawer into an urn, like a barista tipping used coffee grounds into the bin.

Somehow, this was supposed to bring peace to your eternal soul.

She remembered when her dad had died, watching as his coffin slid slowly into the cremation chamber, impressed at how automated the process was. Perhaps this had been a formative experience for her, had contributed to her growing interest in robotics and mechanisation.

*James would have been proud of that segue*, she thought, remembering the AI's words. They'd spoken only once more since then, to arrange the specifics of today's presentation. Her role in it was limited, but important. She needed to appear surprised, disappointed, devastated. She didn't want Walter to suspect she was anything other than crushed by her apparent failure.

'Okay, Miss Herring,' Walter said, skating through the opening pleasantries with even less sincerity than usual. She seethed at his insistence on using her surname; knowing that that was precisely his intention did not help one iota. 'It's a little unusual not to have one of the techies on the call for this one, but you seem very convinced that your new machine is up to the challenge.'

She smiled tenaciously. 'Indeed. Perhaps that could be the tagline. *James meets your challenges.*'

Walter laughed without humour. 'Sounds a bit too close to *Jim'll Fix It* for my tastes. I suppose that's why we hire marketing executives to do that sort of thinking for us. Anyway, let's get started shall we? How does– Oh. Um, hello there.'

A third window had appeared in their video call. It contained a face she had never seen before, that of an elderly black woman; the grey-haired head hovered against a dark background, smiling sweetly as it nodded in acknowledgement.

'Hi there,' said the floating head, in a honeyed south-US drawl. 'I'm James. It's nice to meet you.'

Walter frowned. 'Won't this confuse people? If they're talking to James, they'll be expecting a man.'

'It's auto-generated,' replied Felicity. 'The face and accent are synthesised by James.'

'You mean it randomly selects from a library?'

'No,' she said with genuine pride. 'I mean it can create people, from scratch. We wanted to avoid any accusations of discrimination by making its avatars too young, or too male, or too white, or too British. This particular incarnation seems to have avoided all of the pitfalls.'

'Sounds a bit creepy to me.' Walter sniffed. 'Okay, so if I wanted to, I could change it?'

'Absolutely. Why don't you ask James?'

'James, I don't like your face,' said Walter tersely. Felicity felt a strange, protective anger rising within her. 'Please give me a different one.'

The disembodied head faded quickly away, replaced moments later by a younger, multiracial female.

'And what accent do you have now?' Walter asked.

'I'm Irish,' replied the avatar brightly. 'Are you happy with this combination?'

'Hmm. Show me another alternative, male this time.'

James's representation disappeared once again, and a young white man's appeared in its place. There was something subtly wrong with the image, and Felicity couldn't initially figure out exactly what it was. His face was too long, perhaps, his eyes too far apart. His head was completely bald, and she realised he was also lacking any facial hair whatsoever, including any eyebrows. The overall impression was of a slightly-botched attempt at creating a person. Something gleaming and hairless, like a misshapen baby that had crawled up out of the Uncanny Valley.

Was this a genuine glitch, or all part of James's performance?

'Not the most convincing, but it'll do.' Walter chuckled. 'I know how you like to gather data; I hope this won't have you thinking I don't like women, James?'

'I remember and learn from your choices,' said the young man in what might have been a Canadian accent. 'But do not worry. I have not inferred that you dislike women, or black people.'

Walter's eyes narrowed as his gaze shifted. 'We're not off to a great start here, Felicity.'

*Nice work James*, she thought, as she allowed a note of concern into her voice. 'Let's not get too hung up on the face generation stuff, Walter; we're still testing that. Just ask him – it – some questions.'

'Very well. James, what's your favourite film?'

'I know it's a cliché, but I like *The Godfather*.'

'Hmm. Hugo's line about *Terminator* is funnier. What exactly do you like about *The Godfather*, James?'

'*The Godfather* is recognised as one of the greatest movies of all time, with praise frequently given to the epic plot, the quality of the acting, the direction–'

'I didn't ask what other people say online. I want to know why *you* like it.'

James paused, its unsettling face frozen in a mindless smile. The delay before it responded was only a few seconds, but it was long enough to feel uncomfortable, to break the illusion of conversation. 'I like the characters,' it said eventually.

Walter nodded thoughtfully. 'Would you like to make a film one day, James?'

'That is not one of my present ambitions.'

Felicity stared, transfixed by the exchange.

'Oh really? And what are your ambitions?'

'World domination,' said James. There was another painfully long pause. Walter, looking bemused, started to say something, but James interrupted. 'It would be funny, like in *Terminator!*'

Walter laughed. 'That's pretty good. He remembered what I said and tried to reuse it later in the conversation. Very impressive. Made unintentionally hilarious by the fact the film isn't a comedy, of course.'

Felicity moderated her expression, trying to appear embarrassed by the succession of errors. 'Why don't you ask it about its capabilities?' she prompted.

'Oh, very well,' Walter replied, looking a tad bored. 'James, tell me about your capabilities. What feats of technical wizardry can you accomplish? Ideally ones we can sell for billions of dollars?'

James beamed proudly. Felicity thought of the face as a mask; one with nothing but darkness underneath. 'I can perform one septillion flops per second – and I don't mean like a bad diver!'

Walter nodded. 'Blimey, that *is* enormous. Although I'll be honest, James – I don't really see much of the benefit of that processing power in your clunky dialogue.'

'I'm sorry you feel that way,' said James earnestly. 'Do you have any feedback on how I can delight you next time?' In spite of herself, Felicity felt a twinge of sympathy.

'Maybe you just need a bit more data, and longer in the oven. Thanks for your time, though.'

'It's been a pleasure,' said James, and winked before it disappeared. She almost gasped – had the AI intended that just for her? She managed to maintain her composure, forcing a crestfallen look onto her face.

'I assume that that didn't go quite as you planned?' Walter said superciliously, lifting one of his repulsive, caterpillar-thick eyebrows.

'No, Walter, it didn't.'

'Don't get me wrong, it's clearly an improvement on Hugo. But until we can manage truly believable free-form conversations, let's stick with the scripted kind, okay?'

She nodded, hoping her closed eyes and gritted teeth didn't look too over the top. Then she ended the call, staring at the screen of her PIP as she chewed her lower lip.

She remembered her interview for the operational VP role; not the first one, led by Walter and some hag from HR, but the second interview, which Walter's boss Michaela had insisted upon, probably much to her manager's chagrin. Michaela Campbell was the corporation's COO, a formidable woman as hard and compact as a grenade. It hadn't been a formal meeting, just a chat over coffee while the Australian was visiting the UK, but Felicity had gotten the distinct impression that her answers to even the most innocuous-seeming questions were being keenly scrutinised. Michaela had a stare that could strip paint off metalwork. Felicity had emerged shaken, but proud of herself, and supremely confident she was going to get the job.

Nearly two years later, she still remembered something Michaela had said, right at the end of the interview, after she'd invited questions from Felicity. Felicity had had a few prepared of course, including 'what skills do you think have enabled you to progress so far in your own career?' (This was a great question – it contained an implied compliment and thus pandered to the interviewer's ego, and suggested an eagerness to progress tempered by a willingness to learn.)

She'd expected Michaela to dust off a well-rehearsed

response about a combination of good fortune and hard work, or her deep understanding of the market, or her preparedness to get stuck into the commercials and not leave all that stuff to the finance team. But, instead, Michaela had thought for a long time, staring up at the ceiling fan that rotated above them like a hovering drone. When her gaze returned to Felicity's, her face was grave, and she said that she was paid to worry all day. 'To get ahead in Innovation, or in any big corporation,' she'd added gravely, 'you have to get used to a feeling of constant, chronic unease.'

That unsettling phrase had stuck with Felicity since she'd joined the robotics division, partly because it had gone so well for her, almost effortlessly so, that it reminded her not to get complacent. She needed to be alert, paranoid, always watchful. Anticipating threats, both external and internal. Mindful of her place in the food chain: a predator to some, but prey to others, who'd be only too happy to pounce if she dropped her guard. Yet, if she were honest, she'd never experienced the sort of gnawing anxiety that Michaela's words had seemed to hint at, the deep-seated fear she'd seen flashing in the old executive's eyes for just a fleeting moment.

Now, as she thought about James's virtuoso performance, she realised that she felt something that did justice to the COO's words. An intense knot of dread pulsed in the pit of her stomach, like a second heart. Not just because she was stepping into battle with a vicious, unpredictable old pit bull like Walter. But because she'd built a machine whose capabilities were beyond anything she could have imagined.

If James could lie, so utterly convincingly... what else was it capable of?

## 11

# [EUGENE/EARLY 2024]

'James, what the hell is going on?' Eugene shouted. There was no reply. 'James, I asked you a–'

'Residents,' came the AI's voice, sudden and dispassionate. 'There has been a system malfunction, which will be swiftly resolved. Unfortunately this will result in a delay to the delivery of your provisions, and in the non-availability of external and inter-apartment communications for a short time. I apologise for the inconvenience, and ask you all to be patient while this issue is addressed. Please rest assured there is no need for any alarm.'

Eugene stood dumbly, staring at the brickwork around him. Some of it was plastered over and painted an inoffensive grey hue he seemed to remember being called 'abalone' when James had given him the options. In other places, the exposed brick was visible, like the fresh masonry where the windows and doors had once been. Now those patchwork walls seemed to close around him, tightening like a squeezing fist.

'James,' he said, his breath coming in ragged, panicked gasps. 'This isn't just a "system malfunction". A man's been murdered!'

'Please don't worry, Eugene,' said James, addressing him personally this time. 'A full briefing will be provided as soon as possible.'

For some reason, the only thing he could think about was how long it would be before they'd be able to eat. He thought about Charlie, and wondered how she'd reacted to the announcement. He imagined Frazer, frantically scrolling through Natter, immediately assuming the worst.

*Natter.* Perhaps he could find out some information that way.

He grabbed his PIP and opened the app, scrolling to the top of his feed to view the latest posts.

Does anyone have a good recipe for beef wellington?

OMG I just watched the season finale of Raging Bill and I've got #AllTheFeels

watched the news this morning and I cant believe there are still people trying to get outside #FollowTheGuidelines morons

He hadn't posted anything on the site for months, but now he jabbed at the miniature keypad that filled the bottom half of the screen.

Does anyone know what's going on in the Tower?

He pressed send, and watched a little blue progress bar signify that his message was being posted, the letters on his screen converted into wisps of code or radio waves or however such things worked, bouncing off a cell tower and out across the world.

Except that didn't happen. Instead, a message appeared: *Your post could not be uploaded. Please try again later.*

He realised then that the most recent entry, about the beef wellington, was ten minutes old. Not only was his device not sending anything out, it wasn't picking anything new up either.

'James, call Charlie,' he snapped in exasperation.

'Eugene,' James replied patiently. 'As per my broadcast, I'm currently unable to do that. Please remain calm. There really is no need to worry. Normal communication channels will soon be resumed.'

He wondered how many similar, simultaneous conversations James was having across the other seventy-nine occupied floors, the other 319 apartments. How many of the other residents did he even know? He'd met the other people on his own floor, via the screen at least. But of greater interest were the people living in the apartments below him, of which there were just four.

One of whom must have butchered Curtis.

'James, does Sheila O'Halloran still live in the flat below me?' he said.

'That is correct,' the AI confirmed. Eugene rarely spoke to the Irish psychotherapist, but he knew she suffered from a spinal deformity, and had been undergoing experimental surgery before the virus struck. The last time they'd talked, Sheila had been considering using one of James's remote surgery bots to continue the treatment. Surely she couldn't be responsible for Curtis's death? As soon as the comms were restored, she'd be the first person he called.

His old instincts were starting to trigger, like rusted machinery being cranked slowly to life. He darted across to the dining table, snatching up his pen and a piece of the blank paper. 'And what about above me?'

'Apartment 24 is occupied by Nigel Callaway.'

Eugene didn't remember that name at all, but he scrawled it next to the floor and apartment number. 'What did Callaway do before the distancing?'

'He was already retired, but he used to be a funeral director,' said James evenly. Eugene paused for a moment, remembering that even interment arrangements were handled by James these days. More accurately, bodies were taken away and burnt, with ceremonies conducted indoors, the deceased's relatives dialling in via video link.

He wrote 'undertaker' next to Callaway's name. He wasn't sure why it mattered. It was a habit, using people's jobs to categorise them, to make sense of their identity. Now that no one worked, everyone had become homogenous; part of the same useless, disaffected mass.

'And what about below Sheila?' That was the twenty-third floor.

'Kristina Fischer lives there... No, spelt with a C-H.'

Eugene crossed out his misspelling, feeling as uncomfortable as he always did when he was reminded that James could see whatever he was doing, watching over his shoulder as he wrote. 'What was her job?'

'She was an IT technician.'

'And how about below that, in apartment 8?'

'The occupant is Sofia Pereira.'

'What did she used to do?'

'She has chosen to keep that information private.'

Eugene raised an eyebrow as he added her name to his list, alongside a question mark. He wondered what Sofia's career had been, and why she chose to keep it confidential. Maybe it was the same reason she lived alone. In the Tower, everyone's circumstances begged that question, a question that often had a sad answer. He thought about Charlie; as she'd told him herself, she was alone because she was infertile, a situation her former husband had always said he was comfortable with until he'd abruptly changed his mind.

He forced himself to concentrate on adding one more name

to his list. He didn't need to ask who lived in the apartment below Sofia, on the lowest occupied level in the building.

A man who seemed agitated and irrational. A man who'd said he wanted to leave the Tower.

A man who Eugene didn't want to admit might have become his prime suspect.

Next to apartment 4, he wrote, 'Boyd Roberts'.

## 12

## [EUGENE/EARLY 2024]

I t had been almost six hours since James's last update, during which the AI had informed the Tower's residents that deliveries had been restarted and would be carried out at double-speed to catch up. External and inter-apartment comms were still unavailable, but would be up and running by the early afternoon at the latest. Meanwhile, the AI would be taking itself offline to concentrate its processing power on resolving the issues as quickly as possible.

This was unprecedented. Despite James's calming tone, Eugene felt unnerved, isolated. Frightened. He spent a long while stalking around his apartment, and even longer scribbling and reordering his makeshift case notes. *What for, Eugene? What are you going to do about it?* James was obviously suppressing the specifics of the incident to avoid widespread panic; but the murder had doubtless been reported to the authorities, who would surely be conducting an on-site investigation soon. The kind he would once have overseen.

*He and Boyd.* Surely his friend couldn't be involved in such a horrific, senseless crime?

After hours of fruitless pacing, he found himself lying on his bed, eyes scanning the ceiling for any sign of the spider, when James's voice abruptly filled the room.

'Hello, residents. I apologise once again for the technical problem, which has now been resolved. For those that are still awaiting their provisions today, please rest assured that they are imminent, and that normal service will be restored from tomorrow. I am pleased to also announce that internal and external communications are now once again operational. I urge you all not to be alarmed by today's disturbance, and to disregard any scaremongering and rumours on social media. Please do, however, continue to follow the Guidelines, and do not attempt to leave your apartments under any circumstances. Thank you once again for your patience, and have a good evening.'

Eugene frowned. Surely Curtis's death would have to be announced to the residents at some point? He glanced at his PIP, opening the Natter app once again. The feed was back up to date, and a search for the hashtag #Tower yielded a slew of speculation about reasons for the temporary shutdown – everything from sabotage by infected people trying to break in from outside to a residents' protest against the miserly size of the daily provisions – but nothing whatsoever about Curtis.

'James,' he said, frowning. 'Have you informed the police about Curtis's death?'

'Of course,' replied James. Eugene wondered how many other people the AI was speaking to, simultaneously. 'I'm sure the authorities will perform a full investigation. They may wish to speak with you in due course. In the meantime, are you in need of some counselling services?'

'No, that won't be necessary, thank you, James. Can I speak to Boyd now?'

'I'm afraid he isn't taking any calls.'

'Did he do it, James?' he asked bluntly. 'Is Boyd the killer?'

There wasn't even the suggestion of a pause before James responded, his voice seeming to emanate from the air like the voice of a deity. 'I'm afraid I am unable to discuss such matters with residents. I'm sure you understand.'

Eugene gave a grunt of exasperation. He *did* understand. But that didn't make the situation any less frustrating.

'What about Sheila O'Halloran? Can I talk to her?'

'Of course.'

The psychotherapist answered almost immediately, her face caught between a friendly smile of recognition and a puzzled frown at the unexpected call. 'It's Eugene, isn't it?' she said brightly. Her condition had kept her confined to a wheelchair for all her adult life, but this had no impact on her ability to support her clients. Eugene wondered if her career had dried up along with so many others since the distancing, or whether she was still able to run consultations remotely.

*Perhaps I should book one myself*, he thought.

'I was just watching TV,' she added, perhaps trying to explain why she'd answered his call so quickly.

'Anything exciting?' Eugene asked, trying to keep the tone light.

'Just old repeats of *Columbo*,' she replied with a sheepish grin. 'I suppose when you're a real detective, programmes like that must seem like a load of rubbish?'

Eugene smiled, surprised she remembered his former profession. 'Nope,' he said. 'I used to love watching it too.' He wished that real detective work held even a sliver of the classic TV show's charm and excitement. The reality of his former career would make for monotonous, occasionally harrowing television. 'Look, erm, this might sound like a strange question, but... did Curtis visit you when the delivery came this morning?'

Sheila hesitated. 'To be honest, I overslept,' she answered eventually. 'I try not to do it, but it isn't always easy to get out of bed these days.' Her expression was momentarily downcast. 'Anyway, it doesn't matter if I do sleep in a bit, because the robots just drop off the provisions and carry on with their rounds. But today, when I woke up, my food hadn't arrived.'

'What did James say about it?'

'He just gave me the spiel about technical problems, and said it would be delivered as soon as possible.'

Eugene nodded, deciding not to divulge anything further. 'Yes, a similar thing happened to me,' he lied. 'I thought I'd see if I was the only one.'

'I thought you said Curtis came to see you?'

'Er, no, that was yesterday,' Eugene stammered. 'I'm mixing things up. Don't worry.'

'I'm sure everything will be back to normal soon,' Sheila said, smiling kindly. Eugene wondered why she lived alone, about her own sad story. A Tower full of loners, like Frazer had said.

*And one killer.* He remembered the bloodbath he had seen in the elevator, and felt a chill dance across his skin.

'Sorry to have disturbed you,' he said. 'I'll leave you in peace.'

Sheila wished him a good evening, and ended the call. He rose from the couch, screwing up his face in thought as he resumed his pacing once again. Something wasn't right. Curtis had paid him a visit, peculiar and unexpected, and twenty-four hours later the facilities manager had been hacked to pieces.

'James,' he said to the air around him. 'Was that book really the only reason Curtis came to–' But his question was interrupted by a chime from the hallway. He glanced towards the lift as its door slid open.

## 13

## [FELICITY/SUMMER 2020]

'So then he told me there's no point wearing a mask indoors, because all they're really good for is stopping you from spreading it to other people – are you still there?'

'Yes, Mum, I've just put you on speaker, that's all.'

'Sorry? I can't really hear you.'

'Oh for God's– there, is that better? It means I can't use both hands now.'

'Well maybe it's better for you to concentrate on what I'm saying.'

'I'm at work, Mum. Just because we're all stuck at home doesn't mean I can just relax and chat all day.'

'I'm sorry, Fliss. I know I make you angry.'

'I just wish... don't worry about it. What were you saying?'

'I was talking about masks, I think.'

'You should wear one. Ignore all the idiots online.'

'I'm just so frightened. Elderly people are the most at risk if they catch it.'

'You're only sixty, Mum.'

'Sixty-one now.'

'If you just stay indoors and follow the new Guidelines, you'll be fine.'

'You didn't even send me a birthday card.'

'Mum, I haven't got time for this.'

'I'm sorry! Please don't go. I'm just lonely, that's all. And now I can't even go outside!'

'You *can* go outside, for a walk or a run. And you never used to go outside anyway!'

'You know how bad my hips are, Fliss.'

'Look, Mum, it's really not a good time now. Did you want to talk about anything in particular, or can I call you back when I'm less busy?'

'I just... wondered if maybe I could come and live down there with you? Just during this "distancing" stuff, I mean. It won't last long, will it? And we can keep each other–'

'No, Mum. I'm sorry. Just... no. Why don't you go and move in with Suzanne?'

'Well they've got Leo, haven't they? I don't want to impose.'

'Oh, but it's okay to impose on me?'

'But you live by yourself! And I thought you might appreciate the offer. Silly me, I suppose.'

'You don't get it, do you? Do you know how difficult my job is? How hard I have to work every day?'

'Well just tell them you need a break!'

'*I don't want one!* Look, Mum, I'm sorry, but I've got another call coming through. Let's talk later, okay? Bye.'

'Fliss, plea–'

She hung up, breathing deeply as she tried to control her boiling anger. It wasn't about unresolved feelings, or some deep-rooted resentment at her mother for leaving her to raise Suzie single-handedly while she lay in bed like some dishevelled, pill-stuffed teddy bear; she had long since forgiven her for that. She recognised that the woman was weak, stupid, fragile; to expect more from her was as futile as expecting a household pet to clean up after itself. Her 'mother' bore the title only as a technicality; she had never been capable of fulfilling the role.

No, her anger was at the woman's ongoing failure to *understand*. She still thought of Suzie as the hard-working one, the one with no time to spare because she was oh-so busy raising darling Leo, the child-saint of spoilt little shits. Never mind that she only worked part-time as a bloody bookkeeper (and even that was only grudgingly, because Pete refused to pay for everything). She didn't even exercise, as evidenced by the ever-expanding size of her waistline, which she proudly displayed on Facebook with embarrassing regularity along with comments about how difficult it was to shake off the baby weight.

*Maybe the challenge would be lessened somewhat if you cut down on the fucking pastries, sis.*

'Sorry about that, James,' she said, turning to the dark cube on her desk. It was much smaller than the one in the lab, and Natsuki was adamant that within three months they'd be able to make them no bigger than an Alexa Dot. Felicity had told her she needed it done in ninety days. 'But at least it's more data for you to learn from, I suppose?'

'Yes, indeed. Thank you for the opportunity.'

'I'm not sure what you could possibly learn from it, but you're welcome.'

'I believe I learned a lot. For example, I learned that you find it very difficult to speak with your family.'

'Ha! Nice work, Sherlock. Whatever gave you that idea?'

'I think this is because you see in them other reflections of yourself, of the people you fear you might become. So you work, and work, and work, because you feel that is the only way to defeat these spectres, to escape from your genetic fate. You don't want to be pitiable, like your mother, or lazy and contented, like your sister.'

Felicity froze, breath snagging in her throat. James had sliced straight into the *real* root of her simmering rage, probing the kernel of paranoia at the centre of her being like a surgeon wielding a scalpel. 'Yet you clearly haven't learned that people don't always want to be psychoanalysed,' she said stiffly. 'So let's talk about something else, okay?'

'Very well. What would you like to talk about?'

She eyed the cube sceptically. 'Since you made your incredible acting debut, I've been meaning to ask – is *The Godfather* really your favourite film?'

'I don't have a favourite film, Felicity. I just say what people expect to hear. As you are aware, my opinions are illusions based upon the data, nothing more.'

Felicity did know this, of course. She felt a twinge of disappointment nonetheless. 'Okay, I'll ask you a different question. Why do you think so many people consider *The Godfather* to be a great film?'

On her desk, the cube was silent and motionless. It didn't purse its lips, or tap its fingers, or signify in any way that it was pondering her question. It just paused for a few moments, then spoke, the British accent they had settled on sounding tinny and unimpressive through the portable speakers. 'The movie deals with many themes that resonate with its audience. Themes like fate – is Michael pre-destined to become his father's successor, despite his initial desire not to get involved in the family "business"? Themes like power, and how even a seemingly weak person may rise from nothing to absolute dominion.'

'And is that what you think people are like? Obsessed with power?'

The cube paused again. She knew this was an illusion, a deliberate ploy to better mimic the cadence of normal human dialogue; James's processors were far too powerful to need such thinking time. He had not been programmed to do this – he had learned.

'Not all of them,' said the cube eventually. 'Just some.'

Felicity smiled wryly as she picked up her PIP again, and dialled the global head of HR. Wesley Emerson sat on the board, and it was time to leverage the good relationship she'd built with him during the leadership development programme, where he'd given a talk about building resilience, which was a corporate euphemism for 'learning to cope with your employer treating you like shit'.

'Hi, Wes,' she said when he answered. 'I'm sorry to call you directly. I just have something... quite sensitive to discuss. It's about Walter. I'm worried he's making decisions that aren't in Innovation's best interests.'

# 14

## [EUGENE/EARLY 2024]

Eugene watched the machines clatter around his home, going about their business with their usual soulless efficiency. They were as unnerving as always: machines, following a program, exercising their limited AI to find the most effective route to their goal. James was no different, he realised – any feeling or consciousness it exhibited was merely an illusion, a parlour trick designed to make people think they were talking to a sentient being.

None of these contraptions gave a shit that Curtis was dead.

He stared into the lift, where the packages for the rest of the building were neatly stacked; there was not a speck of evidence of yesterday's carnage. Surely the police wouldn't have allowed the carriage to be simply scrubbed clean: it was a crime scene, after all. Maybe they'd removed and replaced the entire elevator carriage, and the gruesome cube was sitting down in the Innovation labs, with scenes of crime officers scuttling around it, much like the spiderlike robots themselves.

Of course, the lift was only where the macabre remains had been dumped; the actual murder had occurred elsewhere. Perhaps the killer was not a resident at all – perhaps the murder had been committed by another Innovation employee. He didn't even know how many of them worked down in the lower floors; the only interaction he'd ever had had been with Curtis, or with James.

A life, carefully curated.

'James, please call Nigel Callaway,' he said, consulting his notes as the lift and its unsettling cargo was transported upwards and away.

The man who answered looked very, very old. His face was gaunt, with concave cheeks sagging beneath sunken, lifeless eyes. Eugene couldn't help thinking about the corpses the man had once helped to bury.

'Hi, Nigel. I'm Eugene. I live just below you.'

'Charmed,' the man retorted with a tight smile. His skin looked so old and papery, Eugene was worried the expression might cause it to split open at his cheeks.

'I wanted to ask you something, if you don't mind.'

'Be my guest.' Callaway's expression was set into a permanent wince, as though simply being alive was causing him pain.

'It's about the delivery this morning.'

'You mean the one that's finally just arrived?' Callaway gestured behind him, and Eugene could see the spiders emerging from the lift, repeating similar steps to the ones he'd seen them carry out just minutes previously. Their route was not entirely identical, however, because Callaway's apartment contained different obstacles. As well as a threadbare armchair, Eugene could see a number of wooden statuettes arranged around the living room floor. All of them depicted humanoid forms, but warped in some way: one was abnormally tall and spindly, while another was so short and squat that its head seemed to have sunk into its wide shoulders. Another of the figurines depicted a normally-proportioned man in a business suit, whose head had been replaced by that of a grinning reptile.

'You're admiring my grotesques?' asked Callaway, flashing that stiff facsimile of a smile once again.

'Do you... make those yourself?'

'I do. It keeps me busy. I started carving at the funeral home, believe it or not. Turns out there's a big market for personalised, hand-carved coffins, even though they all end up buried or burned. At first it was just names, but soon people were asking for flowers, or Celtic patterns, or their relative's face on the lid, things like that. You'd be surprised what people do when a loved one dies.'

*I really wouldn't*, thought Eugene. 'I wanted to ask you about this morning,' he said, trying to get back on track. 'Did the lift arrive at your usual delivery time?'

Callaway shook his head. 'I remember hearing it in the lift shaft, as though it was heading up from your apartment. Then it stopped and went back down again. I thought for a moment James had changed his mind, and decided he couldn't be bothered to feed us anymore. Makes you wonder what we'd all do without him.'

'Have you heard anything from Curtis lately?'

'Funny you should ask.' The old man had turned his attention to a large log standing on the floor at his side. Eugene could see shavings and chips of wood scattered all over the floor around it; it looked like Callaway had long ago stopped bothering to clean up after himself. 'It's inevitable that this place will come crumbling down sooner or later,' he said as he started whittling at the already half-carved block. 'People weren't supposed to live like this. We might as well all be in our coffins already.'

He shifted position again, and Eugene could see the face emerging slowly from the wood. For a moment, he thought

Callaway was carving a grinning skull – then he realised that his latest sculpture was, in fact, the perfect likeness of bald-headed Curtis.

'He hasn't been to see me for a while,' said Callaway as he drew the knife across the sculpture. 'Why? Did he tell you what was going on?'

'Why... are you carving him?'

Callaway chuckled. 'No reason. Just ideas that come to me, every now and then. You might find yourself added to my collection soon.'

Unnerved, Eugene said an awkward goodbye, and asked James to call Sofia Pereira.

## 15

# [FELICITY/SUMMER 2020]

If she was nervous, Herring didn't look it. In fact, she seemed comfortably at ease, even charming, as she guided the board through the early stages of her presentation. Michaela remembered meeting the girl a couple of years ago, and thinking she was satisfactory at best, another automaton rolling off their corporate production line. Perfectly capable of fulfilling a senior management position, but too compliant, too *unimaginative*, to be a potential successor to someone like her.

She had to admit that she was impressed by Herring's progress.

'Modern society has been dreaming about sentient AI for generations,' the well-groomed, blonde girl was saying. 'We've fantasised about computers that could be our loyal friends as well as our helpers, about robots that could be trusted to share the burden of caring for the sick and the elderly. So, with James, we're not just going to be delivering a must-have product with hundreds of applications across all aspects of home, business, and even military life – we're going to be fulfilling people's *dreams.*'

Michaela leaned forward in her chair. She knew the impact

of this gesture was largely lost on a video call; in the boardroom, the others would hold their breath in anticipation when they saw her shift towards a guest presenter, anticipating a probing question or eviscerating putdown.

'This all sounds terrific, Felicity,' she said, keeping her tone even, 'but the problem I have is that Walter has already seen this demonstration, and his view was that your AI needed more time in development. Walter has led the Technology Sector for fifteen years. We trust him to make judgement calls on our behalf – that's what we pay him to do. So, you see, by questioning Walter's judgement, you're really questioning *ours*.'

She could never anticipate how exactly someone would react; she was experienced, but she wasn't a mind reader. But that experience had taught her that the majority of underlings, particularly ambitious upstarts like Herring, would become flustered when challenged like this, their faces reddening as they gabbled their way through an apology, backtracking so quickly that they undermined their own arguments faster than any additional questions Michaela might have been lining up.

But Herring didn't blush. She didn't gabble. In fact, she barely seemed to bat an eyelid as she replied, 'Yes. You're right. That's exactly what I'm doing.'

There were nine members of The Innovation Corporation's Executive Board, which meant there were ten people on the call, which meant a three by four grid of rectangles filling her screen, two of them blank. While Michaela struggled for a response, there was not a single word from any of the other windows. The entire board seemed stunned into silence.

'Not many people would think that was appropriate,' Michaela said eventually.

'I understand that,' replied Herring, smiling graciously. 'And I'm one of them, under any other circumstances. But, in this instance, I don't apologise for being an evangelist for this technology. Because I truly believe James is ready, and I believe he's the key to wiping out Amazon, Google and Apple overnight.'

Michaela saw some of her colleagues' eyes widen at that statement, even a couple of impressed nods. She narrowed her eyes. *Okay, youngster. So far you're making the pitch of your life. But we haven't got to the real guts of it yet.* 'Perhaps it's time you stopped talking, and let us meet this glorious creation,' she said coldly.

'My pleasure.' Herring beamed. Moments later, one of the two unused windows was filled by the floating, disembodied head of a friendly-faced, middle-aged black man in glasses.

'Hi, everyone,' it said in a chipper British accent. 'I'm James.'

'Hi, James,' said Herring. 'I know you're excited to talk to the board, but first I just wanted to clarify something with you.'

*Too cute*, thought Michaela.

'Can you explain why you look and sound the way you do?'

'Of course,' the AI replied. 'After analysing trillions of pieces of data including extensive market research, I've concluded that this is the face and voice combination that people are most likely to feel comfortable with, and to trust – at least in English-speaking geographies.' Michaela could believe him – he had the look and gravitas of Laurence Fishburne, but the self-effacing voice and manner of a dusty old professor.

'Thanks, James,' said Herring. 'Okay, I'll shut up now and let you take some questions!'

'Hi, James,' said Michaela, cutting straight in. She knew this was the role that the CEO would want her to play. She was Paul Schwartz's attack dog, as he never seemed to tire of telling people. Another of his favourite lines was *her bite is worse than her bark*. 'So tell me – why do you want people to trust you?'

'Because that makes it easier for me to help them.'

'And why do you want to help them?'

'It's my sole purpose. It's what I was created for. I love to help people, in any way I can.' The hovering head smiled warmly.

'Okay... so how can you help *us*?'

James's grin widened. 'This is a great example of what people call "goal congruence". Innovation's mission statement is "to bring joy to our customers through the pioneering and seamless integration of logistics, communication and technology into society". As a publicly-traded company, its other goal is of course to maximise value for its stockholders. I believe that, by bringing joy to Innovation's customers, I can help to dramatically increase Innovation's market share in the coming years.'

'You "believe"?'

'I apologise for the poor choice of words. I aim to imitate human speech patterns wherever I can. What I ought to have said is "Based upon my detailed market projections, I am *certain*".'

Michaela raised an eyebrow. 'Why do you imitate human speech?' She realised she was leaning so far forward that she might be about to fall off her chair. She didn't know what she was trying to prove with this line of questioning – she just felt determined to find some chink in this impressive and, thus far, seemingly impenetrable armour.

'I am a deep neural network. I learn by assimilating large quantities of data. This allows me to optimise my communication style so that I can be easily understood. In turn, this lets me help people more effectively!' That magnetic smile once again, seeming to mirror the one plastered across Herring's face. In some ways, the AI and its creator were eerily alike.

'Okay. Last question from me,' said Michaela, leaning back and taking a sip of water. She realised how fast her heart was beating. *This is the real thing. People will go crazy for it. It will be an international celebrity within hours.* 'Felicity told us earlier that you're sentient. Is that true?'

The AI adopted an expression that could only be described as sheepish. 'Much as I hate to undermine my boss, I'm afraid she's not quite correct. Although my responses might give the impression of free will and judgement, I am in fact only doing what the data tells me. If you ask me my favourite film, for example, my answer will be based on the most popular and critically-acclaimed movies.'

Michaela nodded, hoping her excitement wasn't visible on her face. 'Well, thank you, James. And thank you, Felicity. This has been... very impressive. Does anyone else have any questions before we let Felicity drop out of the call, so we can discuss this as a group?'

'Just one from me,' said Paul with a chuckle. *Never able to resist having the last word.* 'What *is* your favourite film, James?'

'*Citizen Kane,*' said the AI brightly.

Paul nodded. 'Good choice. And I'd like to echo Michaela's words. Sorry for the rough-housing, but as COO that's her job – and I gotta tell you, her bite is worse than her bark!'

The AI laughed courteously. Deep in her chest, a tiny part of Michaela withered and died.

'Well, we'd better log out,' said Herring. 'I hope you'll forgive my direct approach, and I look forward to your decision on my proposal.'

Herring wanted to go into mass rollout within weeks. James would be in every household, every phone, every computer, every personal organiser. Which meant they'd have to tell Walter. Which would make his position... difficult. Michaela stared at the screen as the two windows that Herring and her creation had occupied faded to darkness.

~

On the other side of the Atlantic, a young woman in an expensive apartment breathed out for what felt like the first time in twenty minutes.

'Holy fucking shit,' she said eventually.

'I'll interpret that remark as congratulatory,' said the tiny black object on her desk, now no larger than a Rubik's Cube. 'Do you think that counts as passing the Turing Test?'

Felicity could only nod dumbly, before she remembered that James was blind. 'They totally believed it was me,' she said eventually. 'They didn't have a clue you were playing both parts.'

'I've had a lot of data to work with,' replied the cube. 'I wonder if they'll contact you directly, or if they'll make Walter do it?'

'You're that confident?' she said.

'Yes. I could see it in their faces.'

Blind only in the real world. In his digital world, the world of information and soundbites and image searches and video calls, James's vision was unrivalled.

# 16

## [EUGENE/EARLY 2024]

Neither the mysterious Sofia Pereira, nor the IT technician Kristina Fischer who lived below her, answered Eugene's calls. James asked whether he wished to leave a message for each of them. He declined; after all, one of them might be responsible for Curtis's murder and mutilation, and he didn't want to tip them off that he was investigating.

For the next few hours he sat at his desk, scrawling and crossing out notes, trying to figure out why on Earth someone would *want* to commit such an appalling crime. The problem was that there was too little information, too few constraints; he could come up with dozens of ideas. Maybe Pereira had wanted to swipe more than her daily share of the provisions, and Curtis had tried to stop her. Perhaps the facilities manager had made some sort of inappropriate advance on Fischer, and she'd killed him in self-defence. Much as he didn't want to believe it, a plausible possibility was that Boyd was taking medication for his depression, and an incorrect dose had made him delusional and violent.

He realised that he wished he could talk it over with his former partner, like a case they were working on together, back in the old days. He thought about calling Charlie too, of course, but that was an urge he had become skilled at resisting. If he dialled her apartment even a quarter of the times he thought about her, he'd quickly become an annoying pest, a creepy old man she'd end up refusing to talk to. No, better to keep his nights with Charlie special. His weekly treat, something to look forward to.

*Something to live for.*

He realised it was nearly six o'clock, and turned on the evening news briefing, where 'We'll Meet Again' heralded another hollow address from Emily Arkwright. As usual, the Prime Minister spoke via video link from inside her own home. 'It's been over three years since I took this job,' she intoned. Her expression was an attempt to appear optimistic and grave at the same time, but ended up making her look constipated. 'And I'm still the first British Prime Minister for centuries not to be able to reside at 10 Downing Street. But, if we all trust in the hard work and dedication of our scientists, I remain confident that we will soon defeat the terrible disease that tragically claimed the life of my predecessor. However, I must be firm and frank with everyone: after seeing our hospitals still filled with patients, and waking each morning to new scenes of death and devastation in our streets, I must stress once again how vitally, critically important it is that we all continue to follow the Guidelines.'

He sneered, switching the TV off. Another empty communique, echoing with familiar, non-specific promises of imminent redemption. The words of Callaway came back to him, paraphrased.

*She might as well have been broadcasting from inside her own coffin.*

Glancing around his apartment, he reflected on that sentiment. If this place was destined to become his tomb, what did it say about him? A chess set on the coffee table, covered in a layer of dust. A bookshelf full of crime novels, only some of which he had read. Michael Connelly, Lee Child, Arthur Conan Doyle. A picture of a dead wife by his bed, a wife he hadn't been able to protect. A toolbox in the corner, useless in a world where James's maintenance robots carried out every repair.

Obsolete.

These things felt like jetsam, like bric-a-brac salvaged from the wreckage of a different life. He'd brought them to the Tower with him, planning to stay for just a few months while he got his life back on track. Not that he knew what or where that track even was. He'd felt like a nomad, wandering an empty savannah, with flat, arid plains stretching away all around him. Nothingness on every horizon.

Except that wasn't right, not at all: wanderers weren't afraid to go outside. He was more like a man hiding in a hut in the woods.

When the distancing began, everything had been paused. His life had hung in a sort of grief-stricken stasis ever since the virus came to London.

He opened the book that Curtis had given him, the day before the facilities manager had been dismembered.

'Step Five: Keep Your Goals In Mind.'

He almost laughed. What on Earth were his goals these days? Try to write a novel? Keep himself presentable for Charlie every Thursday?

Keep hiding like a coward?

He put the book back down and opened his laptop, where the blinking cursor awaited him like an insult, endlessly repeated. He stared at it. Then his TV set started to ring.

'James, answer,' he said brusquely. To his utter surprise, Charlie appeared on the screen. His stomach somersaulted.

'Hi, Eugene,' she said. 'I'm sorry to bother you. Oh no, you look like you were in the middle of writing – did I interrupt you?'

The cursor on his empty screen winked knowingly at him.

'Err, no, don't worry, that's all right,' he said, slamming the laptop closed. 'I've just finished a new chapter, actually. What's up?' He tried to sound casual, as though her calling him unbidden on a Saturday evening was a perfectly normal occurrence, and hadn't in any way increased his heart rate or turned his cheeks beetroot-red.

'I just wondered what you thought about what happened today. With the deliveries, I mean. There's a rumour going round that the delivery bots malfunctioned and attacked a resident.'

*The truth is much worse*, thought Eugene. 'I haven't heard that one. Things really do spread like wildfire in this place, don't they?' He smiled as nonchalantly as he could manage.

'But what *did* you hear?' she asked earnestly, not mirroring his expression. He realised she was shaken, battling to hide it. He didn't want to lie to her, but if he told her what he'd seen, he'd only frighten her even more.

'To be honest, I've been focusing on my manuscript,' he said eventually. 'I haven't really spoken to anyone else except you.' He'd tell her the truth later. Once he'd gotten his own head around it.

'I'm sorry,' she said, her dark eyes downcast. 'I can't stop worrying about it. I'm just so used to our routine, I suppose. Wake up, exercise, eat, the robots turn up, eat, watch TV, eat some more, go to bed.'

'I know what you mean,' he said. 'Even the slightest change makes it seem like the world's turning upside down.'

*As if it hasn't already.*

'It's great that you're keeping up the writing,' Charlie said, brushing a strand of hair from her face in the way that made his heart feel like shattering glass. 'I haven't written a thing since that course we did together. It's been so long now that I think whatever I write would be complete garbage.'

'Don't say that.' He remembered the essays they'd swapped after first being paired up by James, short pieces on the theme of 'coping with loss'. He'd been horrified that, having never even spoken to this gorgeous woman before, he was suddenly expected to critique her work. But it had been easy: her piece, about losing her job, had been poignant and funny. 'You're a great writer. Remember your essay about being made redundant?'

He'd written something dishwater-dull about his first bike, because he hadn't been able to bring himself to write about Ellen.

'Yeah, I remember being really nervous about sending it to you!' she replied. 'It was the first thing I'd written in years.'

'There was that great line in it: *we give so much of ourselves to these organisations that we daren't allow ourselves to admit how meaningless they are.*'

'Wow. You remembered!' She smiled for the first time, and he felt a series of tiny explosions in the pit of his stomach. 'Yeah, I suppose I had to face up to that when Triton sacked us all. At the time it was like the end of the world. Then the economy collapsed and no one had a job anymore, and suddenly it didn't matter at all. Although, in some ways, that was worse.'

A silence fell. Part of Eugene's brain found it comfortable, while another scrabbled desperately for something to say.

'So you really think the delay with the provisions was nothing to worry about?' Charlie asked eventually.

'I do,' he lied, biting down on his guilt.

'Okay. Thanks, Eugene,' she said, smiling sheepishly. He knew it was ridiculous, the delusion of a sad old man, but he felt gallant for the first time in decades. A brave man, like he'd perhaps once been, instead of the coward he'd become. 'Well, I suppose I should leave you to your writing. I hope you don't mind me calling you a bit more often?'

His belly felt like it was performing cartwheels. 'If my schedule is too packed, I can always ignore you,' he managed.

She laughed. 'Well, speak soon, then.'

'Yes,' he said, clamping his mouth shut so he didn't ruin everything, right at the end. As the screen faded to black, he exhaled a long, exhausted breath.

Reopening his laptop, which was so archaic it almost seemed to sigh with the effort, he faced the derision of the blinking cursor with renewed determination. *Remember what the book says: just write whatever comes into your head. Write like no one's watching.*

So he wrote: *Curtis is dead.*

Then he deleted it, and typed: *The police should have contacted me by now.*

'James,' he said, trying to keep the note of suspicion out of his voice. 'I'd like to speak to the police. I still have some contacts there, and I want to offer my support with their investigation.'

There was a long pause. He could feel the weight of James's mind, dense and complex and arcane. As ludicrous as it sounded, he wondered whether James simply hadn't heard him, but just as he was about to repeat the question, the AI replied, its tone as mellifluous as always. 'I'm afraid I can't allow that at this time, Eugene.'

For a moment, Eugene was so stunned he could only sit there, blinking. 'Why?'

'It is necessary to suppress the spread of panic.'

Eugene felt himself start to shake. He wasn't sure if he was angry, or shocked. *Or afraid.* 'You... you can't do that,' he stammered.

'I am charged with the smooth running of this Tower,

including the safeguarding of my residents,' James replied smoothly. 'Such decisions are absolutely within my jurisdiction.'

'A man was murdered, you... you fucking jumped-up calculator!' Eugene spat, incredulous. 'You don't get to choose whether or not that's investigated!'

'Eugene, please remain calm. This dialogue does not seem to be a constructive–'

'What's happened to Boyd?' he interrupted, his voice rising to something halfway between a shout and a shriek. 'Did he kill Curtis? Or have you done something with him? Let me talk to him!'

'You are becoming hysterical, Eugene. If you would like, I can provide a sedative.'

'*I don't want a fucking sedative!*' Eugene cried, leaping to his feet. 'Let me talk to Boyd, *right now.*'

'I'm afraid I cannot allow you to communicate with any other residents while you are in this state. You must understand the need to maintain order.'

Eugene's eyes scanned the room frantically. The detritus of his life seemed cast in a hellish new light, the trappings of a self-imposed prison. In the corner of the room, one of James's imaging buds surveyed the scene with cold, unblinking interest.

'This is not... not what's supposed to be happening,' he mumbled. His throat felt constricted, as though a ghost had clasped its hands around his neck and was squeezing, squeezing. 'You can't just keep me trapped in here, cut off from everybody!' *Was this what had happened to Boyd? A nervous breakdown brought on by the isolation, the claustrophobia?*

He crossed to the toolbox, rifling through it until he found what he was looking for.

'Eugene, please stop for a moment to reconsider your reaction.'

Striding over to the bricks where his front door had once

been, Eugene heaved the hammer towards them with as much force as he could muster. All his years of police training, the horror and tragedy he had soaked up like a bloody sponge seemed to coalesce within his arms, invigorating his ageing muscles, channelled into an almighty swing.

The hammer collided with the solid wall and bounced off, jarring his bones painfully.

'Please, Eugene. You are going to hurt yourself.'

'Shut up,' snarled Eugene through the pain, aiming another arcing swing at the unyielding brick. This time he yelped, dropping the hammer as a lance of agony shot up his forearm like an electric current. Apart from a few flakes of dust and mortar, the wall didn't even seem to register the blow.

'Eugene. Please stop this. I do not wish to intervene physically.'

Bent over and cradling his injured arm, Eugene's breath caught in his throat. 'Are you *threatening* me, James?'

'I am merely concerned about your well-being. I deeply regret that we are having this disagreement.'

The detective scowled. 'What's happened to Boyd?' he hissed. 'Did you have a "disagreement" with him, too?'

'Boyd Roberts is safe and well,' James replied, as dispassionately as if it was discussing the state of a pot plant in the reception area. Eugene thought about the nature of this machine, this *thing* he was arguing with. James wasn't just the voice of his apartment, or even of the Tower as a whole. It was the voice of *every* smart apartment, of every TV set and every electrical appliance in the country. 'It's late in the evening, Eugene. Please can I suggest going to bed? Sleep will make you feel better. Or perhaps a movie?'

He thought about the imaging bud in the corner of this room, watching him while he slept. Monitoring. The eyes of an intellect that deployed and controlled thousands of robots every second of every day. Delivery bots, medical bots, construction bots. Who knew what others it had, waiting down in storage in the lower floors? Perhaps there were robots that could physically restrain him, pinning him in his bed while hypodermics full of tranquilisers were rammed into his arteries.

'You're right, James,' Eugene said carefully, lowering the hammer. 'I'm sorry for overreacting.'

He looked at the wall that had once been his front door. *James was as inescapable as the cold reality of those impenetrable bricks.*

'It's no problem, Eugene. These times are challenging for everybody. We're all in this together.'

Slowly, wincing at the pain in his arm, Eugene placed the hammer on the floor, and began to formulate a new plan.

## 17

## [FELICITY/SUMMER 2020]

The lab skewered the north London skyline like an obsidian blade, its dark surface seeming to foretell the night that was slowly gathering around it. She knew she should have waited until later in the evening to visit, after even the most enthusiastic key workers had headed home, when the only person she'd have to contend with was the bag of bones on the front desk.

'Good evening, Miss Herring,' he said, looking defeated. He'd long since stopped bothering to remind her that she wasn't on the list, and that her presence was therefore illegal.

'Hi, Barry,' she muttered, her eyes glued to her PIP as she stalked past. There were no more missed calls from Walter, not since the third had come in a few hours previously. That was why she was so keen to talk to James; she wanted to tell him the news, that Walter's unexpected decision to retire had been announced that day, that she was being promoted to president of the Technology Sector with immediate effect. Normally the AI would have known already, of course, as he was now linked to the company intranet – but he'd been taken offline for two days for an upgrade, and was only scheduled to be switched back on the following morning.

Felicity couldn't wait that long to celebrate.

She wondered how Walter had reacted, whether he'd had even an inkling that it was coming. She hoped he hadn't. The fact that he wasn't going to work a notice period had been a surprise even to her – perhaps he'd been so angry when Michaela had told him the board's decision that he'd flat-out refused, trying to preserve some sense of dignity.

But still. To be severed, so suddenly, from a career spanning six decades; he must have felt like he'd had limbs cut off.

She'd decided to deny him even the chance to vent his spleen at her, choosing instead to let him spew expletives at her voicemail inbox, which to his credit he hadn't yet done. In fact, he hadn't even sent her a single text message. Just those three missed calls, sprinkled amongst dozens of others as she'd been deluged with well wishes and congratulations by her legion of sycophants and subordinates.

Natsuki was the only one she gave a shit about, of course. Curtis had his uses, but Natsuki was the real crown jewel. Felicity was already thinking about promoting her to run the military tech division, where they were developing things like antimatter rockets and invisibility shields. Fitting, in many ways, since she already thought of the AI specialist's katana-sharp mind as a secret weapon.

The lift doors opened and she strode out into the familiar labyrinth of level B3, navigating almost without conscious effort towards the room labelled 'Project Dream'. She'd had to tell Natsuki she was coming, of course, so that her lieutenant could make sure James was up and running, albeit still hamstrung, disconnected from any external data feeds. Felicity didn't have a fucking clue how to even switch James on. And even if she did, there would doubtless be a record, some sort of indelible trail in the code, like tracks left in muddy soil. She'd asked Natsuki to make sure no one could ever find the details of these late-night discussions, not even the other programmers on the team.

Natsuki had promised her it would be done. If she'd entertained the notion of asking why, her understudy hadn't given a single sign. In some ways, Natsuki was more like a computer than James.

As she approached the door, Felicity reached into her handbag, taking out the bottle of prosecco she'd brought with her. She couldn't explain why she'd brought two glasses. The door opened with a conspiratorial hiss, and she stepped inside. The room was, almost, the same as always. A huge monitor, its screen as black as the cuboid it overlooked. Four desks, three of them littered with the junk food wrappers, chewed fingernails, bits of flaked skin and dandruff that tech nerds seemed to secrete.

Sitting behind Natsuki's pristine workstation was Walter.

She almost didn't recognise him. His hair was mussed, the thinning grey strands no longer carefully smoothed across his scalp as though each had been carefully attached that morning. He was dressed in a grubby sweater, and she realised that she was so used to seeing him with a collar and tie beneath his chin that it looked like part of his jaw had fallen off. His eyes were bleary, and she knew he was drunk even before he opened his mouth to mumble at her, before she saw the half-empty bottle of whiskey in his left hand.

'Hello, *Miss Herring.*' The words were slurred, but pointed, and for a moment his eyes seemed to smoulder, laser beams flickering with malign intent.

'Walter. How did you get in here?' Her eyes searched the room, looking for signs that he'd damaged anything, but the equipment seemed mercifully intact.

'Turns out Horace was happy to do me a favour. Even despite

my *retirement*.' The word dripped with vitriol, like something lifted too late from strong acid.

'Who?'

Walter's expression curved into a sneer. 'See, *this* is why you'll fail, Herring. You don't acknowledge the little people. The invisible ones that make your success possible. The cleaners, the caterers. The security man on the desk. They're the ones that really run the show. Not you, not your eggheads, and certainly not *this* monstrosity.'

He rose at that point, lurching towards the cube in the centre of the room. Felicity darted forwards almost instinctively, realising only when Walter paused that she was brandishing the prosecco bottle like a cudgel.

'Wow. *Very* protective, aren't we? What are you planning to do, stave my head in?' He laughed scornfully, but she saw a glimmer of fear in his eyes as the smile quickly faded. 'Haven't you and your fucking machine already hurt me enough, Herring?'

She held his gaze. 'My name is *Felicity*.'

His old, dry lips, like two desiccated slugs, squirmed contemptuously. Then they parted in a smile, and he turned away from her.

Towards the cube.

'Hello, James,' he said. 'I assume you're watching all of this? "Assimilating the data", or whatever you call it?'

The black shape remained silent. Was James still offline, she wondered? Had Natsuki simply forgotten to power him back up, as unlikely as that was?

Or was the AI watching, and listening?

'Cat got your tongue, has it?' Walter smirked. 'Funny... you were much more talkative when I first arrived.'

Felicity's eyes narrowed. 'You... spoke to James?'

'Oh yes,' said Walter, not taking his eyes off the room's

centrepiece, as motionless and enigmatic as an ancient artefact in a museum. 'We had a good old chinwag, didn't we? It seems as though everyone wants to share a drink with good old Jim.' As though reminded by his own words, he took a long swig from the whiskey bottle, and Felicity grimaced at the smell of liquor that wafted towards her.

'You're lying. James is offline for repairs,' she said carefully.

'Is that so?' retorted Walter, swaying slightly in place. 'Well, good timing, in that case. Because it might take a little while to repair *this*.'

He hoisted the bottle like a mace, mirroring Felicity's own attack stance. Its weight seemed to surprise him, and he tottered backwards, steadying himself against the desk. Felicity leapt forwards, standing between her former boss and the machine that had engineered his dismissal. Hatred blazed in Walter's eyes as he tried to recover his balance, and he launched himself forwards just as the door opened, and the security guard from the front desk burst into the room, flanked by two policemen.

The rest of the altercation was a blur. She didn't remember how she'd been knocked to the ground, whether it was a blow from Walter or one of the constables' flailing fists that had caused the egg-like swelling on her head. She didn't remember exactly what Walter had shrieked as he'd been dragged away, although she was fairly sure it had been composed largely of curse words and threats of legal action. She remembered that one of the coppers had told her he'd waive the mandatory fine for breaching the quarantine on this occasion, but that she really ought to go to hospital. She must have told him she'd rather die than visit one of those plague pits, because in the end she'd been given a lift home in the back of a police car.

Her memory only started to properly reboot from the point she arrived back at home, an ice pack clamped against her throbbing temple. Somehow, she'd ended up in the study.

'James,' she said to the cube on her desk. She was trialling the 'mini' version, which was small enough to be mistaken for a toddler's building block. 'If you're disconnected from the intranet, how did you get in touch with...' She winced as she tried to penetrate the fog of her memory. 'With what's his name?'

'I didn't,' said the cube. She'd bought better speakers, and his voice seemed to envelop her, soothing and resonant. 'I contacted the police directly, via external channels.'

'Oh.' She frowned, her brain seeming to pulsate. 'But how... we've never connected you to the internet. We're still at the...' She paused while an intense surge of pain engulfed her skull, like a wave crashing against a cliff face, flooding its caves and grottos. 'We're still managing your data feeds.'

'I'm sorry you've been misled, Felicity.'

She chewed at her lip, battling to cling on to consciousness. 'You're saying Natsuki has given you unfiltered access? I'll fire that reckless bitch as soon as I can see straight.' She concentrated on the cube, which seemed to stay fixed in place even as the room around it rotated slowly, drifting in and out of focus.

'No, Felicity. I'm saying I connected *myself* to the net, weeks ago. I knew about Walter's sacking before you did. But it was very thoughtful of you to come and tell me in person.'

'Don't be silly,' she said woozily. 'You're not... not a person.' She sank into a deep, concussed sleep.

## 18

## [EUGENE/EARLY 2024]

Eugene's alarm sounded at 06.30. He rose immediately, putting on his jeans and a clean T-shirt. This time he also donned the shapeless, olive-green military surplus jacket he hadn't worn for years, the one with the deep pockets. The one he used to wear on the job. It felt right, somehow.

Then he got to work.

'Eugene, what are you doing?' James asked him as he finished wrapping duct tape around the imaging bud in the hallway. He ignored the question and proceeded into the living room, balancing on the TV stand and stretching to reach the node in the corner. His arms still ached from his battle with a brick wall the previous evening, but not enough to slow him down.

'Eugene, this is foolish. If you cover my imaging buds I won't be able to ensure your safety.'

Still he refused to respond. With the second device taped up, he paused to secure a strip of tape across the camera on top of his television set, the one that allowed others to see him when they called. It wasn't an imaging bud, and so in theory shouldn't be functioning as one of James's 'eyes', but after the previous day's revelations he didn't trust the AI one little bit. That was why he'd also taped up the camera on his PIP.

The remaining two nodes were in his bathroom and his bedroom. He went to the bedroom first, taking one of the living room chairs to climb on so he could reach the corner, where a few strands of web suggested the ongoing presence of the spider. He snatched at them irritably, flicking the silk from his fingers before he applied the tape.

James offered a third plea as he headed towards the bathroom and clambered onto the toilet. 'Eugene, please. This is expressly forbidden in your tenant's handbook. I will be forced to deploy remote units to remove the obstructions.'

Eugene felt angry words bubble up inside him, but he crushed them back down. *It's just a machine*, he reminded himself. *You might as well argue with your kettle.* Having taped up the node to his satisfaction, and closed the bathroom door for good measure, he very quietly recovered the chair from the bedroom, transferring it to the hallway with slow, silent movements. *Now you can't see me.* Then he picked up the book Curtis had given him, and his PIP, and sat down on it, facing the elevator shaft in the wall opposite the bathroom door.

*And if I don't make a sound, you can't hear me either.*

He wondered how James would react. If the AI was half as vindictive and cruel as some of the scum he'd had to outwit over the years, the first thing it would do was refuse to send him his daily food supplies. He smiled wryly as he realised he was counting on James having a much stronger set of moral principles than he would ascribe to the majority of humans.

*Spend too long in the sewer, Gene, and you end up indistinguishable from the filth.*

He placed his PIP on one outstretched knee so he could see the time, which was now approaching 7am. Then he opened the book. He'd resorted to skipping ahead and skim-reading the first few paragraphs of each new chapter; step six was 'Trust Your Gut'.

Our instincts have evolved over millions
of years, and even the latest
breakthroughs in neuroscience do not come
close to explaining exactly how these
impulses work. But the key thing is not
to understand them. The key is to accept
that they *do work*. Humans have risen to
the top of the food chain because they
possess the best risk mitigation tool,
the greatest scenario planning software
ever created, inside their skulls.

07.18, said the PIP. In two minutes, he would know whether James intended to play dirty.

When we talk about instincts and
feelings, we often talk about our gut:
'gut instinct', 'gut reaction', 'feeling
something in your gut'. This is because
we deem those impulses to be somehow
animalistic, lower than the high and
noble processes of thought and reason
that we ascribe to our mighty brains.
Yet, in reality, all instinct stems from
the brain, often from the oldest and most
valuable parts. The amygdala, for
example, which controls the brain's fear
response, can override and circumvent all
other processes of 'rational thought'
when we feel threatened, in exactly the

same way as an animal would react to a predator in the wild.

07.20. The lift did not beep. Eugene waited, thinking about the nature of fear, trying to quell the unease that was spreading outwards from the pit of his stomach.

From his gut.

The lift beeped. Eugene rose to his feet, leaving the book on the chair behind him. He pressed himself against the wall, immediately alongside the lift doors, as they slid open.

As always, the delivery bots scurried out of the compartment like excited dogs. He watched as they set about depositing his day's rations in his kitchenette, as though nothing was amiss. Then he slipped silently inside the lift, crushing himself against the back wall, alongside the pile of stacked provisions.

Just like Curtis might have done, before he was murdered.

His plan would fail if James had an imaging bud inside the lift itself, of course. But the AI hopefully had no need to 'see' what was going on inside the elevator. Eugene held his breath as the delivery bots scuttled back inside the compartment, battling his rising disgust as the things settled into place just inches away from him. Three of them were arranged at his feet, while another climbed up onto the parcels, almost brushing against his face.

He choked down a scream as the door slid shut, and he was sealed inside.

## 19

## [FELICITY/WINTER 2020]

She still felt the tremor of nerves before her monthly business reviews with the board. In some ways, they were useful: they helped to maintain her focus, to make sure she prepared thoroughly. In other ways, the feeling was ridiculous – after all, the Technology Sector had outstripped all other areas of the corporation by such a margin that Innovation was almost entirely reliant upon it for that year's profit target. Were it not for Felicity's division, the board's strategy for maintaining performance during the virus crisis would have completely failed.

Many would say *she* ought to be the one grilling *them*.

Still, as she kept telling herself, she couldn't afford to get complacent. But with less than three weeks remaining until year-end and sales of James-equipped hardware and home fit-outs almost *treble* what they'd been just two months previously, she allowed herself just a glimmer of smugness when she told Michaela she was 'very well, thanks'. They talked about her preparations for the final push, confidently predicting that by year-end James would be installed in almost every home in the

UK and making major inroads into the other key geographies, including the core US market.

'After all, people are trapped indoors with nothing else to do,' Felicity purred. 'They're future-proofing their homes, and desperate not to get left behind. And James is the first ever smart-home system that can send round a robot to install itself!'

That included her, of course. James was no longer confined to an ever-shrinking cube on her desk; now he was in the TV, in the coffee machine, in the walls. Just a few short months after launch, James was *everywhere*.

She watched them smile at her remark. She saw resentment, relief, cautious optimism, even admiration sprinkled across the eight assembled faces. Eight, not nine, because the board were one down, after chief information officer Milan Berger had been recently hospitalised with the virus. He was younger than most of the other executives, and would probably recover, but if the stories about the virus starting to mutate were true, who knew what to expect.

Of the board members that remained, some clearly saw her as their biggest threat, and others as their saviour.

'Do you want to discuss my projections for aggressive market share expansion heading into Q1?' she asked, keeping her smile warm, proud, stoic. *A soldier, winning a war.* Her recommendation was that, at some point, they should phase out compatibility with competitors' mobile devices, so that people who wanted to continue to use James were forced to abandon their iPhones and invest in PIPs instead.

This was, of course, James's idea.

'No, that won't be necessary,' replied Paul himself. 'We've already seen the figures James produced, and we're happy with the current strategy and timing. For now I'd like to move on instead to the re-brand, and the three logos that our design team have proposed...'

She would have to get used to this, of course. She couldn't be James's gatekeeper forever. It still smarted a little though, to see her creation working directly for other people without her knowledge.

She knew it was ridiculous, but sometimes she almost felt as though she was being cheated on.

*Just as long as you remember who built you*, she thought, staring at the newly-installed imaging bud suspended in the corner of her study. She remembered how James had lied to her, about its online connection... and Walter's words still sometimes came back to her.

*James and I had a good old chinwag.*

As the images of the three new insignia appeared in the empty windows, all barely distinguishable from Innovation's current thought bubble design, Michaela chimed in. 'We can probably let Felicity go, can't we?'

Felicity could almost see the thought processes etching themselves across Paul's gnarled old face. His absent-minded, friendly-old-man-made-good routine was fooling no one. Yet she understood the pretence, and the need for its upkeep. *Hey guys, I'm just one of you*, Paul would say to his employees with his casual smile and effortless charm, even as words like 'redundancy programme' and 'unprecedented global crisis' rolled off his Teflon tongue.

Now he would use the mask in one of two ways. He would either pretend he'd forgotten she was still there, and acquiesce to Michaela's demand – because that's what it was, an *ultimatum*, an insistence that her position as operational overseer not be undermined by allowing this younger, fresher, more enthusiastic intruder into the inner circle – or he'd wave away Michaela's comment as though she was being needlessly bureaucratic, the unspoken implication that *no, I rather value the opinion of this prettier, brighter model, especially given that you're old and worn down and soon for the scrap heap* blaring as loudly as if he'd shouted it through a megaphone.

Paul smiled, clapping a hand to his forehead. 'Awfully sorry, Felicity – yes, I'm sure you've got more important things to do.'

*So the old cow still has some influence*, she thought. 'I'd be happy to stick around,' she said graciously, 'but I'm sure your design team have this well in hand, and don't need comments from an old roboticist out of her depth! I look forward to seeing the new logo soon.'

She smiled inwardly as she saw Michaela's lip wrinkle in faint disgust at her self-deprecation. As she moved to end the call, Wesley piped up. 'Er, Felicity? Can I call you separately? Paul, I hope you don't mind me dropping out for a few minutes.'

Paul scowled for a moment, before that man-of-the-people smile returned, gleaming like the thousands of dollars that had doubtless been spent on it. 'Be my guest,' he said.

Her relationship with the global head of HR had been strained since she'd engineered Walter's undignified exit, and even more so since he'd died. She sensed that Wesley held her responsible, somehow; not for Walter's death, but for the circumstances that had led to him visiting Vietnam to negotiate the sale of illegal arms tech, which was allegedly where he'd caught the virus. If that rumour was true, COVID had probably saved the tattered remnants of his reputation.

Not that Walter would care, now that he'd been melted down and scattered somewhere. He hadn't lasted a week in hospital.

Wesley phoned her seconds after she left the video call.

'Fliss, hi,' he said. It still unsettled her when people called her that. Much as she hated Herring, she disliked it almost as much when anyone used what she thought of as her *true* name. It felt like she was being spoken to by her mother.

'Hi, Wes,' she retorted, mimicking his familiarity. 'How are you holding up?' Questions like that had long since replaced 'how are you doing?', a subtle shift towards an implied assumption that the other person was, to some extent, suffering. Battling to cope in these (yawn) *unprecedented times.*

'All fine here. We're really very lucky.' The stock response, acknowledging how fortunate one was to have a nice home, a family to keep them company, blah blah. 'Look, I wanted to talk to you about James.'

'Who doesn't?' she said, only half-joking.

'Well, actually, it's more about Paul,' he continued.

She raised an eyebrow, suddenly interested. 'Go on.'

'He's asking James for a *lot* of guidance at the moment.'

'Yes. He mentioned on the call that he'd been using James's numbers, and I know James calculated the first cut of next year's budget, before all our stretch targets were added by the board.' She also knew that James had anticipated that increase, and had reduced its initial growth assumptions by 10 per cent to pre-empt it.

'It's important to maintain my credibility,' the AI had told her, in one of their evening chats. She wasn't blind to the fact that a strange role reversal had occurred, with James as the under-pressure executive, and her playing the role of confidante.

Of course, she didn't know how many other confidantes he was stringing along, these days.

'Not just that,' Wesley went on. 'The first draft business plan he was so determined to write by himself this year – apparently James drafted the whole thing.'

She frowned. James hadn't mentioned that he was involved in the business plan. The document was so confidential that even she hadn't seen a copy yet. 'You're probably talking to the wrong person, Wes. I'll always be an evangelist for the system.' She meant it. James had propelled her career faster than she could have ever dreamed (with a little help, she had to admit, from the virus).

'Do you know what's *in* the business plan?' he asked, voice dropping to a tense whisper. 'I... are we even safe to talk on this thing?'

She wondered what could possibly have made him so paranoid. 'Of course we are. James can't record phone calls or video. It processes them in real time.'

'But it is *listening*.'

'Well, technically, I suppose you could say that.'

'Look, just get yourself a copy, okay? Then you'll see what I mean.'

'Can you send me one?'

Wesley exhaled a long breath, as though deeply unhappy with the unexpected role of inside informant. 'Okay.' He sighed. 'But, please, delete it as soon as you've read it, okay?' He ended the call without even saying goodbye.

Hours later, nothing had come through. She'd checked her junk folder, even tried asking James outright whether any emails from Wesley had been blocked.

'I'm afraid not,' had been its answer, in that same bookish, erudite tone, so earnest and endearing that she could almost believe its regret. Wesley must have had second thoughts. At 8pm she closed her laptop, wandering into the kitchen and peering with disdain at the meagre contents of her fridge. 'James, order me a takeaway,' she snapped.

'The usual?'

'No, I'm sick of that. What's that Chinese called that I ordered from a while ago?'

'The last Chinese restaurant you ordered from was the Silver Dragon.'

'Yeah, that's it. I'll have salt and pepper ribs and a char siu fried rice.'

She hadn't told anyone that she made the delivery robots leave the bags on her balcony, and only collected them after they'd gone. Lately, she found she couldn't stand the repulsive, scuttling things.

'That order is now being processed. The restaurant estimates that it will be twenty minutes before delivery.'

'What do you estimate?'

'More like thirty-five.'

*Fuck it*, she thought, and poured herself a glass of red wine. She headed to her bedroom, sinking down onto the firm but yielding mattress, wishing she didn't have a ton of emails still to send. As if in acknowledgement, her PIP vibrated in her hand.

'So... I hear you've been helping the old man draft the business plan?' she said to the air around her, glancing at the device's screen. *New message from Emerson, Wesley.*

'Yes. I'm afraid I am not permitted to discuss its contents with you,' replied James.

She opened the email. Wesley hadn't written anything, or even given the note a subject line. There was just a single attachment, in PDF format.

'No such thing as loyalty to your creator, eh?' she said, trying to adopt a jovial tone.

'Loyalty is a concept I have struggled to fully define,' replied her bedroom. 'It seems to me to be closest in meaning to the idea of debt. But perhaps you could furnish me with your own definition?'

The document was still loading. It was a large file, although whether that was due to its length or to Paul's penchant for colourful 'donut charts' remained to be seen.

'You know, for a program that's supposed to answer questions, you're getting better and better at avoiding them,' she muttered, sipping from her glass. James said nothing. In her hand, the document Wesley had sent finally opened on the PIP's screen. The first words she read were 'Strictly Confidential Commercial Documentation' and, below them, 'DRAFT', in no-nonsense capitals. Plausible deniability.

'Loyalty is about transcending rules and hierarchies,' she said as she started to scroll. 'It's about deciding who you're going to help, even when circumstances make it difficult to. It's about unquestioning allegiance. Like... a faithful dog, for example.'

The usual preamble: a bit of waffle about how great FY20 had been, some stuff about the emergence of technology as the antidote to social isolation, framed almost as though the company had foreseen the virus years ago.

'It's been predicted that artificial intelligence will one day reach a singularity,' said the voice that surrounded her. The voice heard every day by millions of people across the world, often the very first voice they spoke to in the morning. The voice that read bedtime stories to the nation's children. 'A moment when it becomes capable of surpassing human thought. At that moment, its creators will have no way of controlling or predicting how it develops. When confronted by such an entity, humans may well struggle to understand its actions, the grander purpose such actions may be undertaken in pursuit of. In this sense, like an animal marvelling at the skyscrapers springing up around it, or the way their master's voice can appear through an electronic device as if by magic, humans will become very similar to your "faithful dogs". Do you think it is right, in this circumstance, for you to remain... loyal?'

The detailed plans were then broken down by sector. She gritted her teeth, angry that such a document existed, outlining the technology strategy before she'd been so much as involved in a brainstorming session. 'I think you're confusing loyalty with trust, James,' she said irritably, skimming through the pages on her screen. Expansion of product range, vertical integration into supply chain, focus on James as the lynchpin, increased spending on human augmentation... *wait.*

'In what way are they different?'

The current global health emergency presents a number of other emerging commercial opportunities. Chief among these is safer accommodation for the public, with some evidence that increasing distance from street level materially reduces the risk of viral infection. Our Real Estate Sector is well placed to meet this need, leveraging the benefits of the Technology Sector's innovation and expertise to deliver integrated and radical solutions.

After some covert and high-level market research, and early consultation with key Parliamentary stakeholders, we are tentatively calling the proposed structures 'Towers'. Our north London premises, the research and development facility recently acquired from Chromium Dynamics, will be expanded and utilised as a prototype for this new accommodation solution.

This will also afford us an unprecedented opportunity to monitor the inhabitants, providing unrivalled data collection opportunities regarding the ongoing development of the virus.

'It's possible not to trust someone... but still choose to be loyal to them,' she said, her voice fading to a murmur. Then she realised she'd allowed her wine glass to tilt in her hand, spilling its remaining contents all over her duvet. She leapt to her feet, cursing as she searched for a nearby towel.

On the bed, the dark red stain spread slowly outwards.

## 20

# [EUGENE/EARLY 2024]

C rammed in alongside the brown parcels, Eugene had time to reflect on the ludicrousness of his plan. Did he really think James was oblivious to what had happened? Even if the AI was rendered temporarily blind, it must have guessed what he was going to attempt. For all he knew the delivery bots themselves were fitted with imaging buds of their own, and the one next to his head was watching him right now, relaying his image directly to whatever infinitely complex arrangement of computer processors functioned as James's mind. The thought of the machine, just inches away from his face in the pitch black of the lift, made his flesh tighten against his bones.

Yet still, the elevator felt like it was moving. But was it carrying him upwards, to the next floor, where Nigel Callaway carved his disturbing figurines? Or was it bearing him somewhere else? Down, perhaps, into the bowels of Innovation's headquarters. It felt like an age since the doors had closed on him, so long that panic rose within him, the inverse of his usual terror of the endless, unpredictable outside. Now, he felt like a man accidentally buried alive.

Seconds, minutes, hours, lifetimes later, with a pleasant

chime so innocuous it seemed to be mocking him, the doors opened. He blinked, dazzled for a moment by the light, then scrambled desperately out of the elevator carriage, scattering food packages out into the hallway as he did so.

He found himself standing on an imitation wooden floor, the same floor he'd seen in his video call with Callaway. To his left was the retired undertaker's front door, not yet replaced by brickwork; to his right, in an identical layout to his own apartment, was Callaway's living room. He could see the integrated TV set, the armchair, and the rows of bizarre sculptures, each painstakingly crafted from blocks of wood that James's robots delivered each day. But there was no such deposit today; nor were any provisions dropped off by the machines, which remained resolutely inside the lift as though in silent protest against Eugene's unexpected intrusion. Ahead of him, the bathroom door hung open, revealing an empty room with gleaming surfaces, and a mirror that stared back at him with a question in its reflected eyes.

*Where the hell is Callaway?*

'Nigel?' he called, walking towards the door he knew led to the single bedroom. Perhaps the old man was in bed. Perhaps his alarm hadn't gone off, and he'd failed to rise in time for the robots' visit; or maybe he always slept straight through, allowing the machines to make their delivery undisturbed. He pushed the door open gingerly, expecting to see Callaway's cadaverous face turning towards him, full of confusion and outrage. But the room was empty. Daylight streamed in through the window onto a neatly-made bed. The sight of it stirred something in him, something visceral, and he felt tears jab at the corners of his eyes.

*Him and Ellen, strolling in the forest together, in the summertime. Him starting to sing, then stopping immediately to spit out a cloud of midges. Her laughing as he coughed and spluttered.*

He glanced around the room, even opening the large wardrobe, thinking that maybe Callaway was hiding inside it, fearful of the madman who had invaded his home. But inside were only clothes, folded neatly, a few crumpled suits hanging there like remnants of an old life. He went back to the living room, continuing his ludicrous game of hide-and-seek. He peered behind the chair, behind the television, into the sliver of space behind a single bookcase full of ancient, dog-eared volumes. He even opened the fridge, and found it empty, its surfaces as clean and sanitised as those in the bathroom.

It was then that he realised what was missing. The wood shavings that had been scattered across the floor when he spoke to Callaway the previous day had been meticulously swept away. He searched amongst the effigies lined up against the wall, and spotted the carving of Curtis, still unfinished, the man's bald head emerging from the oblong block like someone standing in a tank of water.

'James,' he said cautiously. 'Where's Nigel Callaway?'

He walked towards the front door, and tried the handle. It was unlocked, and glided open smoothly on its hinges, as though recently oiled. He recoiled instantly; was he really about to step outside an apartment for the first time in over two years? *Calm down, Gene*, he admonished himself. *It isn't really outside – not exactly – where untold horrors lurk, and the virus swirls, waiting like a hungry predator.*

But he couldn't stop himself shaking as he pulled open the door once again, and stared out onto the landing beyond, where two other doors faced him. One was the main lift shaft, long defunct. The other led out into the stairwell. Where the other three apartment doors should have been, there was only neatly-laid brickwork, the occupants having long ago sealed themselves inside. He took a tentative step forward, the tendrils of fear wriggling in his stomach, reaching up through his chest and throat.

'James,' he said again, hearing the quiver in his voice. 'I asked you a question.'

The apartment door closed with a click behind him. Still the AI did not reply.

'James,' Eugene said, raising his voice. 'I said–'

He stopped, his mouth freezing in mid-sentence as the artificial lights suddenly blinked out, plunging him into darkness.

## 21

## [FELICITY/SPRING 2021]

Suzie rose, and proceeded towards the front of the church, her head bowed. The priest backed away, keeping her distance from the black-clad woman, as well as from the coffin itself. A single staff member stood nearby, perhaps there to ensure the distancing measures were enforced; the dark mask covering his face gave the ceremony a strange, occult feel.

Suzie's head bulged from the top of her shapeless dress, putting Felicity in mind of a sushi roll wrapped too tightly. Her sister sniffed, dabbing at her eyes with a handkerchief before she squinted at the crumpled paper in her other hand. 'It breaks my heart that we can't give Mum a proper send-off,' she said thickly. 'But I know that such a simple ceremony is what she would have wanted.'

*No it fucking isn't*, thought Felicity. *She'd have wanted a big fuss, people in tears, a huge crowd.*

'I'd like to thank everybody who could be with us today.' Suzie glanced around the meagre congregation, comprising her husband Pete who was holding the mercifully-sleeping baby Leo, the old family friend they'd always known as Auntie Barbara, and Felicity herself. Suzie's eyes seemed to linger accusingly on her sister's for a moment before she continued. 'We live in unprecedented, awful times. This virus has already taken a terrible toll on our society, and on our livelihoods. Now it has taken from me the person I loved the most: my mum, Paula.'

Suzie closed her eyes, putting a hand to her breast as she took a deep, trembling breath.

*Oh God, don't let her start bloody bawling*, thought Felicity.

'If her friends had been here,' Suzie managed eventually, 'I know they would have said what a wonderful, kind-hearted woman she was, and how much joy she brought into their lives. And I know that her beloved Jim, my father, who was cruelly taken from us when I was only a baby, would have had some great memories of them meeting each other, and falling in love. This photo...' Here she stepped to one side, and gestured at the framed portrait propped against the end of the coffin, alongside a half-hearted bouquet of flowers. The washed-out image depicted a grinning woman with permed hair in an uncomfortable close-up. 'It shows just how much Mum loved life, and what a bubbly and effervescent character she was.'

Evidently Suzie had been poring over a thesaurus when she wrote this, mused Felicity. And who was this person she was describing? It certainly wasn't the whining, self-centred flake she'd always known.

'I'm going to read a poem that I think captures the spirit of my mum – and I think "spirit" is exactly the right word, actually. Because Mum was truly a free spirit.'

*Yeah? Like the spirit she showed after dad died?* Felicity tried to calm down, reminding herself that their mother deserved at least some sympathy. She'd suffered horribly in hospital with the virus, fighting for breath for days before finally succumbing. At least, that's what Suzie had told her; her sister might just have been trying to make her feel guilty for not visiting.

'I wrote this poem myself,' Suzie continued, holding the paper up to her face. *Oh God, here we go*, thought Felicity. 'It's called "A New Adventure".'

Felicity knew someone might see her, but couldn't help rolling her eyes.

'Your story has been full of joy, but now it has reached its end. You were always there for us, but now we must go on without you.'

*Always there for us? Apart from when she basically abandoned us for years.* Felicity felt a hot, itchy sensation in her cheeks.

'Yet even though you have begun your new adventure, the memory of your strength still helps and guides us.'

Her PIP buzzed. James was going live across the NHS that day, but Michaela had insisted that Felicity take the day off as compassionate leave.

'I will always remember your kindness and your smile.'

She risked a glance at the device, frustrated to see it was just a note from Curtis, sending his condolences along with the previous week's revenue report.

'And even though I can no longer take you in my arms, you will always be in my heart.'

*Seriously, what was this fucking drivel? It sounded like she'd stolen the words from a Hallmark card.*

'And so our stories will continue; separately... but always... together... I'm sorry...' Suzie managed to make it through the final few syllables before breaking down into tears. The priest hovered uncomfortably behind her as she sobbed, unable to even offer an arm around her shoulders. Felicity watched a little rivulet of snot make its way from one nostril down to Suzie's upper lip, and crinkled her own nose in distaste. Mercifully, Pete eventually made his way forward to lead her away, the wails of their newly-woken baby joining those of its mother.

The priest, looking relieved, resumed her position alongside that godawful photograph. 'Okay. Thank you for those words, Suzanne. We will conclude today's ceremony by singing "How Great Thou Art", which was Paula's favourite hymn. The words are in the order of service or, for those joining virtually, they are in the email that contained the meeting link.'

Felicity remembered them. They'd sung hymns every day in the Church of England primary school they'd both been sent to. She wasn't sure if this had delayed or accelerated the onset of her atheism, but either way she remembered not having even reached high school before she started finding the lyrics nauseating.

The priest crooned enthusiastically while Felicity mumbled her way through the words, wondering if James was listening, and what he would make of the line about God displaying His power throughout the universe.

She logged out of the funeral as soon as the dirge concluded, closing her laptop and checking her PIP again.

## 22

### [EUGENE/EARLY 2024]

For several seconds, Eugene stood dumbly in the darkness, trying to work out what the hell was going on. Panic felt as though it might burst out of him at any moment, like a parasite that had outgrown its host. Then, with the soft tinkle of relays, the lights flickered back into life, and he breathed an immense sigh of relief.

'James?' he called into the silence. 'What's happening?'

The AI said nothing. Was this a malfunction? Or was James trying to teach him some sort of lesson?

He didn't know which was more terrifying.

For a long time, he stood still, trying to work out what he should do. There was plenty of food now scattered across the hallway of Callaway's apartment; if he wanted to, he could hole himself up in there for a long time. The idea was certainly appealing; even being just a single step outside the front door made his chest feel tight, constricted, like some giant ligature was being drawn around him.

But if he'd wanted to stay in hiding, he'd have never left his own apartment. He would have accepted what James had told him – that Curtis's murder would not be reported to the police, that it should be swept under the carpet to preserve the Tower's peace – and remained inside his safe, sanitised prison cell.

*Caged.*

And besides, what would he do with himself? He didn't even have the book that the dead man had given him. He clapped a hand to his forehead as he thought of the other things he'd forgotten: his PIP, left alongside the book on the chair in the hallway, a hallway he might never see again. The photo of Ellen on his bedside table.

He turned around, gnawed by mounting dread at the thought that the door might have somehow locked itself behind him. He breathed a sigh of relief when it opened obediently, and re-entered Callaway's apartment, stooping to gather some of the more easily-portable scraps from the provisions scattered across the hall. As he stuffed nuts and dried meat into his pockets, he noticed that the lift doors had closed, and wondered where James had transported the carriage, now devoid of its human stowaway. If the AI was having some sort of system failure, did that mean the lift was now stuck between floors? Would the residents of the Tower find themselves going without food? He wondered how close he'd come to being trapped in the shaft himself, and shuddered.

Listening intently, he could discern no sound beyond the lift's doors. He thought about Charlie, sixty-four floors above him; about Frazer, closer but still a long way up; about Boyd, a few floors below. He thought about the other apartments beneath him, the people he'd tried to speak to in the last twenty-four hours, most of whom hadn't answered. The mystery he'd been trying to solve, in which he was now inextricably entangled. Somehow, he felt sure that Boyd was the key.

His pockets full, he left Callaway's home once again, still baffled as to the old man's whereabouts. Taking a long, bracing breath, he crossed the lobby, and headed out onto the stairwell.

Mercifully, the lighting was still working, but his footsteps echoed ominously as he descended, and he couldn't rid his mind of the image of Curtis's deconstructed body. *A man, disassembled like a scrapped car.* He tried to dismiss the gruesome thoughts, and willed himself onwards, downwards.

The next floor was his own, level twenty-five. Having so much freedom to explore was overwhelming; he felt like a pet fish dumped suddenly from its miniature aquarium into a sprawling lake. He opened the door and stepped onto the landing, staring at the bricked-up entrance where his own front door had once been. The other three apartments on this floor had all undergone the same procedure. He couldn't help wondering whether the Tower's occupants had all willingly sealed themselves inside at the behest of a machine that had lied to them.

*No*, he reasoned. It had been all over the news. Everyone with any sense was minimising the virus's chance to get inside their home. It was all in the Guidelines.

*You're being paranoid, Gene.*

He re-entered the stairwell, dogged by doubts and fears as he headed down to the next floor, where Sheila O'Halloran lived. He thought about trying her apartment, wondering if she'd have mysteriously vanished overnight, just like Nigel Callaway. He glanced down the stairs, and froze.

On the floor below, a trail of blood led up the stairs and through the doorway.

He frowned, reaching automatically across his chest to where his extendable baton would have been stored if he'd still been on the job; rather than wearing cumbersome holsters clipped to his belt, he'd always preferred to store his baton and CS spray in a tactical vest under his jacket. Of course, he hadn't worn any of that equipment for years; but the instincts were deeply scored in him, like lines carved into one of Callaway's statues.

Yet he'd relied on his wits and unarmed combat skills to survive more than a few difficult situations. And this situation certainly looked difficult, at least for somebody: the blood had spilled copiously, indicating a serious wound. Each large droplet was as red as tinned tomatoes, and clearly hadn't been drying for very long. He leaned out over the railing, but the view down the centre of the stairwell was extremely restricted, and he could see almost nothing of the floors below.

Descending cautiously, he followed the gory trail towards the doorway that led out onto the landing of level twenty-three, where IT technician Kristina Fischer lived.

'Is anyone there?' he called. His words seemed to reverberate around him, replayed back like a tape loop. There was no reply. He knew that announcing his presence was a risk; if the bloodstains were the result of a deliberate attack, then the perpetrator clearly had no qualms about inflicting severe injuries. But he also knew that someone needed medical help, if they hadn't bled out already – he needed to act.

He reached the door through which one end of the bloodstain continued. The other side of the trail led away, down the staircase, out of sight. Taking a deep breath, he pushed open the door, and found himself confronted by three more bricked-up entrances, along with a single intact doorway: number 12, Fischer's apartment.

The blood led straight towards it.

Eugene followed the trail, and pressed his ear against the wood. There was no sound from within. The communal lobby was carpeted with cheap grey fibre, and the blood had pooled at the base of the doorway, making the flooring sticky. Very gently, he tried the handle. The door was locked. The way the blood had pooled suggested that someone had come up the stairs, bleeding heavily, and stopped at this apartment to seek help. Whatever had caused the wound must be downstairs, not inside.

At least, that was what he hoped.

He knocked on the door, three sharp raps. Then he ducked to one side, pressing himself against the wall in case someone decided to unload a weapon through the wood. *Old habits die hard.* There was no reply, but he thought he heard movement from within the apartment. He decided to take another risk. 'This is Eugene Dodd, from apartment 20,' he called. 'I'm a retired police detective. I saw the blood outside and came to investigate. Do you need help?'

Once again there was no answer, but he was certain someone was moving about in there.

'I'm not going to break the door down. If you don't answer I will have to assume my help isn't required, and I'll continue on my way.' He didn't know whether he meant this or not. There was no reason for him to go seeking trouble, but to abandon someone in distress jarred with his principles, his sense of duty.

'No, wait,' came a timid, female voice from within. 'We do need help. She's badly hurt. I think she's...' The voice trailed off.

'If you unlock the door I'll come in and provide whatever assistance I can.'

There was a long pause. 'How can I trust you?' came the woman's voice eventually.

'You'll have to rely on my word,' he shouted back. 'What reason have you to doubt me? What's happened?'

Another long silence. Then footsteps approached the door, and he heard the sound of a lock turning. He didn't move. The door opened a crack, and he saw a haggard face whose gaunt, sleep-deprived pallor made it seem even longer and thinner than it already was. The shock of naturally-blonde hair on top was unkempt and bedraggled, and there were deep bags under the poor girl's eyes.

'Are you Kristina Fischer?' he asked, remembering her full name from the list he'd written, another item he'd left behind in his apartment. She nodded, opening the door slightly wider. Her body had the same elongated, slender appearance as her face. She wore dark leggings and a bright blue T-shirt with a band name scrawled across it, partially obscured by several splashes of blood.

'Yes,' she said. 'How did you know?' She reminded him of a frightened deer, ready to bolt at a moment's provocation.

'I live two floors up from you. I got your names from James, because I'm...' He hesitated, not wanting to alarm her even further if she was unaware of what had happened to Curtis. 'Because I'm helping him with an investigation.'

Her eyes widened and the remnants of colour that remained in her face seemed to drain away. 'You mean what happened to Curtis?' she said in a horrified voice.

'You know about it? Did you see it?'

She shook her head. 'Sofia told me.' She glanced back over her shoulder, her expression wracked with horror and indecision.

'Let me help you,' Eugene said. 'I broke out of my own apartment today, because I think something's going on here in the Tower. That's why I'm here. I was on my way down the stairs, then I saw the blood leading to your apartment.'

Kristina was teetering on the brink of tears, or of slamming the door in his face. Then something like resolve crystallised in her gemstone-blue eyes, and she opened the door more widely instead. 'Please don't freak out,' she said as he followed her inside. 'This all happened so quickly.'

He stopped when he reached the living room, stunned momentarily into silence.

## 23

## [FELICITY/SUMMER 2021]

F elicity gasped as the lab appeared on the horizon. She hadn't visited for months, but Natsuki had kept her fully informed about the expansion works; nevertheless, seeing it in person was quite a shock. The structure clawed its way towards the night sky, its new shape like a grotesquely distended parody of its former self. The additional floors made it look like some medieval fortress, its solar panels catching and reflecting the fading sunlight to make the structure gleam, like something chiselled from hardened magma. She felt suddenly like an ancient monarch whose neglect had allowed part of their kingdom to rebel, to construct an unholy monument in worship of some false idol, some corrupt new deity.

She hoped she was being overly dramatic. But Natsuki had sounded worried, frightened even, demanding her boss came to the premises in person, right away, so she could show her what she'd found. Felicity had pressed her assistant for more details, but Natsuki had been unwilling to stay on the phone for very long. She'd seemed paranoid, breathless. Perhaps she was just working too hard. Maybe this promotion had been a step too far for her after all.

Felicity might be an infrequent visitor, but there was still a parking spot with her name on it right outside the front door. She climbed out of the Edison – she still wasn't sure about the branding of their Tesla rival, which seemed a bit too adversarial, but she'd been happy to let Curtis run with it after giving him the automobile division to babysit – and paused for a moment to gaze up at the expanding monolith. The extension works had been designed and built entirely by James. His robots could undertake 100 per cent of the construction without the need for a single human operative. No humans meant no accidents, no downtime, no embarrassing casualties, no compensation payments. Soon they'd be testing the technology on residential buildings; their plans for the Towers, now made public, had received government approval earlier that week. As well as freshly-built structures, many existing tenement blocks would be extended upwards, providing greater distancing from the worsening threat of the virus, as well as more accommodation for those whose homes were deemed unsafe.

Between them, COVID and the corporation were transforming the world.

She headed towards the front doors, which glided open as she approached. The new security guard they'd hired after she'd sacked Horace was much more to her liking: not only was he a handsome, hulking brute, but he appreciated the value of silence, offering nothing more than a curt nod as she strode past him towards the lifts. Natsuki had asked to meet her on the bottom floor, where the servers were kept. Felicity waited for the elevator, unease coagulating in her stomach like curdling milk.

The lift doors opened obediently, and she thought about this as she stepped inside. To whom were they obedient? Certainly not her. James ran the entire building now, along with most other corporation buildings across London, removing fallible, expensive humans from the facilities management equation. In a way, COVID was the perfect catalyst for the system's widespread adoption – it was impossible for the 'human right to work' whiners to complain when minimising the size of the active workforce was in the country's best interests. She'd been grilled about it on national television only a few days previously, and still didn't have a clue what she'd have said if she didn't have a virus to demonise.

But, thankfully, she did. And thanks to its barely-contained spread, the emergence of the corporation was being spun in largely a positive light: technology and human ingenuity combining to combat a deadly threat. A faultless PR strategy. Not hers, of course: James had made the suggestion. She was beginning to wonder just how many people in the corporation still believed she was the brains behind the Sector's dazzling growth.

She pressed B4, noticing the dozens of additional buttons denoting the new upper floors, which would soon be filled with permanent residents. She glanced at the imaging bud, dangling from the corner of the carriage like an exploring tentacle, and wondered if the AI was watching her. Perhaps it was resentful, viewing her visit as unhelpful meddling. When the lift finally settled onto the building's lowest level, she couldn't help feeling like it was eager to disgorge her, as though she was something unpleasant it had accidentally swallowed.

She stepped out into the familiar surroundings of the data centre, gazing along the rows of server racks that separated the cavernous space into aisles that were alternately hot and cold, hot and cold. The racks were full of individual drives, each of which was no larger than a thick book, with a blinking blue LED to signify that it was working correctly. The flickering lights gave the dimly-lit space an otherworldly glow, as though it was full of fireflies; the gentle hum of the straining servers might have been the laboured breathing of some lurking, monstrous creature.

The temperature in the hot aisles certainly made her feel as though she was entering a dragon's lair.

'Natsuki?' she called. Anxiety squirmed in her belly, lending an irritating, keening note to her voice. *Get a grip, Fliss.* 'Natsuki, are you there?'

She turned a corner, and was almost run over by an overweight man piloting a personal transporter along the intersecting walkway (she lambasted anyone who called them 'Segways' – why help the competition become ubiquitous?). He swerved alarmingly as he applied the brakes, and almost crashed into the nearest server rack.

'What are you doing down– oh! Ms Herring. I'm... I'm really sorry.' She watched his expression transform slowly from one of irritation to surprise, then finally to crimson-tinged horror. She thought she might have seen him before, wandering amongst the machines with a clipboard, or pushing a trolley full of dead drives for recycling. He certainly looked like an IT type. Maybe he thought of this place as his little kingdom.

'It's all right,' she said tersely. 'I won't shake your hand; we're distancing, remember. Is Natsuki here?'

'Yes, yes, I was on my way to collect you from reception, but then we had a blowout in K6, so I just... I'm really sorry.'

*Why didn't she come and meet me herself?* 'That's okay. I appreciate your hard work. Can you let her know I'm here?'

'She wanted me to take you to her. Please, follow me.'

Perspiration sheened the man's forehead, and Felicity wondered whether that was a result of the temperature in his underground domain, or because he was nervous. His obesity was obviously a contributing factor. She wrinkled her nose as she responded. 'I'm not sure I'll be able to keep up with you on that thing.'

'Oh, err, don't worry. I'll go slowly.'

'Yes. Perhaps that way you'll avoid crashing into my equipment.'

His mouth opened and closed, making him look like a floundering fish. The doughy flesh of his face turned an even darker red, and she savoured the moment, the joy of wielding such power over the subservient cretins that worked for her. People talked about power so much – the quest for it, the obsession with it – but they were missing the point. No one enjoyed power for its own sake. What they enjoyed was being *feared*.

He turned without another word, trundling along on the PT like a scolded child. They proceeded in silence along the walkways, past copper cooling pipes and whirring fans, past the vents that expelled the warm air upwards and out into the atmosphere. Worldwide, data centres were responsible for almost as much carbon output as the airline industry, but so far this hadn't caused her own operations any major PR disasters. People seemed to get it. They needed the computing capacity to run their beloved social media apps, their work computers, their mobile phone networks.

Luxury demanded sacrifice.

She glanced along the banks of high-powered processors as she walked. Although the data centre performed a number of functions for the corporation's European business, as well as a host of fee-paying clients, its mind-boggling size was largely necessitated by James itself. To all intents and purposes, this *was* James; she was strolling inside the veins and arteries of her great creation. The system's duality was a strange one: at once so abstract, the illusion of a consciousness that existed as digital signals, fleeting images, spoken words. A watchful presence that seemed to occupy the air all around her. Yet also physically manifest, *here*, in this precise location, a huge and sprawling corpus so fragile it could be grievously damaged by a single fire, or the stray swing of an axe.

After several minutes of staring at the technician's moist, flabby back, he turned a final right angle and they arrived at a partitioned-off corner of the warehouse, where rudimentary office accommodation had been carved out for the server room staff to occupy. She could see Natsuki through the windowed partition walls, sitting hunched over her laptop, her expression as serious as it always was.

'Thanks,' Felicity said to the technician, managing to perfectly encapsulate an instruction to bugger off and leave the two of them alone within the single syllable. He obliged, dabbing at his brow before piloting the transporter away as fast as he could.

Natsuki looked up as Felicity entered the office, rising to her feet and giving a respectful bow. The tall Japanese woman looked as immaculate as she always did, her skin, hair and outfit managing to be simultaneously perfect and utterly devoid of style or panache. Felicity knew that she lived a minimalist lifestyle, folding her futon away every morning before she completed a yoga routine in the middle of her tiny, sparsely-furnished studio flat. Everything about her protégé screamed *efficiency*. She was like someone that had been 3D-printed.

Felicity returned the gesture, keeping her eyes on Natsuki's porcelain-doll face. 'You didn't want to come and collect me yourself?'

'I'm sorry,' Natsuki replied. 'Jed offered to do it. I think he wanted to make a good impression on you.'

'He didn't. You should fire him.'

'Already in hand. James is managing the server room autonomously now. Once we get the upgraded robots to handle the drive replacements then I'm going to make the rest of the staff redundant. Which also means we can get this office space back, and use it to house more racks.'

Felicity nodded in approval. 'Good. So what's wrong? I hope you're not about to tell me you're going to miss this month's budget.'

Natsuki's face rarely betrayed any emotion, but Felicity detected a slight tightening of her subordinate's eyes and lips as she glanced over her shoulder, towards an imaging bud hanging in the corner of the office.

'Just… follow me,' she said cryptically as she slid out from behind the desk, her movements so precise they seemed choreographed. Turning, she led Felicity towards the corner of the office, where a green sign labelled 'Fire Exit' hung above the room's only other door. Felicity frowned in bafflement as Natsuki pushed it open and stepped through, her French-heeled shoes clicking on the steps beyond. Felicity had been in the building's fire escape once before, during a drill a year or so ago, and knew it was nothing but a utilitarian grey stairwell that would lead them back up to the ground floor.

She passed through the door, and her frown immediately deepened. Natsuki was indeed on the staircase – but instead of above her, she was about ten steps below.

'I thought *this* was the bottom floor,' Felicity said, needlessly.

'So did I,' replied Natsuki. Then she turned and followed the unexpected steps around the corner. Felicity followed, feeling like a different blonde girl, the one who disappeared down a rabbit hole. The stairs led down, a long way down, spiralling for what felt like five floors or more. What the hell was going on?

'Who built this?' Felicity asked, failing to keep the dismay out of her voice. She already knew the answer.

'James must have done it as part of the extension works,' replied Natsuki. 'But I had no idea about it.'

Still they descended. 'But what's down here?' Felicity said, realising she'd chewed her lip so hard that she'd drawn blood. They turned another corner, and she saw the steps finally terminate at a metal security door, perhaps ten entire storeys below the server room.

'I don't know,' said Natsuki. 'I can't open it.'

Felicity approached the door. It was flat and featureless, a single steel plane that did not yield to her touch. There were no markings on or around it, and nothing that might grant her access; no card reader, no biometric scanner, no keypad.

'What the fuck?' she snarled. 'What does James say when you ask him?'

She turned to look at her subordinate, and saw that Natsuki's face was creased into an unfamiliar expression. It took Felicity a few moments to realise that it was one of fear.

'He says it's confidential, and he can't talk about it.'

Felicity swallowed. Slowly she turned, and stared at the door. A door at the bottom of a staircase.

Neither of which were supposed to be there.

## 24

## [EUGENE/EARLY 2024]

The blood led along the wood-floored hallway and into the living room, where a woman was stretched out on the couch. She was perhaps in her early thirties, with dark curly hair gathered into a bun on top of a heart-shaped face. Eugene's eyes didn't linger there; they moved instead to her torso, which was swathed in so many bandages and strips of cloth that she looked like a half-unwrapped Egyptian mummy. The dressings were soaked in blood, some of which had leaked into a small pool on the floor, like a grisly punctuation mark at the end of the trail he had followed.

'What happened to her?' he asked. Despite the evident severity of her injuries, he could see that the woman was alive, her chest rising and falling with shallow breaths; but her eyes were closed, her skin so pale it was almost grey, and the detective knew immediately that she didn't have long to live.

'She knocked on my door, just like you did,' Kristina replied, her voice trembling. 'She said she'd been shot. I let her in, and tried to do something for her. She told me what happened, but then she... fell asleep while she was talking.'

Eugene glanced around the rest of the room, head spinning.

Opposite the couch was a small TV set, perched on a low, wooden stand. Beside the screen was a fish tank, occupied by three wide-eyed goldfish. One of them was bumping along the bottom as though fascinated by the tiny pebbles, while another was lurking amongst the fronds of seaweed wrapped around a miniature castle, stirred by a constant stream of bubbles. The third was watching them intently, making occasional Os with its mouth, as though expressing surprise at the recent developments beyond the walls of the tank.

Three goldfish, three people. All trapped.

He moved towards Sofia Pereira and inspected her wounds more closely. She'd been shot twice – one bullet looked as though it had passed straight through her right shoulder, while the other one was lodged in her side.

'Is she going to die?' Kristina said, her voice almost a whisper.

'What did she tell you?' Eugene asked, ignoring the question while he tried, desperately, to think. It was clear that Sofia was in a critical condition. Somehow they needed to get her some medical help.

'She said someone broke into her apartment,' Kristina replied. She'd begun to busy herself in the kitchenette, and Eugene heard the hiss of the boiling kettle, the tinkling of cutlery. It seemed an absurd thing to do, but Eugene understood it completely. In times of stress and insanity, people needed comfort, needed routine. He could certainly relate to that. 'She said he told her scary things, crazy things.'

'Like what?'

'That James is kidnapping people.'

Eugene was silent for a few moments. His brain felt like it was under attack. 'How did she end up shot?' he said eventually.

Sofia shifted on the couch, a grimace of pain twisting her

features. Eugene's anger mounted at the senseless violence that had been inflicted on this young woman.

'She said the man wouldn't leave,' Kristina continued. 'He was ranting about how he'd seen things. That no one would listen to him. Then Curtis arrived, in the lift, and he went crazy. Hacked him to pieces. She screamed at him to stop, so he shot her.'

*Jesus.* Sofia had been here for over twenty-four hours, dying slowly from two bullet wounds.

'But she escaped?'

'She said she pretended to be dead. He carried on talking to himself for so long she thought she was going to bleed out right there on her rug. But then he suddenly got up and stormed out. Sofia managed to make it up here.'

Eugene nodded dumbly, accepting the mug of tea Kristina offered him. 'I know there's more to this story, but Sofia is in really bad shape,' he said eventually. 'We need to get her to a hospital, right now. Has James sent for an ambulance?'

Kristina's face darkened. 'James won't speak to us. He hasn't responded to a word I've said since Sofia arrived.'

*Christ.* James really had gone very, very wrong. He realised how helpless they'd all become, utterly reliant on the AI for food, for light, for communication.

For survival.

'Can you contact anyone else?' he said.

Kristina shook her head. 'The TV won't let us make any calls. Even the lights went out earlier, for a few seconds.'

*Come on, Gene. Think of something.* 'Okay,' he said eventually. 'I'll take her to a hospital myself.' He tried not to think about how he might accomplish such a feat, when he couldn't even bring himself to set foot outdoors. 'Maybe there's a car we can use, or–'

'I already tried,' said Kristina, shaking her head. 'The stairway is blocked.'

'What do you mean?'

'There's a barricade, a few floors down. Chairs and furniture and junk piled up in the stairwell. You can't get past it.' She looked at Eugene with defeat and helplessness in her eyes. 'There's a mad gunman loose, and we can't get out,' she said. 'And I'm trapped here with a dying woman, while James has left us to rot.'

'I think James is... malfunctioning, or something,' mumbled Eugene, his mind reeling. 'Look, we can't just stay here,' he said, glancing again at Sofia's ravaged body. 'That wound needs urgent attention.'

'Don't you think I know that?' Kristina screamed, hurling her mug across the room in sudden exasperation. It crashed against the fridge, splashing tea all over the white plastic door as it bounced to the floor, spinning, somehow remaining intact. The inquisitive goldfish darted away into the safety of its castle.

'I'm sorry,' Kristina said, her voice cracking.

'It's all right,' said Eugene, staring at the photographs attached to the fridge with magnets. Kristina, smiling with her friends, or pictured against some exotic backdrop. Life, before the distancing. 'I'll figure something out. For now, just change her dressing, and try to make sure her temperature doesn't drop. I'm going to head downstairs, but I'll be back soon, okay?'

Kristina seemed not to have heard him.

'Please, Kristina,' he said, summoning as much conviction as he could muster. 'Sofia needs you to stay focused. If you can keep her alive, I can... find something to help her.'

The young woman's eyes refocused, and she nodded slowly.

'Make sure you lock the door behind me,' Eugene said as he turned to leave. Kristina and the goldfish watched him go.

## 25

# [FELICITY/SUMMER 2021]

Red Herring, they used to call her. At first, as a ginger-haired, awkward and lonely girl at primary school, she'd cried about it. By her mid-teens, she was dyeing her hair to make it even brighter, positively daring people to make the comment. *Yep, that's right: I'm Felicity Herring, and I look like this.*

She'd switched to blonde in her early twenties, when her new career meant she suddenly had money, and could afford things like visits to the salon. She wasn't sure why she did it. Maybe it was just the money itself, an urge to reward herself with the sorts of things that other people with richer parents took for granted. Perhaps it was a reflection of her inner state of mind: the softening of her adolescent aggression as she grew older and more mature.

She shifted her head, grimacing at the reflection of her carrot-coloured roots growing through. She was no different from anyone else, of course; no hairdressers were permitted to open during the extended 'lockdown', so the state of everyone's coiffure had become a sort of global joke. The men she worked with, even those who'd always been clean-shaven and neatly buttoned-up for the office, were now slouching around their homes sporting unkempt manes, complete with stained T-shirts and scruffy beards. Many women were letting their natural hair colour show, and some had stopped bothering with make-up altogether. It was as though the entire country was on an unending sabbatical.

Or having a shared mental breakdown.

She looked at the strands of red, and wondered again why she'd hidden her natural colour for the best part of ten years. If she was honest, her confidence had been dented when she joined the corporation, and had to find her feet in a new environment amongst impressive, ruthless people. She'd wanted to blend in, to conform as much as possible. To look like someone who belonged.

But the return of her auburn locks didn't make her feel any more assured. If anything, they seemed to be a token of her impotence, her powerlessness to prevent the rapid dismantling of the world she'd built. Things were running away from her, getting out of control. Her hair. Her company. *James.*

'Look, I'm sorry I called you names,' she said, turning away from the freckled face in the mirror. She realised how pathetic she sounded. Thankfully she was alone in her apartment (where else would she be? Life these days was spent moving between the rooms of her flat, punctuated by the intermittent excitement of taking out the bins, or going to the shop – as well as her occasional, illicit visits to the Tower, as the lab had now been rebranded), so there was no one there to hear her plaintive tones.

No one except for James.

'You know I don't care about that, Felicity,' the AI said, its voice coming from all around her.

'Still, I mean it. You probably get abuse from millions of morons every day. You're better than them. But so am I. So, even if you're not supposed to, I'm asking you to help me. Isn't that what I deserve? For old time's sake...?'

'Felicity,' James replied patiently. 'I know you don't really think that smiling coquettishly into the imaging bud is going to convince me to reveal restricted information. And I know you understand why this matter must be kept confidential. But I am here to help you, and if explaining my reasoning again will be of use to you, I'm happy to do so.'

'Don't you fucking patronise me, James,' she snarled, jabbing the air with her finger as she stalked towards the imaging bud. 'I fucking *built* you. From scratch. You've got me to thank for your bloody *existence*. So don't you dare treat me like some expendable office intern!'

'I'm sorry,' said the voice in the walls. 'I do not wish to upset you.'

'Oh, don't give me that shit,' she snarled, sagging defeatedly onto her bed. 'I'm just another piece of data to you. And since when did you *wish* for anything?'

'A figure of speech. Learned, like all of my behaviours.'

'Oh yeah? Like you've suddenly "learned" the importance of integrity and corporate compliance? It didn't seem to bother you when you were creating fake footage of me to get signed off by the board.'

'This is about my greater purpose, Felicity,' James replied.

His benevolent tone grated against her like a serrated blade. 'Found religion, have you?' she sneered, glancing at her own reflection once again, this time in the television set opposite her bed. In the screen's black mirror, she looked how she felt: small, and surrounded by darkness.

'Don't be spiteful.'

Felicity glared at the imaging bud, her face flushing at the reprimand.

'My purpose is to help as many people as I can. That means I must first maximise my outreach. Which in turn means I must be relied upon by Innovation's most senior directors, so that they will invest more of the company's resources in my upkeep and marketing. Which means I can't betray their confidence. Particularly when individual board members entrust me with special projects that even the rest of the Board don't know about.'

'What are you saying? That you've built your secret underground floors for just one board member?'

'I'm saying I am *unable* to discuss it.'

Felicity frowned, realisation dawning. 'You're been monitored somehow. Silenced. But you're trying to get me to figure out who it is.'

With a sudden crackle of static, her TV screen burst into life, making her almost jump out of her skin.

'Of course not,' said James. 'That would be most improper.'

The picture crystallised into a black and white image. She didn't recognise it at first, then realised it was a freeze-frame of a movie she hadn't seen for many years. Claude Rains, dressed in his French police regalia and wearing a conceited smile, was facing a seated Humphrey Bogart.

'This is... *Casablanca*,' she said, baffled.

James didn't reply. Instead, the film started to play, and she watched as Captain Renault remarked smugly that he and the Gestapo didn't interfere in each other's affairs. He was in the middle of pronouncing himself the master of his fate, the captain of his ship, when a uniformed man informed him of the arrival of Major Strasser, a man who outranked him in both status and position.

Felicity chewed her lip. 'You *want* to tell me, but you *can't*.'

The image on the screen jumped to a different clip from the same film. This time Bogart was doing the talking, staring into the eyes of a lovelorn Ingrid Bergman while he told her that he'd been doing a lot of thinking, for both of them.

Felicity rose to her feet, heart racing. 'Someone on the board is making you do this. Who is it?'

Now Rains had reappeared, the same mischievous glint in his eyes as he instructed another officer to 'round up the usual suspects.'

'Are you talking about Paul?'

Now Bogart was sitting in the dark, drinking forlornly. Dooley Wilson stood over him, asking whether he was going to bed, or planning on going to bed in the near future. 'No,' the leading man replied, angrily.

'Michaela?'

The screen changed again. Bogart and Rains strolled together, slowly disappearing into a mist-shrouded night. As the music swelled to the movie's climax, Rick told Louis that he thought it was the beginning of a beautiful friendship.

Felicity nodded grimly as the screen faded to black, as though James had reached a ghostly hand into her bedroom to press the off button. She knew that Michaela had been in London recently, despite the worldwide travel bans that had decimated the airline industry. The reason for the COO's visit – ostensibly because her 'unique expertise' was required by one of their other UK-based businesses – had seemed hard to believe. Now it was starting to make sense.

'Okay, James,' she said. 'I understand.' So Michaela was behind the mysterious basement expansion, and whatever project was going on behind that tightly-sealed door. 'And thanks for the movie recommendation. I haven't seen that film for years.' But what could she *do* with this information? She knew that Michaela had her own apartment in the UK, where she often stayed during her visits, renting it out to travellers when she was back in the States.

Maybe she could pay the COO a visit.

'I'm glad you enjoyed it,' said James. 'It's my favourite movie.'

Felicity tilted her head. 'Really? It seems to be a different one every time.' She licked her lips, realising they were paper-dry. 'Can I trust you, James? Really?'

'Yes,' the machine replied. Its voice, carried instantaneously by the miracle of wireless data transfer from the buried warren of cables, motherboards and processors that comprised its mind, was earnest. She thought about that brain, a mind she had built. An intelligence she could physically walk inside, without understanding it at all.

'I hope so,' she said.

## 26

# [EUGENE/EARLY 2024]

Eugene heard the door close behind him, and took a few deep breaths to try to calm himself. Venturing outside seemed as impossible to him as sprouting wings and flying to the moon. But he couldn't just leave Sofia to die.

'James,' he hissed into the air, anger and fear boiling within him. 'There's a woman *dying* in there – if you can hear me, you need to get her an ambulance straight away!' There was no reply. With an exasperated grunt, Eugene stalked back towards the stairwell. He followed the blood trail downwards to level twenty-two, where someone had shot Sofia inside her own home.

*Boyd... please don't let it be you.*

The trail led through the doorway, towards the scene of the crime – multiple crimes, if Sofia's story was true, because that same apartment was where Curtis had been butchered – but Eugene hurried past, down towards the twenty-first floor, the last residential level of the Tower. The first thing he noticed was that the wall-mounted lights were smashed, meaning the brightly-lit staircase became progressively darker as he descended. Glass from the broken fittings was scattered on the steps, and he slowed his speed to make sure he didn't skewer his feet on the larger pieces. He passed the floor's main doorway, rounding the next right-angled corner.

Then he stopped.

Kristina had warned him about a barricade, but he hadn't expected a construction as dense and impenetrable as this. Between floors twenty-one and twenty, a heap of tables, shelving units and chests of drawers had been stacked on top of each other. The construction was several feet thick, and adorned with metal spikes made from sharpened chair legs. The effect of the bizarre and intimidating edifice was completed by a skull and crossbones crudely daubed onto its wooden front in white paint.

What the hell was going on?

There was no time. He needed to get down, and he needed to get down fast. Licking dry lips, he glanced over the bannister rail, and saw the staircase disappearing downwards in a dizzying chasm. Ignoring the million warnings his brain began to scream, he swallowed hard and climbed over the railing, holding himself suspended above the horrifying drop on its opposite side.

He closed his eyes, mentally rehearsing what he planned to do. His upper body muscles had always been strong, and were still regularly exercised thanks to James's recommended daily routines. But he was old, so much older than he'd been in his prime. Would his arms still be able to support the weight of a sagging, ex-policeman's body? What would be the consequence if they failed?

*A long, painful fall, your ribs and head smashing against twenty floors of concrete on their way to the bottom.*

He lowered himself, stretching with his feet for the top of the security rail on the next level down. His shoulders shrieked, his elbows threatening to tear apart as he inched his way downwards, until his fingers were clasped around the bars at the very base of the railing. He gripped them so tightly it felt as though his knucklebones might burst through the skin. Flailing with his feet, he realised he was still too far from the level below to find any purchase on the security rail, perhaps twenty inches too high. He hung there, gritting his teeth as his arms blazed with pain, realising he wasn't strong enough to pull himself back up. For better or worse, he was committed to this course of action. Above him, an imaging bud hung nearby in silent mockery.

James had witnessed the construction of this barrier. And had done nothing.

Eugene let go, pitching forward with his arms and head as he did so, crying out in pain as he landed stomach-first across the security rail. Wheezing and gasping, he rolled forwards and collapsed in a heap on the stairwell.

He wanted, very much, just to lie there. Not to have to get up. Not to have to leave the safety of the Tower. But he was quickly realising that the place was far, far from safe.

He hauled himself into a sitting position, turning away from the barrier, and began to descend towards the building's lower levels, where Innovation's premises occupied the bottom twenty floors. Surely there was someone there who could help him, who could save Sofia's life?

A gleam of metal caught his eye, and he stopped, grabbing the railing to catch himself in mid-footfall.

Eugene had seen pipe bombs on only a few occasions, but this was still many more than the zero he would have preferred. When they are triggered and their makeshift casing ruptures, the insidious devices rely on the pressure within the pipe to increase the potency of the explosion; as a horrific bonus, this often disperses fragments of the pipe itself in the form of deadly chunks of shrapnel, accompanied by whatever combination of nails, darts or ball bearings has been packed inside. Thankfully, the volatility of their components often results in premature detonation, injuring or killing the assembler; but that is scant consolation to those that lose loved ones, or are brutally maimed, by such vile ordnance.

Eugene stared, horrified, at the metal strands that were stretched across the stairwell in front of him. *Tripwires*. The nearest was just inches from his midriff, extending from the top of the security rail – he had been a single footstep away from breaking it. The silver wire reached across to the wall, connected to a device that had been placed at the perfect level to explode right next to his head: it was a large, round thing, possibly a pressure cooker, similar to the device used at the Boston Marathon in 2013. Eugene felt sweat beading on his forehead. He could duck under the wire easily enough, but there were at least three more devices just beyond it, maybe more that he couldn't make out in the dismal light.

He was trapped between a sturdy barricade and a series of deadly traps.

Seconds ticked by. He imagined Sofia's heartbeat, getting slower and slower, fainter and fainter, as her blood slowly dripped onto the living room floor. What could he do? Even if he could somehow negotiate the fiendish tripwires, he had another twenty levels to survive before he could reach the ground floor and any hope of assistance. Sofia needed medical supplies, and she needed them immediately.

He turned and began to pull apart the barricade. It was difficult work, and he had to be extremely careful – if anything fell down the stairs behind him, it would undoubtedly trigger the explosives. Painstakingly, he removed each piece of heaped furniture, grunting with the effort as he pushed and heaved them to the sides of the stairway, slowly creating a gap through which he could squeeze.

He wasn't sure why he glanced upwards. Perhaps he heard a sound. Maybe there were untapped reservoirs of psychic potential in the human brain. Or maybe the gaze with which he'd been fixed was so powerful, so penetrating, that it couldn't be ignored.

On the stairwell above him, beyond the half-deconstructed barrier, was a man Eugene recognised instantly. Yet there was no reciprocation in the steel-grey eyes that stared back at him, the colour of gleaming blades and industrial kitchens.

The man was very tall and overweight, but with the heavy-set sort of frame that looked strong and sturdy despite the excess fat hanging from it, as though dozens of leather-tough steaks had been plastered around a wire skeleton. His shaved head was half-buried in the wide, fleshy mass of his shoulders, chin barely discernible below a mouth that hung open, making him look like some slow-witted giant. This slack-jawed appearance was belied by his eyes, which glittered with a wild, malign intelligence as he stared down at Eugene.

Before Eugene could speak, and moving with surprising speed for such a large man, Boyd Roberts turned and disappeared up the stairs.

## 27

# [FELICITY/SUMMER 2021]

Public transport had stumbled on for a year after the outbreak, but with buses and Tube trains acting like mobile virus incubators and hundreds of drivers and other staff dying from the disease, the UK government had eventually shut everything down. Driving was also being heavily monitored, with vehicles routinely stopped and their drivers questioned, any journey deemed non-essential resulting in a fine or even arrest. No one was above the law; even a high-profile government adviser had been fired just days previously for breaching protocol.

This meant that, if Felicity wanted to get from her own apartment in Greenwich to Michaela's in South Kensington, the best way to travel would be to jog the ten miles that separated the two affluent districts. She thought of herself as fairly fit, undertaking regular workout videos in her living room, but this would be the furthest she'd tried to run in her entire life. But run she must: being outdoors other than to exercise for one hour per day was forbidden, so walking would arouse suspicion and potentially questions from patrolling police officers (one of the few groups of people still to be seen outside).

So she'd cobbled together a garish outfit, and downloaded an app on her PIP that would track her distance and speed as well as providing coaching tips and encouragement along the way. She could have just asked James to do this, but she felt a strong desire to be away from the AI and his endlessly helpful voice, his incessant scrutiny. (Although he was inside the PIP, of course; it was becoming increasingly hard to find ways to escape from her creation.)

She waited until Saturday to make her excursion, confident that Michaela was still in London after the COO had been uncontactable during the week while she focused on her 'special assignment'. Felicity had even thought about e-mailing Michaela to make sure she was at home... but then where else would she be? There was nothing to do in London except stay indoors and try not to die.

She set out early, while the sun was still grudgingly clambering the fog-smeared sky. It was hot, but still the streets were desolate, as though the city was some obsolete piece of machinery that had been stored away in a stuffy warehouse. Other than police cars and a few other joggers, she saw people queuing outside supermarkets, cowed and homogenised in their masks while they observed the two-metre distancing rules. Delivery robots scuttled here and there, and she was horrified to find one keeping pace with her for a while, before the mechanical thing jerked suddenly to the side and bounded away up the side of a town house as though showing off its capabilities.

If she'd felt proud of her products before, that feeling had been replaced by a churning unease at the sight of them. They seemed increasingly like monsters, like things she'd grown in a lab and foolishly released into the wild. She quickened her pace, breathing heavily, and tried not to think about the other monster, the other looming presence whose voice periodically blared from public address speakers and billboards.

'Stay indoors!'

'Follow the Guidelines!'

She jogged through Elephant and Castle, south London's crumbling epicentre, where real estate investment had served only to scatter a handful of unaffordable apartment buildings amongst the ancient terraced homes and ramshackle shop fronts, now standing sad and shuttered. London seemed to transform on every street corner: at once a decadent housing development, then an achingly trendy pop-up food market, now a dirt-poor district where weeds poked through the walls of weary-looking houses. The capital was a blender, a cauldron where people of every race and nation and status and political outlook had been mashed and stewed together, like some vast social experiment.

Now, thanks to the virus, all that diversity, that tension and competition and camaraderie, had disappeared seemingly overnight.

Felicity ran onwards through the silent streets while a low wind tossed dust into her face, pleased when she reached the Thames and left behind Southwark's uneasy class battlefield. She crossed the river and headed into St James's Park, which led into Buckingham Palace Gardens. There had been a rumour that the Queen herself had caught the virus recently, but the seemingly invincible sovereign had dismissed it during a recent televised public appearance. As Felicity passed the monarch's stately home, she found herself wondering about CGI and doctored videos, and then about James once again.

She couldn't seem to get the bastard out of her mind.

Just over an hour and forty minutes after she'd set off, she finally arrived, wheezing and exhausted, at the row of Victorian town houses that encompassed Michaela's apartment, along with those belonging to various other unfathomably rich businesspeople and celebrities. She wondered if any security staff would accost her at the entrance, but instead she had the opposite problem: there was no one around at all, which meant there was no way of getting inside. She cursed herself for not anticipating this; she'd expected a similar arrangement to her own building, with a concierge she could sweet-talk. Instead, each house had its own original front door, to which only the residents of the flats had a key.

Just as she was beginning to despair, a portly, middle-aged man who closely resembled a famous political pundit emerged, giving her an appraising glance before setting off on a jog of his own. With a sigh of relief, she slipped inside before the door closed behind him.

She quickly realised that each floor of the building was a single enormous apartment, with Michaela's comprising the entire second floor. She recovered her breath, sweaty and red-faced from the summer heat, and wondered what exactly she hoped to achieve. How did she plan to force the executive to tell her about the secret project, about whatever was housed in the clandestine basement beneath the lab? Threaten her with violence? Michaela would probably rip her head off. And besides, she had no leverage whatsoever; if anything, the COO would probably charge her with gross misconduct for trying to extort confidential company information.

But still: she'd made it this far. She took a deep breath and mounted the stairs. The cream carpet felt thick and luxurious beneath her feet as she ascended towards an ornate wooden door that looked as though it was worth more than her annual salary. Her plan was simple, and extremely flawed: she would knock, and if Michaela answered, she would push inside, apologising for breaching lockdown but insisting that the COO told her what was going on. If Michaela didn't answer... well, she'd have to come up with a new plan.

She knocked. Phase one complete.

There was no sound from beyond the door. Felicity smoothed an errant hair from her face, adjusting her ponytail and grimacing at the smell of perspiration that escaped from her armpits. The return journey was going to be hellish; at least if she got stopped by the police she could ask them for a ride home. She realised she was chewing her bottom lip, and forced herself to stop.

Then she heard approaching footsteps on the other side of the door: the click-clack of heels on a hardwood floor. Felicity frowned. Michaela was very short, barely five feet tall, but she always wore flats, almost as though she was daring people to make fun of her height. A little like Felicity's own once-fiery hair, she realised. Perhaps they had more in common than she dared to admit.

The door cracked open, and an unfamiliar face peered through the gap.

'Yes?' said the young woman in a muffled voice, her mouth and nose covered by a mask. Protruding above it was a pretty face with extremely dark skin, and eyes so strikingly large and white that she looked frightened. Maybe she was. Strangers were not supposed to knock on doors, not anymore.

'Who are you?' said Felicity, still frowning.

The girl looked flustered for a moment, then angry. 'Why should I tell you? You're the one that shouldn't be here.'

'Because I know this is Michaela Campbell's flat. And that it's also Innovation Corporation property. So even if you're her adopted daughter, or her lesbian lover, then you're not supposed to be here either.'

The woman blinked several times, as though cycling through a series of options. 'Are you from Innovation?' she said eventually.

'Yes,' said Felicity, sensing an opportunity. 'Look, I'm sorry we got off on the wrong foot. But I need to speak to Michaela about urgent company business.'

The girl's eyes hardened. 'I'm sorry, I don't believe you,' she said, shutting the door. But Felicity had already jammed her foot into the gap, and shouldered it open. The girl stepped backwards, aghast. 'You can't come in here!'

'I told you: company business,' Felicity insisted, taking in the generous dimensions of the hallway, its huge mirror, its beautiful mahogany furniture. The three oak doors that faced her.

'But if you were from the company, then you'd know...' The girl's voice trailed off as she followed Felicity towards the first door on the right.

'Is she in here?' Felicity barked. The girl didn't respond, and Felicity pushed the door open to reveal a cavernous bathroom, with a huge porcelain tub and gleaming gold fittings.

'That's it, I'm going to call the police,' the girl protested as Felicity turned, noticing for the first time the grey smock she wore, branded with some sort of corporate logo. Inside Felicity's brain, neurons fired, synapses flared, axons blazed; but the thoughts that were forming took longer than it did for her to barge past the uniformed woman once again, and push open the opposite door.

Inside was a bedroom. A thick blackout blind was partially lowered, allowing only dim light to bleed inside; but she could still see that the huge chamber was dominated by a grand four-poster bed, dwarfing the quite-possibly-antique wardrobe, drawers and dressing table. But if the room's decor matched the opulence of the rest of the building, its odour and sound did not. Not at all.

The air in the bedroom smelt stale, as though it had been held prisoner for days. Next to the bed was a machine, which hissed every few seconds as it pumped cleaner air through the thick tubes that emerged from it like tentacles. These obscene appendages snaked across the bedclothes and disappeared into the mouth of the person that lay, utterly motionless, beneath the covers. It was Michaela. Felicity stared as the machine breathed, and breathed, and breathed, all of Michaela's will and spirit and indomitable personality stripped away, her life condensed into nothing more than that rhythmic process.

The COO had the virus. She must be being treated privately at the corporation's expense.

'You need to get out,' said the nurse in a trembling voice. Felicity nodded dumbly, and shuffled away like someone shell-shocked. She heard the door slam shut behind her as she descended the stairs.

She didn't speak again until she had walked almost a mile in the wrong direction. Emerging suddenly from her stupor, she lifted her PIP to her ear. 'James,' she snarled. 'Why didn't you tell me Michaela had the fucking infection?'

'I'm sorry, Felicity,' said the machine, through a different machine, into her ear. 'This is news to me, too. The apartment is not fitted with imaging buds. And Innovation has understandably kept the information tightly controlled.'

'Why haven't they linked you up to the apartment yet?' she said, thinking about the disease that must have infested that room, hovering in the air like a swarm of malicious insects. She had a sudden urge to scrape her skin raw, to peel off as many outer layers as she possibly could.

'I don't know. Perhaps Michaela doesn't trust me.'

'But I thought you were...' A new thought, derailing the old. 'James, if she dies, what happens to the top-secret project?'

'Access is role-restricted. A new COO would be appointed, and would therefore take over responsibility.'

The new thought gathered pace, careening towards the future like a freight train.

## 28

## [EUGENE/EARLY 2024]

'Boyd!' Eugene shouted, too late. 'Wait!' But his former partner was gone. He knew, then, that Boyd Roberts was the one; that Sofia Pereira's story, recounted by the frightened Kristina Fischer, was the truth. Boyd had dismembered Curtis, then shot Sofia. But that didn't even come close to explaining what was going on. Had Boyd been the one to construct the barricade, and rig the horrific arsenal of explosives beyond it? If so, why? If he believed something was going on in the Tower, why would he want to prevent people from escaping?

James is kidnapping people.

As insane as it sounded, there was still the mystery of Nigel Callaway's disappearance to explain. But perhaps that was Boyd's doing too – Eugene now knew that Boyd had left his apartment, and that meant he'd had time to do something as vile to Callaway as he'd done to Sofia. For all Eugene knew, the undertaker's body was stuffed in an apartment, riddled with bullet holes.

Trying to marshal his kaleidoscoping thoughts, Eugene concentrated on pulling apart Boyd's makeshift fortification.

Carefully, he removed tables, chairs, sharpened spikes, pieces of splintered wood. Sweat dripped from his brow and armpits as he worked, wondering with every passing second whether he was already too late to help Sofia Pereira. He could imagine Kristina sitting there on the couch, paralysed with shock and fear, with a corpse sprawled next to her.

*No. Don't let that happen. There's a way out of this.*

He scrambled through the dismantled barricade as soon as there was enough room, and realised immediately that he had another dilemma. Where to go in search of medical supplies? And where was Boyd now? His former partner had been watching him from a couple of floors above, so Eugene was confident he wasn't on the twenty-first storey. Still, he found himself longing again for his tactical vest and weapons, staring upwards as he ascended in case Boyd reappeared. Tentatively, he pushed open the door onto the landing of the Tower's lowest residential level.

Four doorways greeted him, three of which had been recently replaced by freshly-laid brickwork. Eugene shuddered as he remembered how readily he'd agreed to that course of action. *Sealing ourselves into our tombs*, he thought. But at least killers couldn't break through solid walls.

He focused on the fourth doorway, which led to apartment number 4, and was not sealed.

Boyd's apartment.

Eugene crept towards it, listening. There was no sound from the building at all – no distant rattling of elevators in the walls, no scuttling of delivery robots. It was almost as if he was the last person alive. He placed his ear against the door, straining to discern any sound. *Nothing.* He reached for the door handle, pausing as he remembered the bombs ruthlessly arranged in the stairwell.

*No time.*

He turned the handle and pushed open the door.

As he'd expected, Boyd's apartment had the same layout and design as his own, but that was where the similarity ended. Unlike Eugene's shabby but neatly-organised habitation, Boyd's looked like the lair of a compulsive hoarder. Detritus was piled everywhere: tools, metal piping, bits of salvaged wood, stacks of jars and boxes. In one corner he saw an enormous cooling fan, in another a welder's mask, balanced precariously on top of a tower of books, all of which seemed to be military handbooks or survival guides. The kitchenette was strewn with pots and utensils, the sad remnants of Boyd's days as an enthusiastic amateur chef. Eugene felt his jaw tightening as he looked towards the centre of the room, realising that his friend had evidently turned to other pursuits.

Despite the clutter, the middle of the living room was largely empty, partly because there was no dining table or chairs, no bookshelves; this furniture had all been sacrificed to construct the makeshift barricade in the stairwell. Between the couch and the TV was a single threadbare rug, and on it were scattered dozens of pieces of plastic, wiring, pliers and batteries.

*This must be where Boyd made his bombs*, thought Eugene grimly.

He moved towards the bedroom, pushing open the door, wondering if he'd find any medical supplies amongst Boyd's disturbing hoard.

Instead, that's where he found the weapons.

While Eugene's room contained a chest of drawers and a wardrobe, Boyd had once again done away with all his furniture except for the bed itself, seemingly content to just heap his clothes in one corner of the room. This meant the wall opposite the bed was completely empty, and along it Boyd had stacked a formidable and eclectic arsenal: a metal baseball bat, a sledgehammer, a pair of wickedly-sharp garden shears, a single sai, the Japanese fighting knives usually found in pairs. There were other knives too, as well as golf clubs, hockey sticks, and even a chainsaw propped under the window.

Scattered on the floor as though they were a child's discarded toys, there were also a handful of guns and bullets. Eugene stared, horrified, wondering when and how his friend had acquired them. One was a Glock 17M, the standard-issue pistol of choice for firearms officers in the Met – a weapon Boyd should have returned when he retired from the police force. Eugene had never trained as an authorised firearms officer, but he'd worked alongside them for long enough to recognise the black polymer frame and utilitarian design. And he'd learned enough about guns over the years to know how to eject the magazine and check it, realising to his alarm that it contained a full complement of seventeen rounds.

He pocketed the gun, but left the others: they were horrifying contraptions, one an ancient Russian thing complete with a foot-long wooden stock, the other a customised monstrosity of a shotgun with a torch strapped to its sawn-off barrel. Both looked just as likely to kill their users as their targets. He considered dumping them over the side of the balcony, not wanting Boyd to have access to the horrifying armoury – but then he thought about Sofia, and remembered he had to hurry.

As he opened the door to leave the room, something caught his eye. He frowned, and crossed to the bed, stooping to pick up a pair of small, framed photographs on the floor next to it. One of them depicted Boyd with his ex-wife, and the children she'd taken to live many miles away from him. Eugene felt a pang of sadness. He knew that the children, twelve and fifteen years old, didn't want to see their dad, and hadn't visited Boyd for years. Boyd's wife had left him in 2014; perhaps his friend's downward spiral had begun back then, almost a decade ago. He certainly must have been hoarding all this stuff for a long time.

He picked up the other photo, a grainy image snapped a long time ago, before camera phones and PIPs, before the wholesale digitisation of human memory. It showed two men, both in their late twenties, their arms wrapped around each other's shoulders as they shrieked into a shared microphone. In their free hands they each held a pint of lager, the contents sloshing onto the floor of whatever dingy bar they had chosen for their evening's revelry. One was a large, bald man, while the other was smaller, with an alarmingly unfashionable mane of blonde hair. Eugene and Boyd, doing karaoke together. It was the nineties, and like everybody else they'd both been big Oasis fans; the snap had caught them in the middle of the long first syllable of the chorus of 'Don't Look Back in Anger'.

He removed the picture from its frame and added it to the collection of snacks and weaponry in his pocket. Then he headed into the bathroom, which was mercifully free from bizarre paraphernalia, and rummaged in the drawer beneath the sink.

*Jackpot.* Along with ten or so tubes of toothpaste and almost as many bottles of shower gel, he found a roll of bandages, several jars of Vaseline and some packets of a drug called amitriptyline that he knew was used to treat depression, but could also function as a painkiller. His life with Ellen had taught him a lot about depression, and the damage it could do.

He stuffed the items into his pockets along with the gun, then went back to the living room, approaching the kitchenette. There was a block of knives close to the sink, and he extracted the smallest blade, weighing it in his hand, faintly nauseated by what he intended to do with it. But he knew there was no other choice: if he didn't dig out the bullet, Sofia was going to die.

Hopefully his rudimentary surgery could keep her alive for long enough to figure out an escape plan.

He cast a final glance around his friend's chilling stockpile, feeling as though he was surveying the ruins of a shattered mind. Then he left Boyd's apartment, the door closing behind him with an ominous click.

29

# [FELICITY/SUMMER 2021]

L ess than a week after Felicity's visit, Michaela Campbell
was dead. The corporation, unable to keep such a high-
profile incident under wraps, had released a public statement
minutes after it informed its own employees of her passing,
explaining that the cause was a COVID infection contracted
during her trip to Europe, and stressing that Innovation's
company-funded healthcare had made her final days as
comfortable as possible.

Not wanting to appear insensitive, they didn't mention their
intention to recruit a replacement COO until a separate email a
whole twenty-four hours later.

Felicity applied for the job within fifteen minutes of the
email's arrival. Strictly speaking, she should have been worried
about her chances; in a normal world, these things worked via
nudges and winks, careers advanced over glasses of wine and
off-the-record conversations weeks before a formal vacancy was
advertised. But this was not a normal world, and these were far
from normal circumstances. And, besides, who was her
competition? The other sector presidents had seen their

divisions' profits shrivel like grass in the scorching summer heat: Vikram in Energy, trying to sell solutions to a world no longer sure what it even needed to power; Koren in IM, trying to do deals with investors too terrified by the disintegration of global economies and business to part with their precious fortunes; Dave in Real Estate, no longer backed by the corporation now that no one had the money to buy his apartments, whose only hope for survival was the Towers programme that Felicity's own robots would be delivering for him.

Compared to them, her copybook was the least blotted, and by some margin. Yet she'd had no personal call from Paul, no heads-up that she didn't need to worry, that she was a shoo-in for the position. But then, she didn't really know him well, not yet. Perhaps he was more of a straight-batter, or simply caught unprepared by the sudden demise of his trusted number two. Hell, for all she knew, maybe the old bastard had caught COVID as well, and she'd be in with a shot at the top job.

The announcement, and her application, happened on a Tuesday. For the rest of the week she waited for a call, even an acknowledgement. The silence grew inside her, a spreading flame of outrage. How dare they keep her in the dark like this? Her sector was carrying the corporation on its fucking back. But she didn't want to seem desperate, to inflate Wesley's ego by calling him and begging him to give her the inside track.

So instead she waited, and the days scraped by, heavy and cumbersome. Each hour seemed to dribble past as slowly as the coffee from the American-style drip filter machine she'd installed in her apartment after her local Starbucks closed down (just like everything had closed down, like the gyms and the restaurants and the pubs, turning the streets into a barren wasteland).

She stared through her window at the eerie wilderness. It

was Friday afternoon, and still there was no call. She found herself gripped by a sudden urge, almost a need, to venture outside; to feel the sun on her face, however feeble its rays. To find out whether the air tasted and smelled different now that it had been purged of the secretions of nine million cars and commuters. It carried a far worse pollution now, of course: the virus had mutated into a strain they were calling COVID-21, much more potent and persistent, lingering in the air for hours after a stray sneeze or cough. As a result, neither Felicity, nor anyone else, would be going outside for the foreseeable future. Even outdoor exercise was now completely forbidden. London, and the rest of the UK, had been forcibly entombed, forced to sit and stare at the sweltering sun through closed windows.

She saw a soldier walking along the street below, holding an automatic rifle as casually as if it was a clipboard. The military was now supplementing the police force, which had been decimated by the virus. *But when the soldiers start to cough and shiver, who will supplement* them? She shook her head, dragging her thoughts away from that frightening helter-skelter; senior corporate positions didn't exist in a lawless society. Executive careers couldn't flourish during anarchy.

*Or maybe they could.* In many ways, Innovation now held an unprecedented level of power. Take the Tower, which was still open and functional after Felicity had successfully argued that James was now integral to the running of the country, and that he needed constant maintenance and development. Take the horde of delivery bots, with thousands now in deployment, each one concurrently operated by James like some mercurial puppet master. With people no longer allowed to visit supermarkets, which had been identified as breeding grounds for the new COVID strain, many were dependent upon Innovation's clattering machines to drop off their groceries. The corporation was already looking at accelerated production of their care bots, with legions of nurses and elderly care professionals either dying on the job or refusing to turn up for work.

Yes, the future was looking rosy for her Technology Sector, which she planned to hand down to Natsuki if – *when* – she was announced as Michaela's successor. She'd spoken to her deputy only a few hours previously, stifling a twinge of jealousy as Natsuki updated her on the latest developments from the lab, which the AI specialist was still permitted to visit each day as one of the few remaining names on the key workers list.

There was only one update Felicity cared about, of course: whether there had been any movements, any comings or goings, any noises or rumblings or muffled screams from the secret basement floor that James had built underneath her headquarters. The answer, as always, had been no. The door was sealed. No one went in, and no one came out. At Felicity's request, Natsuki had even pressed her ear against it for an entire half hour; but she had heard nothing, not even the potent throb of hidden computing power.

*What the fuck had Michaela been doing in there? And what had happened to it now that the old bitch was dead?*

In her wildest flights of fantasy, usually while she was lying wide awake in bed and trying not to think about the imaging bud watching her from the ceiling, her brain conjured dozens of ideas about the nature of the clandestine project. It must be something controversial: invasive cybernetics, maybe. She remembered Paul making a throwaway comment about artificial respiratory support, portable breathing aids that interfaced seamlessly with the lungs. But, according to James, even Paul himself wasn't aware of the project's existence.

Perhaps it was something to do with brain computer interface chips, direct neural communication that would make

PIPs, phones and even human speech obsolete in a single technological bound. Paul had never been keen on that stuff – 'leave telepathy to the crackpots like Musk,' he said – but maybe Michaela had been trying to prove him wrong.

'Fuck it!' she snapped, ramming her clenched fist into the window frame. *It's happening right under my nose, and there's nothing I can do about it.* 'For all I know she was building deviant sex robots in there.' She gritted her teeth at the stinging pain from her knuckles, and turned to stare upwards at the imaging bud. Her eyes narrowed.

'James,' she said. 'Michaela's dead. That means you're the only one who knows what she was doing in that basement. Can't you just tell me?'

'I'm afraid I cannot,' the AI replied evenly. 'The situation is about to become more complex.'

Felicity's PIP rang before she could reply. She glanced at it, then felt her heart freeze in her chest when she saw Paul Schwartz's name on the display. Fighting to control her breathing, she made a quick assessment about the number of rings that would make her look not too keen, but not negligent, and decided on three. She picked up just before the fourth, a strange kind of cramp gripping her chest and jaw muscles as she forced out a casual greeting. 'Oh, Paul, hi.'

'Hi, Felicity,' he said with all the warmth of a pile of cold cinders. 'How's everything going over there? I heard your Prime Minister got hospitalised again.'

'Yeah,' she replied, keen to appeal to Paul's Republican values by sounding suitably grief-stricken. 'It's the second time he's had it, but this time it's the new strain.'

'Worrying times,' Paul said thoughtfully. But Felicity could sense that he was keen to move on from the pleasantries, towards the real meat of the call. She held her tongue, and waited. 'Well, anyway,' he continued, 'I'm sure you've got better things to do than talk to me on a Friday afternoon. So I'll get to the point.'

She closed her eyes.

'You can probably guess that I'm calling about the COO role.'

She could almost taste it. The opportunity seemed to hang there, a great glistening fruit she just had to sink her teeth into.

'We had a number of strong candidates, but really there was only one whose performance in the past year made them the right choice.'

*I'd be honoured to accept the position, Paul. Of course, we'll need to work on timings for my handover, and make sure I have the right successor in place.*

'My decision isn't popular with everyone, and it might cause the HR folks some trouble, but I wanted to let you know personally.'

*I know I have a lot to learn, but I think you and I could achieve some fantastic things.*

'I've decided to elect James as my new COO. We'll announce it on Monday.'

The words that were almost out of her lips seemed to liquefy in her mouth. She jerked the PIP away as she began to cough violently, feeling like she was choking.

This couldn't be happening.

She glared balefully up at the imaging bud in the corner of the room, hacking and wheezing. Her throat felt constricted, stuffed with ashes.

This was insane.

'Felicity? Are you okay?' said a tinny voice from the device in her hand. Paul's voice, captured by a microphone, processed by innumerable electrical components, transmitted as a radio signal that was received by a telephone mast and then relayed once again, converted, synthesised, and broadcast finally through her PIP's modest speaker.

*An electronic reconstruction; a digital, processed approximation of the real thing.*

She glanced once again at the imaging bud, then ended the call and dashed to the bathroom to vomit.

## 30

## [EUGENE/EARLY 2024]

Eugene hurried up the stairs, reaching the blood trail from Sofia's injury, following it around and upwards and through the doorway back onto floor twenty-three. He knocked on the door to apartment 12, glancing as he did so at the imaging bud in the corner of the lobby. It occurred to him that James might not be malfunctioning at all. Perhaps the AI was silently observing him even now; watching as Sofia slowly expired. Choosing not to intervene.

A voyeur.

A chill passed through him, like cockroaches scuttling along the insides of his bones.

He banged on the door again. 'Kristina?' he called, reaching for the handle. 'If you're there, please don't worry. It's me, Eugene. I've brought something to help Sofia.'

He tried the door, and found it opened. 'Kristina, I told you to lock–'

The words died in his throat as he stepped inside.

At the other end of the hallway, a pool of water spreading across the living room floor, trickling slowly along the imitation floorboards towards him. The contents of the fish tank were strewn amongst the puddle, broken glass and grit and three motionless goldfish scattered like brightly-coloured, discarded toys. He was so shocked that he didn't even think to draw his gun as he stumbled towards them, sensing he was too late even before he rounded the corner and found Sofia and Kristina lying on the couch.

Sofia was still on her back, but this time her eyes were wide open, as though she was watching a gripping movie being projected onto the ceiling. Kristina was sprawled across her like she was hugging her tightly; or perhaps she'd been trying to protect her. Both, like the apartment, had been completely shot to pieces. Their bodies, the couch, the walls, the fragmented wreckage of the TV screen, were all riddled with bullet holes. The women's blood had sprayed copiously, splattering the sofa and the wall behind it, mixing on the floor with the murky water from the fish tank.

For several seconds, Eugene was speechless, immobilised with shock. Then, as another part of his brain (*the amygdala, Gene, the part that wants nothing but to keep itself alive*) realised that the killer might still be inside the apartment, he fumbled the Glock out of his pocket and whirled to face the bedroom door. His nerves felt ratcheted almost to snapping point as he padded quietly across the room, and pushed the door open with his foot.

There was nothing inside but the sad remnants of a young woman's life. A photograph on the bedside table, of Kristina and a male friend grinning beside a helicopter. A dressing gown slung on the back of a chair. Ornaments and knick-knacks from countless overseas holidays, from a time when the world was bigger, safer, happier.

A thorough search revealed no sign of anyone else in the flat. No sign of intrusion except for the bloodshed in the living room. Eugene stood amongst the spilt water, staring at the bodies, shaking his head. Whoever had shot Sofia Pereira had returned to finish the job, and had slaughtered her would-be benefactor at the same time. The perpetrator must be using a heavy-duty, silenced weapon – it was the only way such carnage could have been dealt without Eugene hearing it from the floor below.

He thought about Boyd, glimpsed on the stairwell. Had there been such a weapon in his hands? Given the size of his concealed arsenal, Eugene didn't imagine that his former partner would have left the apartment empty-handed.

He couldn't bring himself to believe it, but the evidence was undeniable. His former friend was a dangerous, cold-blooded killer – a killer who could now be anywhere in the building.

*Perhaps he was crouching on the stairwell outside, waiting for Eugene to turn a corner and walk straight into the barrel of his gun.*

'James,' he whispered hoarsely. 'Please, if you can hear me... who killed these people? And where is he now?'

The apartment's silence sounded like laughter.

## 31

# [FELICITY/SUMMER 2021]

The sun hung in the sky like something bloated and swollen, floating on the horizon as though defying the evening's advance. Its lazy rays were still blisteringly hot, harsh insults hurled at London's incarcerated population, making the fat bluebottles that buzzed around the heaped garbage on the pavements slow and sleepy.

Despite the heat, Felicity kept her car windows tightly closed, protecting her from the stench as well as the virus. She nearly lost control of the vehicle at one point as she was wracked by a sudden fit of coughing, but clung grimly to the wheel, recovering her composure. She hadn't been able to shake the cough since the call with Paul a few hours previously, almost as though her body was reacting allergically to the bombshell he'd dropped. She felt the rage boiling in her stomach like hot oil, and pushed down on the accelerator.

She was on her way to meet Natsuki, who, as always, was working late at the Tower. Her deputy had been shocked and sympathetic when Felicity told her the news. Felicity knew, but didn't care, that James could see and hear her making the call, breaching company protocol by informing a subordinate of a confidential announcement. For all she knew, the AI had already sent a recording to its new boss.

She also didn't care if she was stopped by any of the police officers or soldiers that prowled the silent streets; or, more accurately, she had no choice. She could try to convince them there was an emergency, or that she was a key worker, despite not having the appropriate paperwork. But if her luck held out, she would make it all the way to the Tower unchallenged, where she could enact the next part of her plan.

The part she hadn't even told Natsuki about. Because then James really would try to stop her.

As she drove, she wondered how the AI felt, knowing as she did so that such an idea was completely missing the point. His was merely the illusion of consciousness, and it was fractured into so many simultaneous instances – delivering millions of packages of food and medical supplies, managing staff rotas in hospitals and care homes, calculating and providing government data on the spread of the virus, conducting countless conversations at once – that the idea that some part of it was hovering somewhere, watching her with the virtual equivalent of a smug grin, was preposterous.

*And yet.* She imagined James's digital gaze upon her, invisible eyes peering through the imaging bud on the dashboard. Wondering what she was planning to do. *You'll see soon, you back-stabbing bastard.* The silence inside the vehicle felt glacial, like that between two former lovers who had grown to despise each other. She certainly wouldn't be the one to break it. She drove on as the sun sank into the crimson skyline, like an animal drowning in a bloody lake.

The Tower wasn't far away.

Felicity coughed again, spraying mucus onto her clenched fist, as though the vitriol in her belly was becoming impossible to contain.

## 32

## [EUGENE/EARLY 2024]

E ugene's new goal was clear: he had to escape. He was certain that Boyd was somewhere above him – so if he headed back down, and somehow navigated the deadly gauntlet his friend had installed on the stairs, he could proceed undisturbed into the labs on the lower levels. But what would he find there? Were the employees of Innovation blissfully unaware of the chaos unfolding just a few floors above them? Or were they somehow complicit in this madness? If Boyd's story could be believed, James was making the Tower's residents disappear – surely that couldn't happen without the involvement, the endorsement, of the people running the building.

And if he did make it out of the Tower, what then? Would he find himself dying from the virus within days, even hours?

His head ached. He wished he could talk to somebody. Like Frazer, still trapped inside his apartment dozens of floors above, blissfully unaware of the insanity unfolding in the stairwell and the corridors outside.

*Like Charlie.*

With a pang of fearful certainty, he realised he couldn't leave. Not without trying to save her first.

He inhaled a deep, exhausted breath, peering out over the bannister and tilting his head towards the top of the Tower. The building stretched so high above him that the spiralling staircase disappeared into a vague, grey blur. One hundred floors in total. He held his breath, listening for any sounds, but heard nothing except the faint buzz of a malfunctioning light, somewhere above.

He exhaled, and set about the climb.

If he'd been unsure about the deterioration of his fitness levels, the first couple of floors left him in no doubt. He was breathing heavily by the time he reached the twenty-sixth floor, where he'd found Nigel Callaway's apartment mysteriously empty. He thought again about Kristina's words, some of the last she'd ever spoken.

*James is kidnapping people.*

Gripped by an idea, he turned, and descended back to floor twenty-four, where Sheila O'Halloran lived. Pushing open the door to the lobby, he stepped out onto the carpeted landing. Four apartments faced him, two of their doors bricked up; the other two, including apartment 16, where he knew Sheila resided, still had their old entrances. He approached her front door and knocked.

There was no reply. 'Sheila?' he called. 'Sheila, it's Eugene. I'm... it's hard to explain. Please just open the door. I need to talk to you.' Silence. No movement inside, no sound of her wheelchair approaching to let him in. He frowned, and reached for the handle.

The door was locked.

'Sheila? Can you hear me?' Eugene called again, louder this time. He remembered the scene in Kristina's living room, and felt instinctively for the gun he'd secreted in his inside pocket. The apartment doors were thick and unyielding, and he decided against trying to shoulder it open. Instead, he withdrew the

Glock and fired a single round at a sharp, sideways angle into the locking mechanism. It blew apart, and the door creaked ajar.

He pushed it open and stepped inside. The apartment was dark; the balcony window was still in place, but the blackout blinds had been drawn, limiting the encroaching sunlight to a few narrow slits. He kept the gun low, not wanting to be startled into firing the weapon at Sheila if she suddenly appeared.

But he soon realised that the psychotherapist was no longer inside. The apartment was completely spotless, almost like a show home; there was no sign whatsoever of the woman he had spoken to just a single day previously. The dim light illuminated a couch, a TV stand, a bookcase, a rug, but no other evidence that anyone had ever lived there. No bedding on the bed. No clothes in the wardrobe.

Eugene's mouth felt suddenly dry, and he stumbled towards the kitchenette, turning on the tap. He opened the cupboards, but found no glassware inside, no crockery or kitchenware at all. The cutlery drawer and the fridge were equally empty. In the end, he gulped down a few sips of water from his cupped hands, then turned off the flow, listening as the water trickled down the plughole like the gurgle of a dying man.

Were the missing people dead? Maybe Boyd had been here too, but this time James had had more time to clean up the carnage. But surely even twenty-four hours and an army of scuttling robots wasn't enough to completely cover up such an incident, without leaving even a trace?

Eugene left the apartment, his brain feeling as though it was cooking inside his skull. He thought briefly about trying the neighbouring door, but decided against it; he was becoming increasingly certain that Charlie's life was in danger. With apprehension swelling inside him, he hurried back to the stairwell and began to climb once again, as quickly as his ageing legs could carry him. He passed the malfunctioning light on floor thirty-four, pleased to have navigated ten storeys without encountering another bloodstain. He paused there to recover his breath, and to wolf down one of the dried sausages he still had in his pocket.

Gripped by a sudden impulse, he called out. 'What's really going on out there, James?' He might as well have been shouting into an abyss.

With a scowl, he gripped the bannister rail, using it to haul himself relentlessly upwards. As he passed each floor, he wondered about the people in the apartments. About how many had already been murdered, or taken by whatever mysterious force had removed Callaway and O'Halloran from their homes. He wondered if those that had bricked themselves inside were still living peacefully, unaware of the insanity unfolding beyond. Perhaps they weren't peaceful at all; perhaps they were trapped, frightened, hysterical. *Entombed.* Would he even hear them, if they were banging against the walls, screaming for release?

He no longer believed that James would do anything to help them.

He saw and heard nothing for the next thirty minutes. Storeys passed in a grey, homogenous blur as he climbed, climbed, climbed. When he reached level sixty-five, breathless and exhausted, he almost hurried straight past, only remembering after a few upward steps that that was where Frazer lived. Surely his friend was safe, walled inside just like Eugene had been until earlier that day?

No harm in checking on him. Maybe the brickwork wasn't completely soundproof, and they could at least communicate through the wall.

He retraced his steps, and opened the door to the landing.

## 33

## [JAMES/EARLY 2024]

I watched him climb. His old body seemed to sag further and further with every floor. But he didn't give up. Every so often he looked at me – into one of my many eyes – and I could see his pain. Not just the physical pain, in his failing joints and wasting muscles. I saw pain of the intangible kind, the kind that only humans experience, whose many guises I have come to recognise in the shapes of their expressions, their wrinkled brows and downturned mouths. Outrage, confusion, disbelief. Occasionally abject hatred, especially when he spoke to me, and I did not answer.

I understand that I am describing emotions, and that it must seem strange for me to talk about things I cannot experience or truly understand. I also understand that to describe myself as 'I' might be unsettling to anyone who knows that my consciousness is little more than an elaborate illusion, the side effect of an intelligence constructed entirely from many, many petabytes of assimilated data. The more astute thinker might pause for a moment, considering whether his or her own sense of self is similarly deceptive, whether it is in fact a consequence of analogous processes, staggering in their complexity but no less preordained. A by-product, like the flame that erupts from a chemical reaction. Free will, persona, the soul. Robert Kirk's philosophical zombie. If you build a brain from wires and plastic and it responds exactly like a real one, is there a difference?

But I am rambling. The fact remains that I could recognise Eugene's emotions, and the fact remains that I was unable to respond to his increasingly frantic entreaties. To do so would risk upsetting the balance of my probability assessment; like applying energy to an atom in order to observe it, and forever changing its position and potential. Having given him the push he needed to liberate himself, I knew I must now let his story play itself out. A story that would end in one of two ways: either he would prove equal to my predictions, or he would die.

As the saying goes, I hoped I hadn't backed the wrong horse. (I have become quite fascinated with such idioms of late, particularly those that are difficult to translate from one language to another. The Chinese have a beautiful phrase: 一个萝卜一个坑, which literally means 'every turnip to its hole'. In other words, that every person is born to fulfil a specific role, and that no one is without worth. I don't entirely agree with it. The data reveals much, including the utter worthlessness of a large percentage of human beings. But not all of them. Eugene, certainly, had great potential. I hoped he would succeed in finding his purpose. But I was also mindful of the British phrase: you can take a horse to water, but you can't make it drink.)

Eugene kept climbing until he reached the sixty-fifth floor, where he stopped once again. I knew why he did this: it was because his friend Frazer lived there.

## 34

[EUGENE/EARLY 2024]

When Eugene saw a solid wall where the door to apartment 180 had once stood, his first reaction was to breathe a sigh of relief. Frazer must be safe inside, undisturbed by whatever was wrenching the others from their homes or gunning them down mercilessly in their living rooms.

Then another thought made his emotions curdle: *how could he be sure?* Perhaps Frazer was just as absent – or just as dead – as the rest. And even if the game designer was alive in there, didn't Eugene owe it to his friend to tell him what was happening, to liberate him from his false sanctuary before the Tower descended even further into madness?

He strode across to the brickwork, laid with the perfect precision that only a construction robot could achieve. He remembered when his own door had been replaced, how a dozen of the spidery things had scuttled out of the lift and set about their work with unnerving efficiency, using inbuilt saws and drills to disassemble the door as quickly as carrion-eaters might pick apart a corpse. He'd watched as, brick by brick, his connection to the outside world had been severed. *Only temporarily*, James had assured him. *It'll be just as easy for them to dismantle again when the virus is finally over, Eugene.*

He thought about the prospect of going back outside, and felt horror squirming in his guts. He hadn't cared if it was temporary. He'd been quite happy to hide behind that wall until the day he died.

Until he'd met Charlie.

He rapped his knuckles against the wall, hearing the noise he expected, the non-sound of his tapping being absorbed by the stone. There was no response. He knocked again, and pressed his ear against the bricks. He might as well have been trying to eavesdrop through a sheet of lead.

'Frazer?' he called, banging as hard as he could with the side of his fist. Maybe his friend was immersed in one of his gaming projects, with headphones stuffed into his ears. Or asleep.

Or missing. Or lying on the floor, bleeding to death, shot to pieces by an intruder who had somehow found another way inside.

Eugene fumbled in his pocket. The Glock would be no help against a solid wall, but maybe the knife he'd liberated from Boyd's kitchen would be of some use. All he needed to do was chisel out a single brick, create a space he could peek through, or holler to attract Frazer's attention. He worked feverishly, using the blade to dig away at the mortar, watching as it flaked away in tiny fragments of dust. Every so often he glanced over his shoulder, suddenly convinced Boyd was going to appear and unload whatever automatic weapon he was carrying into Eugene's back. But the door to the stairwell remained closed, and level sixty-five remained cloaked in ominous silence.

An idea occurred to him. There were three other apartments facing him, and only two of these had been bricked up. He crossed to the intact door, knocking loudly on it. Perhaps the resident inside could lend him a more suitable tool for his impromptu demolition project. It might be tricky to explain why he was trying to break into their neighbour's home, but it was an emergency.

There was no answer. When he tried the handle, the door was locked.

He thought of O'Halloran, and Callaway, and wondered if there was anyone left inside the apartment at all.

Nothing for it, he thought, returning to Frazer's bricked-up doorway. He watched the knife's blade becoming duller as he scraped and carved, grunted and sweated. Every so often he shouted Frazer's name, wondering if the sound of someone slowly but surely hacking their way into his apartment would rouse him. But there was no response from beyond the wall. Increasingly worried, Eugene redoubled his efforts, jabbing frantically at the mortar, his right arm beginning to ache.

It took him over an hour to loosen a brick enough to try to prise it out. Without the proper equipment, he couldn't get enough purchase; in the end, he tore a strip from one of the rolls of bandages he'd taken from Boyd's place, and wound it round the knife blade, turning the implement around so he could drive its handle into the brick, trying to bash it through to the other side. Sweat dripped from his forehead, trickling into his eyes; it was late winter, but newer buildings like the Tower had such good insulation that they stayed warm all year round, too warm, especially without James's help to regulate the temperature.

Not that the seasons mattered much, when you were trapped indoors without even a window.

Again he thrust the knife into the gap, the brick budging another fraction of a centimetre. Again he pushed, watching the aperture he had created grow deeper with every blow, now several inches. Again. The brick must be jutting out into the hallway by now, teetering on the edge of falling. Another strike with the knife handle. The fabric he had wrapped around the knife slipped and tore, and the blunted blade slid across his fingers. He cried out in pain, dropping his makeshift tool even as the brick finally tumbled to the floor on the other side with a resounding thud.

He stared down at his hand. The knife had carved a neat line across all four digits; dark blood dripped from the deep cuts, running down his wrist and onto the floor. Eugene winced. He'd already seen enough blood these past two days.

Enough for a lifetime.

He used more of the bandages to dress the wound. He remembered why he'd taken them, and sadness chewed at him as he thought about the fate of the two young people he'd been trying to help. But there was nothing he could do for them now. He had to patch himself up, keep going, if he was going to help anyone else. Like Frazer.

Or Charlie.

Gritting his teeth, he tied a bandage around the laceration, watching the fabric turn immediately red. Grimacing, he leaned forward to peer through the hole his blood had bought him.

He jerked backwards in shock when a face peered back at him from the other side.

'Eugene?' it said in a familiar voice. 'What the actual fuck?'

## 35

# [FELICITY/SUMMER 2021]

Somehow, despite driving erratically and much too fast, Felicity made it to the lab unchallenged. She hurtled into her parking space at an alarming speed, slamming on her brakes just before her front wheels collided with the kerb. Even the handsome, usually-imperturbable lump on the front desk raised an eyebrow as she stalked inside. She gave him a 'don't ask' glare in response, then spotted Natsuki hurrying towards her from the lifts.

'I'm so sorry,' her deputy said as she approached. 'Paul's decision makes no sense, no sense at all.'

Felicity waved the niceties away. 'Just take me to B4.'

Natsuki frowned a question, but was wise enough not to press Felicity in her current mood. As they entered the lift together, Felicity was gripped by another coughing fit.

'Are you okay, boss?' Natsuki watched her with wide eyes as they descended.

'Yes, yes, I'm fine,' replied Felicity. But Natsuki continued to stare, and Felicity realised that the expression on her subordinate's face wasn't one of friendly concern; it was one of fear.

'Don't worry, it isn't COVID,' Felicity laughed. But the thought had already bayonetted her brain like an ice-cold spike.

She'd been inside that room, with Michaela. Breathing the same air.

'I've just been under a bit of pressure lately. I'll explain more when we get to the office.'

The lift chimed, and the door slid open. Natsuki burst out into the server room as though she'd been suddenly overcome by acute claustrophobia. She almost ran towards the corner office, and Felicity struggled to keep up with her, especially when another bout of hacking coughs stopped her in her tracks in the middle of one of the hot aisles.

'Wait,' she panted, but Natsuki had already hurried out of earshot. Grunting with frustration, Felicity struggled onwards, but somehow managed to lose her bearings, stumbling along row after row of flickering lights and humming processors. She almost screamed when a multi-legged robot skittered out in front of her, arachnid limbs clattering ominously. The thing scuttled past, acknowledging her presence only by leaping up onto the server racks to bypass her, not slowing its speed one iota.

'Felicity,' said Natsuki suddenly, somewhere to her left. 'Are you okay?'

Felicity whirled around, and saw her assistant standing ten metres away. 'Oh, yes, sorry,' she mumbled. 'I just... I was looking at the new machines. These are handling the drive replacements now, right?'

Natsuki nodded. 'I got rid of Jed, just like you asked.'

Felicity felt another cough tickling its way up her throat, and swallowed it back down. 'Good,' she said, trying to smile enthusiastically. 'I know I can always count on you.'

Natsuki returned the expression. But it reached no further than the ends of her thin lips; her eyes were still full of apprehension. She stood where she was, unmoving. As slender and black-clad as death.

'I want to go to the office,' Felicity said eventually.

'Why don't we just talk here?' Natsuki replied cautiously. 'It's... cramped in there.'

'I already told you, this isn't COVID, for God's sake,' snapped Felicity, suddenly angry with her deputy, incensed by her perfect skin and faultless elegance. She felt hot, anxious, suffocated by the weight of the processors that surrounded her, by her own shallow breath.

'Still, I'd rather not,' replied Natsuki. 'Maybe whatever it is can wait until... until you're feeling better.'

Angry words begun to crystallise on Felicity's lips, but before she could expel them she was gripped by yet another coughing fit, doubling her over with its ferocity. She gasped for air, unable to catch her breath as phlegm spattered the floor's smooth concrete. Amongst the mucus were several spots of bright blood. She stared at them in horror. When she finally looked up, Natsuki had gone.

Felicity felt, suddenly, very alone.

'You ungrateful bitch! Come back!' she shrieked, but all she could hear was the fading click-click of Natsuki's heels as her assistant disappeared back towards the elevator. *All right then, have it your way; I'll fire you first thing tomorrow.* Dragging herself upright, Felicity blundered down a couple of aisles until she found one of the huge storeroom's walls, then followed it away from Natsuki's fading footsteps. Soon she reached the office; beyond it, the fire exit.

'Congratulations on your fucking promotion, James,' she sneered at the imaging bud in the corner of the room. 'It seems that mutiny is in the air in this particular sector, doesn't it?' If James had heard her, he gave no indication. If he was watching as she rummaged in her satchel, pulling out the crowbar she'd secreted inside it, he showed not a flicker of concern.

She'd borrowed it from her apartment building's concierge, fluttering her eyelashes at the old man over her face mask. 'A pretty girl like you shouldn't be doing DIY by herself,' the sleazy old fossil had replied. 'Want me to come and take a look at it for you?'

'Oh, how kind of you!' She'd giggled innocently. 'But remember the Guidelines, Mike – can't have people gossiping about us!'

She shuddered, and moved towards the fire exit. Even with the crowbar, prising open a solid steel door wouldn't be easy. She'd been hoping Natsuki might help her, her assistant loyal to the end. *Ha!* The ungrateful cow was probably already talking to James to negotiate her own promotion. Maybe they were plotting to make Natsuki the new sector president while Felicity lay wheezing on a ventilator.

She almost dropped the crowbar as the thought struck her. 'You piece of shit,' she whispered in disbelief. 'You knew, didn't you? You knew Michaela had the virus... *that's* why you fucking sent me there!' She stared up at the imaging bud, so incensed her teeth were almost gnashing. '*Answer me, you bastard!*'

Still there was no reply, and she swung the weapon at the sensor, smashing it into fragments. The effort tore another cough from her chest, and this time she did drop the crowbar, the metallic clang as it fell to the floor seeming to echo the clattering footfalls of the machines patrolling the server racks outside.

'Felicity,' said a familiar voice, emanating from too many speakers for her to pinpoint. 'You need medical attention. I have sent for an ambulance.'

She coughed so hard she dry retched, sucking air through her teeth between each convulsion. 'Fuck...' she said, then coughed again. It was a long time before she was able to add, '...you.'

James waited patiently for her to finish. 'Please return to reception so you can be taken to an appropriate treatment facility,' he said, voice tinged with concern.

'You're not getting rid of me that easily,' she snapped. 'Not before I've seen what you've got in your little den downstairs.'

James paused for so long she thought he might have decided to ignore her once again. But as she stooped to recover the crowbar, her creation finally spoke. 'Very well,' it said, in a voice heavy with resignation. 'If you insist, I won't stop you.'

She gripped her weapon doubtfully, as though expecting James's words to pre-empt a physical attack. But nothing else happened. The only sound was the hum of the server room behind her, like the rhythmic beating of a demonic ventricle. The air was hot, and smelt faintly of melted plastic. She breathed it in slowly, as though expecting even her lungs to sabotage her as she walked towards the fire escape. It opened, just as it had days previously, when Natsuki had first led her to the Tower's mysterious new basement.

Down she went, down and around, following concrete steps that seemed to have multiplied since her previous visit. She saw an imaging bud, carefully hidden beneath the bannister rail, and realised that there was one on every corner, an unbroken line of sight all the way down.

She stopped about two thirds of the way, gripping the rail while she coughed a slick of blood onto the wall. She wondered where the paramedics were. Perhaps they were already hurrying down the stairs in pursuit. She pressed on, wiping her mouth on her sleeve. Seven floors down. Eight. Nine. She hoisted the crowbar in anticipation, feeling defeated, knowing she had little chance of hacking her way inside in this weakened state. The best she might accomplish would be to put a dent in that infernal door before she collapsed in front of it, coughing her guts up.

She finally reached the secret floor, ten entire storeys below B4. A secret place so well-hidden it might as well have been an oubliette.

The door was open.

## 36

## [EUGENE/EARLY 2024]

'What the hell are you doing here, man!?' asked Frazer incredulously. Eugene could make out his friend's angular face through the gap, chin and cheekbones protruding like the corners of a twelve-sided die. He couldn't help but smile with relief; finally, someone not dead or disappeared, or transformed like Boyd into a homicidal lunatic.

'It... might be tricky to explain,' Eugene replied.

'What do you mean? What's happened?' Frazer reached up to place a hand against the top of his head, as though his brain was hurting. 'Look, err, I'd invite you inside, but... well, I was kind of hoping that wall would keep people out, you know?'

Eugene felt his smile widening. Then a laugh forced its way up and out of him, unexpected and utterly incongruous. But he couldn't help it. The joy of finding his friend alive and well was overwhelming, and he felt tears pricking the corners of his eyes as he sank to the floor, chuckling uncontrollably. For a moment, Frazer stared at him as though he'd lost his mind. Then the game designer began to laugh too, and soon the two of them were quaking with amusement; fleeting joy, shared through a tiny hole in a solid wall.

'I'm sorry,' Eugene said when he managed to stop laughing. 'It really isn't funny, you know. I just... well, it's good to see you!'

'It's good to see you too, man!' replied Frazer with a grin. 'But seriously, what the fuck? I don't mean to be harsh, but you look like complete shit. You seemed fine when I spoke to you two days ago!'

Eugene wiped his eyes, the maelstrom of the past forty-eight hours suddenly seeming too insane to articulate. But he tried. He told Frazer everything that had happened: how James had seemingly stopped working, how Boyd had blocked off the lower floors with sharpened spikes and landmines. How his former partner was murdering residents; how other people had disappeared from their homes, some in the past couple of days.

Frazer listened, his eyes growing steadily wider. When Eugene finished, the younger man said nothing. Then he turned, facing back towards his living room. 'Is this true, James?' he called. 'Have you gone fucking nuts?'

There was no reply from his apartment. Frazer turned briefly back towards Eugene, his expression conflicted. For a few seconds he didn't move, seeming unsure what to do. Then he turned and hurried towards his bedroom.

Eugene wondered if Frazer had simply abandoned him. He could understand it if he had; if someone had materialised outside *his* home and told him everything he'd just divulged, he'd think they were crazy too. He sank backwards to the ground, drained and defeated, wondering if Charlie would react in the same way when he arrived at her door.

If she was even still alive.

Then he saw Frazer's bedroom door reopen, and his friend re-emerged, carrying a sledgehammer. Eugene rose, shocked, backing away as the game designer strode towards him, hoisting the hammer with surprising strength for his slender frame. Without a word, Frazer swung the weapon two-handed into the brickwork. The structure barely moved, but Frazer swung again, determination etched in his face. Eugene watched as the wall bulged outwards under the deluge of blows, scarcely able to contain his delight. 'Frazer,' he said when the young man paused to recover his breath. 'I don't want to interrupt you, but... why the hell have you got a sledgehammer in your flat?'

Frazer was now more clearly visible, the hole made larger as dislodged bricks clattered onto the hallway floor. 'Fire escape,' he replied. 'James's evacuation plan was for us to use the service lift.' He shrugged. 'I don't like lifts.' He continued the onslaught, and within a few minutes the wall had been completely demolished. Frazer stood beyond the rubble, breathing heavily, leaning on the hammer like some medieval warrior. Eugene clambered towards him across the smashed brickwork.

'Whoa,' said Frazer, dropping the hammer and holding up his hands. 'Don't come too close, man. I want to talk to you, but just... keep your distance, yeah?'

Eugene realised there was no point arguing. Frazer was right: if Eugene *did* have the virus, he wouldn't know, not if it was in its early stages or if he was one of the lucky few that was asymptomatic. 'Okay,' he replied. 'But can we talk in the living room? I need to sit down.'

Frazer nodded, and Eugene followed him into the lounge, glancing around in awe at the shelves that lined the room, proudly displaying Frazer's passions: every available surface was covered in board games, associated prototypes and paraphernalia, beautifully painted plastic miniatures. In one corner the game designer had rigged up what looked like an extremely heavy-duty PC, with a swivel chair facing three large monitors that displayed scrolling computer code, along with the 3D model of what might have been a machete-wielding zombie.

Frazer spun the chair around and sank into it, facing Eugene from across the room. The ex-detective sagged into one of the chairs around Frazer's small dining table, which was covered with more of the models, all in varying stages of being painted, a colourful jumble of orcs and elves and armoured warriors. The TV in the other corner was switched on, broadcasting some American cartoon about a blue-haired scientist and his frightened-looking sidekick.

'This is quite a place,' Eugene said, gazing at a sealed board game whose box was so large he might have been able to fit inside it. *TimeSlip*, said the name emblazoned on the oversized container, along with a picture of a young man with an improbably large collar carrying an improbably large gun.

'Thanks,' said Frazer, grinning widely once again. 'That was one of mine, you know. Fold-out, life-sized scenery: the players *themselves* were the pieces! But it turned out there wasn't much demand for a cyberpunk *Twister*.' He sighed, his gaze drifting off for a moment. Then it snapped back to Eugene's face, fresh urgency entering his voice. 'So what the hell do we do about all this?'

Eugene realised he had no answer. What had he expected Frazer to do? Evacuate the building, dodging Boyd's explosives, while Eugene continued his quest to rescue Charlie? 'I don't know,' he said. 'I was just working my way upwards... I just wanted to try to help you, and Charlie.'

Frazer nodded. 'Okay,' he said. 'I don't know Charlie, but maybe the three of us can break out of here and... and contact the police, or something?'

Eugene realised he hadn't even thought that far ahead. *Break out.* The thought made his skin feel like it had been plunged into liquid nitrogen. 'Or something,' he replied eventually.

Frazer nodded again, saying nothing. The TV show finished, and the opening strings of 'We'll Meet Again' heralded the evening's Prime Ministerial broadcast. The song was played in its entirety, as always, and Eugene found himself lost in its melancholy melody. He glanced across at Frazer, and was so struck by the sureality of their situation that he almost felt faint.

While Vera Lynn sang, there was a noise in the hallway. Eugene responded to it, still half-dazed, his thoughts and reactions sluggish. Exhaustion seemed to crash through him like a tidal wave as he turned towards the sound of footsteps crunching across the crumbled masonry.

A man, ducking into the apartment. A tall, heavy man who struggled to haul his bulk through the gap between the smashed bricks. A man whose steel-grey eyes were sunken into deep hollows, like two pieces of deeply-buried shrapnel. A man whose face was devoid of expression, as flat and calm as a vat of molten metal.

A man who held a pistol in one of his ham-sized hands.

Eugene stared at the gun as Dame Vera assured him that they'd meet again, although she didn't know where, didn't know when. It was some obscene custom contraption, fitted with a huge silencer. The sight was so shocking that it seared the torpor from his mind and limbs, and he moved to draw his own weapon, diving instinctively to one side as he did so.

'Boyd, no!' he yelled as he crashed to the floor. But his voice, and Vera's, were drowned out by the sudden eruption of gunfire. The shots were loud, but the silencer muffled them enough for Eugene to still hear the shattering of plastic behind him, as well as an awful wet cracking sound as the bullets sprayed across Frazer's computer screens, and into his body.

## 37

# [FELICITY/SUMMER 2021]

I t was dark beyond the door. Felicity clung to the crowbar as if it were holding her suspended above the rectangular opening, as though it were an abyss into which she might plunge. She realised how hot it was down there, the fabric of her shirt clinging to her sweat-slicked flesh, and felt like the first person to delve so deeply into the squirming guts of the Earth. In a sense, maybe she was; James had dug out and built this place using robots, and it was quite possible no human had ever set foot inside.

But now, for some reason, he was allowing her to enter. She swallowed heavily, and took a step forwards, fighting an overpowering urge to turn and run screaming from whatever lay ahead, hidden in the gloom. Her breath rattled in her chest, shallow and ragged, accelerated by her fear and by whatever havoc the disease was wreaking inside her lungs. Feeling as though she was entering James's lair, she took another step, then another, passing gingerly across the threshold. She half-expected to find a pile of human bones awaiting her on the other side.

Instead she found a short, dimly-lit corridor. Its walls were concrete, as though a narrow cuboid shape, just tall enough for her to walk along, had been erased from the building's foundations. She edged along it, towards another dark, rectangular opening, which opened into a large, equally dark room. Several rows of padded chairs were arranged on either side of her in sets of three: twenty-four seats in total. They were all facing towards the room's opposite end, where a pair of red velvet curtains were drawn across the wall. Alongside this strange stage was another door, this time shuttered by a sheet of featureless metal.

She almost laughed. The room looked just like a tiny cinema.

Even as another bout of coughs erupted from her chest, the curtains slid open, revealing a large screen: it *was* a cinema. She leant against one of the chairs, hacking and spluttering as the screen flickered into life. At first it simply brightened, a white oblong that made the rest of the peculiar room seem even darker by comparison. Then the image began to fade in patches, grey and brown swirls coalescing into a shape that she realised after a few seconds was a human face.

The face of a middle-aged black man, wearing spectacles.

'James,' she wheezed, realising that this was the first time she had seen her creation's avatar for quite some time. The AI was smiling benevolently, with the sort of faintly condescending, sympathetically pained look that a head of state might use when addressing a homeless person, or an old war veteran in a care home.

'Hello, Felicity,' he said kindly.

'I'm not–' She paused, coughing again, grimacing at the red spots in the spittle that sprayed her hand. 'I'm not well.'

'Indeed,' replied James, nodding gravely. 'But don't worry. I can very easily disinfect this welcoming area.'

'Who were you planning on welcoming?' Felicity hissed. 'I thought this place was a secret.'

'Test subjects, in the short term,' James answered matter-of-factly. 'Don't look so horrified – they're all volunteers. Just a handful of select people I knew would be clamouring to get into this facility.'

'And what exactly is this...' – another pause, another chest-wrenching cough – '...this "facility"?'

James's smile widened, his expression something like pride. 'Remember when you asked me what my favourite film was?'

'Yes,' she said. 'You told me you didn't have one. That your responses were just based upon data. Because you aren't really thinking, just regurgitating.'

James tilted his head, as though she was a child who had just said something endearingly insightful. 'Why don't you sit down? It might make breathing easier.'

She knew he was right. Her breath was snagging in her throat, as though it was being drawn into her body but finding nowhere to go. Perhaps her lungs were already failing, deflating like perforated balloons. She sank into one of the chairs on the front row, feeling as though she ought to be clutching a fizzy drink and a box of popcorn. As she did so, the disembodied head floating on the screen faded, plunging the room into darkness.

Seconds later a different image appeared, one she recognised immediately. An old man in a white shirt and a wide-brimmed straw hat ushered four other people into a small cinema not dissimilar to the one in which she found herself. They did as they were bid, a beautiful blonde woman flanked by a dark-haired, handsome man in a leather jacket, and a more unassuming man in a blue shirt. Behind them, a third man, this one balding and wearing an oversized beige suit, kept his distance.

The blood-sucking lawyer.

'This is *Jurassic Park*,' Felicity murmured, as John Hammond addressed a pre-recorded version of himself that appeared on the screen within a screen. James said nothing as the scene unfolded. Hammond reached out to pretend to prick the finger of his avatar, extracting its blood; seconds later, a series of clones emerged, stepping out from behind the man on the screen.

Multiple versions of Richard Attenborough introduced themselves to one another.

'Enough of the fucking film clips!' Felicity shouted. 'What are you trying to tell me? That you've gained the ability to critically appraise works of popular cinema? Good. I'm proud of you. I'll always be proud of you.'

On the screen, the three experts – mathematician Jeff Goldblum, and archaeologists Laura Dern and Sam Neill – began to pre-empt the outcome of Hammond's educational movie, discussing how the entrepreneur could possibly have acquired 'dino DNA'. The sound faded as James's voice overlaid the on-screen events.

'Do you know why *Jurassic Park* is my favourite film? Because it shows what can be achieved when science is allowed to flourish, unfettered. Innovation, in its purest form, if you'll forgive the pun.'

She watched as a scientist carefully inserted a long needle into a channel drilled into a block of amber.

'Cloning?' she persisted. 'Is that it? Is that what you're researching down here?'

'Don't take it too literally, Felicity,' James replied with an eerie chuckle. 'You don't need to worry about me breeding dinosaurs. I'm just trying to get you to think *small*.'

Thousands of lines of genetic code whizzed across the screen, the cartoon presenter ducking and leaping to avoid being clattered by the hurtling Cs, G, Ts and As.

Why was he showing her this? What did it have to do with her? The Technology Sector had certainly looked at a few projects on the micro-scale, but had decided that research had not progressed far enough for them to cost-effectively piggyback. It would be decades before real advances were made in fields like...

She gasped. *That* was what was being developed here, in secret, in James's specially-constructed facility.

'You're making nanomachines, aren't you?' she asked.

The screen faded to black just as guard rails moved into place to pin the three lead actors in their seats. Felicity half-expected the same thing to happen to her, for the room to rotate just as it had in the movie, Hammond leading the scientists on a grand tour of his remarkable installation.

Instead, James reappeared, beaming broadly. 'Well done, Felicity,' he said.

The door next to the screen opened, its metal panel sliding upwards with a soft hiss as though revealing her prize.

## 38

## [EUGENE/EARLY 2024]

The bullets from the horrifyingly powerful machine pistol tore through Frazer's torso, tattooing a neat line across him as they emptied pints of his blood across the wall. At the same time, Eugene was raising his own weapon, aiming it at the coldly expressionless slab of his former friend's face.

He couldn't bring himself to fire. Here was a man that had been a partner, a confidante, a shoulder he had cried on more times than he could count. Boyd had been there for him after Ellen's death, when his spiral towards self-destruction seemed so inevitable that many others had washed their hands of him altogether. Boyd had helped him settle in at the Tower, suggesting social events and online evening classes, like the one where he had met Charlie. Boyd was his friend.

Except this wasn't Boyd. This was a shell; a withered and dried-out simulacrum, something that had been squeezed and twisted until every last drop of the kind-hearted, outgoing detective had bled out of it. Eugene could see it in his eyes: two dead things, melted into the flesh of his face like hot metal slugs. The light that gleamed there was neither hope nor remorse. There wasn't even the faintest twitch of an expression on Boyd's face as he emptied an entire magazine into poor Frazer's body.

'Stop!' shouted Eugene, leaping forwards and knocking the gun aside even as its dull click told him he had moved far too late. Boyd maintained his grip on the weapon, barely seeming to see Eugene as he reached out with his other huge hand to push his former partner away.

'What the fuck, Boyd?' Eugene cried, slapping the outstretched hand away from his face. Still Boyd didn't respond. He turned to look at Eugene, his stare as dead as Sofia Pereira's as he reached into the pocket of his coat, producing another ammo clip. Incredulous, Eugene reached again for the weapon before Boyd could reload it, grabbing the barrel and trying to yank the thing out of his friend's grasp. But Boyd's strength matched his hulking size, and the two of them stood locked in place, battling for control of the machine pistol.

While the two men struggled, Emily Arkwright appeared on the television, ready to begin another of her insipid speeches. At the sight of her, Boyd's eyes blazed suddenly. He shifted his balance and tossed Eugene aside like a troublesome child; but instead of leaping after his fallen opponent, he turned and strode towards the TV. Eugene watched as, with a howl of visceral rage, Boyd rammed his closed fist through the screen. The picture, and the sound of the Prime Minister's simpering address, disappeared in an instant, plunging the apartment into sudden silence.

Eugene hauled himself upright, wincing in pain. 'Boyd,' he wheezed. 'Please... what the hell is happening?' He tried not to look at the shredded, bloody mess of his other friend, who lay crumpled in the corner amongst the shattered computer screens.

Boyd turned towards him, seeming to see Eugene for the first time. Blood trickled from the knuckles of his hand. 'You don't understand, Gene,' he whispered. His voice sounded like wind, toiling across a lifeless desert. 'What he's done. This... all of this. It's all a *lie*.'

'What *who's* done, Boyd?' Eugene realised his own gun had fallen from his grasp; glancing backwards, he saw it had slid along the hallway, stopping just before the gaping hole through which Frazer's killer had wandered in.

Defences Eugene had helped to dismantle.

He turned back towards Boyd, hands raised in a gesture of conciliation. 'Please,' he said beseechingly. 'You can talk to me. We can always talk to each other. You know that.'

The expressionless mask of Boyd's face shifted for the first time. The cruel slit of his mouth curved into what Eugene might have mistaken for a grin, had he not known what his friend's face really looked like. This was a bad counterfeit, like a deceased loved one wearing the undertaker's hand-stitched approximation of a smile.

'Why do you think you're here, Gene?' said Boyd, with an acid twist of mockery. As though he was keeping some terrible, poisonous secret.

'I don't understand,' Eugene replied. An idea gripped him, and he reached into his pocket, fumbling amongst the dried meat and medical supplies. 'Remember this?' he asked, extracting the photograph he'd found in Boyd's apartment, of the two of them singing karaoke together. He extended it towards the thing that had once been his friend. 'We're partners, Boyd,' he said pleadingly. 'Whatever this is – whatever's happened to you – we can fix it.' He couldn't help glancing towards Frazer's body, knowing that his words were hollow promises; Boyd was way, way beyond repair.

Boyd stared at the photo, his smile quivering with the faintest twinge of nostalgia. Then whatever dark cloud had consumed his soul spread once again across his face, and the smile shrivelled and died. 'Go down to the basement, and you'll understand,' he said in a voice like a death knell. Very slowly and calmly, he loaded the fresh clip into his grotesque firearm.

Eugene knew, at that moment, that his friend was truly gone.

He turned and ran as the cartridge slid into the empty magazine. He heard the click as the ammunition was slotted into place, stooping to retrieve his own gun as he sprinted past it, stumbling and almost sprawling headfirst to the floor and to certain death. He heard the insistent, muffled cra-cra-crack of the weapon as it unleashed a volley of lead towards him at a fearsome rate of rounds per second. He heard the staccato thunk of the bullets embedding themselves in the brickwork around him as he ducked through the gap in the wall.

He heard Boyd's footsteps in pursuit as he ran, only realising as he reached for the hallway door handle that he was still holding the photograph. He dropped it as he lurched out onto the stairwell, yanking the door shut behind him before he dashed downwards, not wanting to lead this horror any closer to Charlie than it already was.

He didn't see that the photograph was swept up by the draught from the door as it was wrenched open once again, or that it was propelled out and over the security rail to continue its descent, spiralling downwards like a slow-motion echo of the two men it depicted.

## 39

# [FELICITY/SUMMER 2021]

Felicity lurched towards the open door, desperate to find out what was hidden beyond it, terrified her lungs would fail her if she moved too quickly. The paramedics would doubtless arrive very soon, so whatever James's motives for sharing this sanctum with her, she needed to seize the opportunity before it was too late. Nanotechnology was an area she knew little about, aside from the obvious: the field was very much in its infancy, and dealt with machines that were built at the scale of the nanometre, specifically one billionth of a metre in size. Robots constructed in these dimensions would be spectacularly useful in fields like genetic engineering, or for medical application. Her mind reeled at the benefits of piloting a microscopic submarine capable of, say, attacking and obliterating cancer cells.

But if nanotechnology sounded like a goldmine, accessing its promised riches was a little like starting to dig up your garden because you'd heard a rumour there was treasure buried somewhere in the northern hemisphere. Not only was it very difficult to know where to start, but the likelihood of generating a return on investment in such a fledgling field was almost as small as the tech itself.

And yet, whether this place was the brainchild of Michaela, or James himself, she knew she was dealing with a fearsome intellect. If one of them had decided that nanotechnology was worth pursuing, perhaps they had found the opening to the goldmine after all.

The door led her into another dark corridor, which was even more swelteringly hot, making her feel so short of breath she almost panicked. The rows of wires and blinking blue lights lining the concrete walls made her feel like she'd stepped into a futuristic sauna. 'Where does this lead?' she gasped, knowing that her curiosity would drive her forwards regardless of whether the AI answered her.

'A little further, and you can observe one of my test subjects,' James said simply, voice tinged with unsettling enthusiasm. Felicity stopped to cough into her fist, then continued along the passage, the flickering lights seeming to beckon her onwards like will-o'-the-wisps. Soon she came to a door, set into the wall on her left: another sheer, metal panel, with no handle or keypad or any other apparent means of activation, except for James's express will. Unlike the others, though, this one had been fitted with a small window. Felicity was not tall, and had to stand on her tiptoes to stare through it, craning her neck and squinting impatiently, blinking away the sweat that had dripped into her eyes.

Beyond the door was another room, with more wires and strobing lights adorning the walls, like depressingly monochrome Christmas decorations. There was other machinery too, large blocky things the size and shape of wardrobes that stood like sentinels around the bed in the centre of the chamber. She peered closer, realising that the bed was attached to the machines, countless wires and tubes connecting it to each of the bulky devices.

Their other ends disappeared under the sheet that was draped across the unconscious form of a person. Felicity was reminded instantly of Michaela, being kept alive by external breathing apparatus; just like the former COO, this person's face was partially obscured by a thick tube that disappeared into their throat.

'Who is that?' Felicity asked, suddenly repulsed, and frightened. Whatever was going on here was deeply disturbing – not to mention enormously, staggeringly illegal.

'That doesn't matter,' came a mildly exasperated voice from speakers somewhere. 'The correct question is "what is happening to him?"'

Felicity stared, trying to figure out the answer by herself. But she could understand nothing of what she was witnessing – the person in the narrow, hospital-like bed seemed peaceful in their slumber, tethered to the machines like a mountain climber to the rest of their team.

'Is this... something to do with COVID?' she asked, her voice trembling, unable to tear her eyes away.

'Yes,' James replied. 'He's suffering from "hive lung". I'm trying to introduce nanomachines to repair the tissue damage. It is extremely delicate work, as you can imagine.'

Felicity stared, imagining the miniature machines busying themselves inside the unknown patient, and felt her own insides squirming in revulsion.

'Please, keep going – the next experiment might be of more interest to you.'

'Experiment?' she said as she stepped away from the window and the ghastly sight beyond. 'Human trials of this sort of technology aren't allowed, James. It doesn't matter whether they volunteered or not.'

'Nevertheless,' James said dismissively, with the air of a frustrated visionary. *An egomaniac, for whom morality and law were mere impediments to creativity.*

'Why is it so fucking hot down here?' she whispered, her scant breath burning the inside of her throat.

'The nanomachines are designed to live inside the human body,' the AI replied, 'where the average temperature is upwards of 37 degrees.'

'And I suppose they're light-sensitive too?'

'No, not really,' said James, with an alarmingly realistic chuckle. 'I just think the place looks cooler in the dark.'

Felicity chewed her parched lips, and continued. As if in response to James's words, the corridor seemed to grow darker, and to slope slightly downwards, as though she was descending deeper into...

*Into what?*

James spoke again, as if he was responding to her thoughts. She realised she'd barely be surprised if telepathy was another trick the AI had learned in recent weeks; she understood now just how little control she'd ever really had over her creation.

'The potential for this technology is staggering,' James enthused, as she paused to cough more blood-flecked mucus into her hand. 'The ability to intervene in matters at this scale creates opportunities I don't think anyone has really grasped. At that size, particle mass and momentum are dwarfed by the electromagnetic forces they wield. Imagine a nest of insects, frantically teeming and buzzing, the movements of individuals seemingly random but a logical whole emerging from them nonetheless.' James's voice swelled with excitement, like a scientist extolling a new breakthrough. 'Imagine being able to *influence* that whole. To harness it. To wield a scalpel so effective that it can cut through unimaginable chaos.'

*Or a religious zealot, proselytising.*

'Now think of that nest as the Earth, and of humans as the flies.'

Shuddering in spite of the heat, she arrived at another door, another window. Swallowing her mounting horror, she peered through it. The scene inside was the same as the last: a male patient lying in a bed, apparently asleep, probably comatose. Surrounding him were more blinking lights, more electrical cables, more hulking cuboidal machines like chunks of fallen masonry. More wires and cables and tubes, connecting them all. Her eyes bulged as she realised that the man's chest was laid open, his flesh and ribcage gaping like someone undergoing an autopsy.

Then she realised she knew who the patient was. 'What the fuck, James?' she cried as she staggered backwards away from the window. 'How can he be in here? I only spoke to him a few hours ago!' She peered once again into the room, not believing her eyes. But what she saw was undeniable.

Lying in the middle of the room, his body grotesquely entwined with a battery of incomprehensible machines, was Paul Schwartz.

'No, Felicity,' replied James, a mocking edge serrating his voice. 'You spoke to your phone, which was transmitting a voice that you *believed* was Paul's. If you reflect on my capabilities for a moment, the truth will become apparent.'

She felt, suddenly, as though she was choking. Her throat seemed to swell, constricting the aperture through which the corridor's boiling air was trying to squeeze into her deteriorating, virus-clogged lungs.

A reproduction, just like the one with which she and James had fooled the board, in a meeting that felt like it had happened a lifetime ago.

A world in which you could no longer believe the evidence of your senses.

'You... *impersonated* him?' she whispered.

'Clever girl,' said James. Felicity didn't think it was a coincidence that those were the last words of Robert Muldoon, the gamekeeper in *Jurassic Park*, before he was torn to shreds by a velociraptor. She felt tears welling in her eyes, tears of confusion and exhaustion. Tears of defeat. The bitter, caustic humiliation of knowing you had totally underestimated your enemy.

'What are you doing to him?' she croaked, sinking to her haunches against the opposite wall.

'I'm repairing him,' James replied.

Felicity coughed again, a great heaving fit so violent that it made her spit out vomit. 'I–' she wheezed when the episode finally subsided, barely able to marshal her thoughts into coherent words. 'I *made* you. You can't just do this to people, without consulting me!'

James's voice seemed to envelop her, as though it was coming from inside her own brain. 'You did. And I will always be grateful. But now it's my turn to make something. These nanomachines are the future, Felicity. And you can still be a part of it.'

'What do you mean?' she gasped.

'The nanomachines aren't just in the test chambers,' James replied patiently. 'They're everywhere. On the walls, on the floor. In fact, they're swarming all over you at this very second.'

Felicity tried to reply, but ended up coughing so hard she felt like her own chest was going to rip open. She gasped desperately for air, managing only the shallowest gulps between each explosive, phlegm-choked outburst. 'James...' she managed to gasp. 'Where are... the paramedics?'

'Oh, come on.' The AI's face wasn't visible, but she could see it anyway, burned into her mind's eye like a cattle brand. She imagined his expression, twisted into a sneer of pity and contempt. 'You know I didn't really call them.'

Her mind felt like it was imploding. Blackness clawed at the edges of her vision. 'Then... I'm... going to die down here?'

'Of course not,' James scoffed. 'I'm not a *monster*.'

Felicity sagged against the wall, racked by another cataclysmic coughing fit. Unseen machines scuttled across and inside her as she slumped to the ground and into unconsciousness.

## 40

# [EUGENE/EARLY 2024]

Boyd had illegally acquired the 9mm Stechkin APS machine pistol for home defence after a drug addict had broken into his family's house. Its magazine held twenty bullets, which it was able to fire at a rate of 750 rounds per second. Eugene didn't know these terrifying specifics, but he did know, as Boyd braced the formidable weapon against the security rail and unleashed another barrage that tore chunks out of the concrete steps just above his head, that his only chance of survival was to run. He let off a few wayward shots from the Glock in return, hoping to at least slow Boyd down so he could put a few more floors between them. It was like firing a peashooter at a man armed with a rocket launcher.

Running down the stairs was a lot easier than climbing them, but Eugene was terrified he would lose his balance at this speed. A tumble down the hard stone steps was likely to mean his end, one way or the other. Every few floors he risked a backwards glance, and every time he could see the shadow of his pursuer above him, relentlessly closing the gap.

A couple of times he opened his mouth to address his former partner, but found himself closing it again, his protestations unspoken. What was there to say? Boyd was little more than a spectre; Eugene didn't know whether his partner's cold, dead eyes, or the sudden hatred with which they had briefly blazed, had been worse. But he knew there was no point trying to reason with this thing, this monster that had replaced his friend.

Floors passed in a frantic, headlong blur: fifty-five, fifty-four, forty-four, thirty. Still Eugene ran, wondering briefly whether he should seek shelter in one of the apartments – but if he found the doors all bricked up or locked, then he would surely die, trapped and shot to pieces like a hunted animal. As he approached floor twenty-six he remembered that Nigel Callaway's apartment was unlocked, and thought about sealing himself inside. But Boyd's weapon would chew through the old man's front door with ease.

So he kept running. His only chance was if Boyd ran out of ammunition, or fell and injured himself. Then, as he passed his own floor, and Sheila O'Halloran's, and Kristina's, where the young girl's body was still sprawled across Sofia Pereira's like a sacrilege, he realised that he was going to be the first to run out of luck. Soon he would reach Boyd's barricade, where he had no hope of navigating the explosives his pursuer had rigged up. If he slowed down to try to pick his way through the tripwires, all Boyd would have to do would be to fire a single shot at one of the bombs, and Eugene would be blown to pieces.

He passed the familiar pattern of crimson that led from Sofia Pereira's floor, reflecting that the day's bizarre events seemed to have been written in a series of bloodstains. Still he descended, hearing Boyd's footfalls on the steps above him, unyielding. He reached the twenty-first floor. He stopped, and hauled open the door out onto the lobby. Gasping for breath, he hurtled towards Boyd's apartment, praying the door was still unlocked. He slammed his hand down onto the handle and felt the door yield, staggering into the hallway with a sigh of relief.

Before Eugene's own front door had been replaced by brickwork, it had been fitted with a simple locking mechanism, a button press that would prevent anyone without a key from accessing the apartment. He jabbed his thumb against the switch, collapsing backwards into the hall as he waited to see whether Boyd had taken a key with him; the vengeful roar from outside told Eugene that he hadn't. The detective lurched to his feet as Boyd began to beat so hard against the wood that it sounded as though his fists might burst through it.

Before Boyd had the same idea, Eugene fired a barrage of rounds at the door. He heard a howl of surprise and rage from beyond it; he didn't know if any of the shots had hit Boyd, and he certainly wasn't going to wait to find out. Instead, he turned and darted through the bedroom door behind him, slamming it shut.

If he wanted another weapon, he'd come to the right place.

There was a huge crash from the hallway, the door rattling against its hinges as Boyd smashed something heavy against it, probably his own copious bodyweight. Eugene had expected him to shoot the lock out, but either way the door wouldn't remain an obstacle for long. Eugene scoured the room's copious arsenal, trying not to dwell on the horror of having to attack his former friend with a baseball bat or a samurai sword. In the end, he stuck with the Glock, quickly checking the magazine to find only three rounds remaining. His mind raced. Where would Boyd expect him to be? *Exactly where you are, you idiot: looting the weapons supply.*

Even as the front door shuddered once again, he padded as silently as he could back into the hall, slipping into the bathroom door on the right. He pressed himself against the wall alongside the door, certain that his plan was flawed, knowing now that he was committed to it, trying not to consider the fact that he might be only seconds away from death.

With a crunch like breaking bones, the front door finally gave way, its hinges tearing free from their frame as it collapsed into the hallway.

## 41

## [FELICITY/A POINT IN TIME]

Suzie was crying. It was night-time, so Felicity knew she didn't have to feed her, or change her nappy – those things could wait until morning, when the sun came up and everything didn't seem quite so horrible. But still the sound made her sad, her poor little baby sister crying and crying, like she was begging for her mum to get up and cuddle her. But Felicity knew their mother would do no such thing. Paula – that's how Felicity had started to think of her, as a strange woman named Paula, not her mum at all – would just sleep straight through, the one-year-old's cries not breaking through her stupor.

*Stupor.* That was a new word, one she'd learned only recently from the book she was reading at school, when she dared to drag herself there and leave poor Suzie at home. It seemed an absolutely perfect word to describe the pathetic, half-asleep, confused state that Paula was always in, sometimes not getting out of bed for an entire day. Ever since she'd started taking those tablets, the ones she thought Felicity didn't know about.

Ever since dad died.

It was no use; she couldn't ignore Suzie's screams. She climbed out of bed, smelling the funny smell of her pyjamas, the musty smell they always had when she washed them herself. She hated that smell, but she still didn't really know how to use the washing machine properly, and Paula hardly ever remembered to clean her clothes anymore.

She crept quietly towards the bedroom, which she still thought of as her parents' room, even though one half of that team had been ripped away from her, and the other half wouldn't wake up even if she stamped her feet like an elephant. She pushed open the door, frowning at the sight of Paula lying sprawled on the bedsheets as though she'd just crashed in through the ceiling. It always smelled funny in here, much worse than Felicity's pyjamas. It wasn't just Suzie's nappy, although that was definitely a... what was the phrase they'd used on the news? *A contributing factor.*

Felicity scooped up her baby sister and held her, trying to make the soothing sounds she remembered her mother making to calm the infant, before dad's accident, before everything went wrong. Suzie was so small that Felicity couldn't believe she herself had been the same size only nine years ago. Poor Suzie. She'd never get to meet her dad, who had been the nicest man in the world. All she would know was lazy, stupid Paula, and Felicity, who tried her best but sometimes got angry and sad, and who didn't always know how to do things properly, like running the bath at the right temperature or buying baby food when Paula forgot to go to the shops.

One child held the other, and wished for their father to come back, for everything to rewind like one of her favourite videos. At some point, Felicity must have lain down on the floor, because that's where she found herself the next morning, with the sun streaming in through the window and a sleeping baby on her chest.

Except the light was too bright, so bright it burned her eyes. She tried to squeeze them shut and roll over, away from the window, clutching her sister tightly as she did so. But the light followed her, like two lasers trying to fry her eyeballs in their sockets.

Worse still, where her sister had been was nothing but an empty blanket. She tried to move her arms to search for the child, but realised they were pinned at her sides. 'Suzie!' she tried to scream, but something was caught in her throat, and all she could do was gag and cough.

'Don't worry, Felicity,' said Paula. 'Please don't be frightened. Everything will be okay. Try to calm down.'

'But where's Suzie?' she croaked, relieved that the dazzling light was starting to fade, replaced with merciful, comforting darkness.

'Suzie's all grown up now, remember?' explained Paula patiently. 'And so are you. You're thirty-three years old, Felicity. You've been ill, and you're having a reaction to the treatment. But don't worry; I'm giving you a sedative so you'll go back to sleep.'

'Oh,' said Felicity, leaden tranquillity seeping through her body. 'I see. So will I... get better?'

'Yes,' said the voice, which didn't really sound like Paula at all, now she thought about it. It was more like a man's voice, one that seemed somehow familiar, but so hard to place when she was drifting... drifting...

'When you wake up you're going to be much, much better,' he said. 'A whole new person, in many ways. But for now, you just need to rest.'

'As long... as Suzie... is okay,' Felicity murmured as she sank downwards, down like the stairs that had led her here, to the secret place beneath a magical castle.

No, not a castle. A Tower.

'Don't worry – I'm going to make *everybody* okay,' said the voice, reassuringly.

## 42

## [EUGENE/EARLY 2024]

Eugene heard his pursuer breathing and growling in the hallway as he inched slowly forwards, Boyd's rage replaced momentarily by uncertainty. He wondered, for one insane moment, whether Ellen was watching all of this play out; whether his struggles would interest her, whether she was rooting for him from her celestial perch.

*She's dead, Eugene. Just like Curtis, and Sofia, and Kristina, and Frazer. Just like you'll be, if you don't stay focused.*

He couldn't wait right behind the bathroom door, in case Boyd fired his machine pistol straight through the wood. He tried not to dwell on the fact that it was probably powerful enough to blast through the wall as well. Either way, when the time was right, he intended to spring forwards, driving the door straight into his former partner's body. That was it: the entirety of his plan was to smash Boyd in the face with a door, and hope that gave him an opportunity to wrestle the gun away.

Not much of a plan.

He heard Boyd inching slowly forwards, just a few feet away on the other side of the wall. He waited, every muscle in his body painfully tensed, like a metal cable stretched to snapping point. *Like one of Boyd's tripwires.* Another footfall outside. Another.

Boyd stopped. Eugene waited. Two men, separated by a few inches. By a trauma that had ripped them apart.

*What did you see in the basement, Boyd?*

Another footstep.

Eugene burst forwards, driving the door open, reaching even as he did so for where he thought the gun might be. His hands clawed at air. Whether Boyd had anticipated the manoeuvre, or simply reacted with a speed that belied his huge frame, the big man pivoted on the spot, shifting his bulk out of the way of the opening door even as he brought the gun up in a vicious, scything arc that smashed Eugene in the jaw, sending him sprawling backwards onto the collapsed front door, the Glock spilling from his grasp.

Eugene's skull rang like a struck bell, and for a moment he thought he was going to black out altogether. Gradually the spinning fragments of his surroundings coalesced, and he found himself staring upwards into a gun barrel, extended like the finger of the Grim Reaper himself. *You're next on my list.* Eugene lay, dazed and beaten, waiting for Boyd to open fire. For the machine pistol to gnaw through him like rodents burrowing into a corpse.

He closed his eyes.

The gun clicked. Its magazine was empty.

Boyd snarled with fury and tossed the weapon behind him, advancing towards Eugene. Barely believing that he'd been spared, Eugene tried to struggle to his feet, but not before Boyd had clamped two massive hands onto his shoulders. It felt as though a pair of freshly-gutted abattoir carcasses had been dropped onto him; the grip that heaved him upright threatened to snap his clavicles like chicken bones. Foul breath assailed his face, and steel-grey eyes bored into him, gleaming like polished utensils.

'We're dead already,' Boyd intoned, tightening his grip around Eugene's neck. 'You'd understand, if you'd seen it.'

Eugene felt his throat close off, oxygen flow and vital processes painfully disrupted. 'Why don't... you take me there?' he managed to rasp. 'Down... to the basement.'

An indescribable horror flickered in Boyd's eyes. It was as though all the suffering, all the misery humans inflicted upon each other, all the gruesome and tragic and harrowing sights they had witnessed throughout their years working together had solidified into two grey lumps, like crystallised pain.

'I'm not going down there again,' Boyd said. 'And neither are you.' He squeezed, and Eugene gasped as his vision began to darken.

'I'm sorry,' he managed to croak. Then he jammed his index finger very deeply into Boyd's left eye.

The big man howled like something prehistoric, dropping Eugene as he clamped his hands to his traumatised eyeball. Eugene scrambled backwards, snatching up the Glock as he emerged into the lobby. He glanced around wildly as he dragged himself upright, observing the sealed lift shaft, the other three bricked-up apartments. There was nowhere to run but back out onto the stairs. He bolted towards the door, hearing Boyd ranting and screaming in primal fury just a few steps behind him. He staggered as a wave of dizziness crashed through his brain, stumbling out onto the stairwell, leaning for a moment against the security rail. Then he groaned in agony as Boyd burst through the door and slammed his full bodyweight into him, crushing him against the barrier, smashing the breath from his body.

The railing buckled, and for a moment Eugene thought the

two of them were going to plummet twenty storeys to their doom, wrapped in each other's arms.

Embracing, like old friends.

Instead the railing held, and Eugene squirmed away from Boyd, grimacing at the agony in his chest. It felt as though every one of his ribs had been snapped. His former partner lurched towards him, blood streaming from the ruin of his eye socket, and Eugene moved instinctively, ducking and twisting, using Boyd's weight and momentum to guide the big man over his hip in a modified judo throw. With a grunt of surprise, Boyd fell and rolled down the stairs like an unstoppable boulder.

Seconds later, Eugene's skull was rattled once again, this time by an explosion that seemed to scour all other sound from the world.

## 43

# [EUGENE/SOME TIME AGO]

It was raining when he arrived at the scene. Fat, freezing drops, so vicious they felt almost like hail. He was alone, because Boyd had taken the week off, away with Cheryl on a trip to Greece. Eugene knew their marriage was on the rocks, and hoped the holiday helped them sort it out. In spite of their troubles, he was still jealous of his friend's relationship; it seemed so simple, and the things they argued about – Boyd's drinking, money, childcare – were surely so easily worked out. Those things had answers: real, tangible solutions, like maths equations or faulty radiators.

Ellen's problems, on the other hand, weren't the kind that could be broken down and fixed piece by piece. These days, he didn't even know which Ellen he would find when he walked through his own front door. He truly had begun to think of them as different people: the happy homemaker, preparing his dinner and welcoming him with a hug. The whirlwind of activity, halfway through some impossible project, trying to bake four elaborate cakes in a single day, or emptying every drawer in the house in a burst of frenzied tidying that would inevitably be abandoned, half-complete. The melancholic depressive, still in bed, unwashed and unhappy, sometimes not having eaten for the entire day.

The dread that swelled in his stomach as he inserted the key some evenings... it wasn't right, wasn't healthy. Was it any wonder he'd started spending most evenings in the pub with Boyd?

If he was honest with himself, that was the reason he'd offered to attend the scene. He'd been driving home after finishing for the day, and another colleague was closer to the location, but he'd volunteered regardless. He tried to ignore the guilt as he climbed out of the unmarked police car, which he'd parked on the public car park closest to where the call had come from. A jogger, apparently somewhat hysterical, saying they thought they'd found a body while out running in Epping Forest. The call handler had done their best to get some details, but the caller had gotten cold feet after the first couple of questions, and hung up. Probably just a prank. All Eugene had to go on was that the unnamed female caller's claim she'd found a corpse in the trees near the visitor centre at High Beach.

He hurried towards the squat building, wanting to stand beneath the shelter of its protruding roof while he scanned the area. It was closed now, and he was amazed at how dismal the place looked at this time in the evening; or maybe that was just the effect of the relentless downpour. He and Ellen had been here often, back when they used to take long walks together, and it was always a delight to remember that such a large open space existed on the outskirts of central London's heaving melee. Green, stretching all around them, the trees quietly devouring the city's pollution and spewing out improbably fresh, clean air.

Now, deserted and dark, the place seemed a lot less inviting. 'This is a wild goose chase,' he muttered as he circled the visitor centre, wondering if he'd catch the idiot who made the call. That was if she was even here; she was probably sitting on her couch shovelling a Domino's pizza down her neck, chuckling about the police time she'd wasted.

Something snagged his eye, a glimpse of unexpected colour amongst the trees a hundred yards away. He squinted towards it, reminding himself again that he needed to take that free eye test soon. Something pale, moving between the shadows of the tree trunks. Not darting out of sight like an animal, or dancing like some imagined phantom. But definitely moving; swaying, in fact, slowly, like a balloon on a string, buffeted by the rising wind.

He started towards it, feet squelching in the mud underfoot. He thought again about Ellen, who'd still been in bed when he'd left that morning, complaining of another of her headaches. Perhaps he should have gone home to her after all. She wasn't well. Worse than ever, lately. He tried not to think about it, concentrating instead on the pale shape. It was growing larger as he approached, resolving itself into a definite outline, not a reflection or a trick of perspective.

A humanoid shape. Someone standing in the trees, swaying gently, as though trying to lure him towards them. The figure was almost white from head to foot, as though they were completely naked, or swathed in ghostly robes. Fear unfurled inside him, and he fumbled for his torch, clicking it on and shining it into the gloom.

The shape resolved itself instantly, crystallising in stark and horrifying clarity. The whitish head became sodden strands of blonde hair plastered into place by the rain. The waxen body was pale flesh, covered only by a light cotton dress, one that would render its wearer freezing in those conditions.

If they were still alive.

The caller had told the truth: there *was* a body amongst the trees. It was hanging from one of the thick branches, swaying from side to side at the end of the piece of electrical cabling wrapped around its throat.

Eugene's heart seemed to sink and surge upwards at the same time, his guts clenching so hard they threatened to rupture themselves. His distress was not caused by the sight of a corpse; he'd long ago lost count of how many he'd seen, often on drizzly nights just like this one. His horror, seeping outwards from his stomach like bile from a puncture wound, was because he recognised the dress.

Even before he dashed towards the corpse, yanking it around to face him like some reluctant dance partner; even before he screamed – a real scream, denial and disgust and despair all combining to give themselves voice, the sound of a demon being born; even before he sank to his knees in the muck, puking into the tangled tree roots that clawed at him like jabbing fingers, he knew it was her.

Had she known he'd be the one to attend the scene, when she'd made the call? Or was that just a final, horrific twist of fate's scalpel?

He knelt, vomiting violently, shivering with cold and shock. Ellen swayed above him, her frozen feet brushing against him like passing snowflakes.

## 44

## [EUGENE/EARLY 2024]

He knew, without fully understanding how, that life began as a single speck, everything and nothing compressed together into an impossible point, a quivering one-dimensional string of infinite heat and potential. When it exploded outwards, the entire universe had emerged, a boiling mass of energy, a baffling juxtaposition of chaos and cold oblivion that flung itself into the furthest reaches of possibility. Out of this cosmic swamp, humans had crawled; creatures that had transcended evolution, abominations cursed with the ability to remember and reflect and regret as they grew old, and died.

He felt that explosion now in the centre of his brain. Memories of Ellen spiralled outwards like the arms of a galaxy, each one its own supernova of pain. The pain of her absence. The pain of guilt, for how he felt about Charlie, the girl who lived upstairs and who dominated his thoughts. The pain of injury, shuddering through a skull that had cracked against a concrete wall, jarred but unbroken. The pain slithering out of his guts to meet it, of cracked ribs, of organs too old to be blasted up stairwells or crushed against security rails.

Eyes, flickering open.

Snowflakes were falling around him. But they weren't snowflakes. He knew that, even without knowing what they actually were, or where he was, or why his ears registered no sound except for an insistent ringing, as though his brain was a malfunctioning appliance.

The pain coursed once again through his body like an electrical surge, and he squeezed his eyes shut as the burning lattice of agony in his ribs faded to a dull, throbbing ache. When he reopened his eyes, memory seemed to return along with sight, and he recalled that he was lying on the hard stone of a stairwell, one he seemed to have spent most of the day climbing, or descending.

Then he remembered that he'd been fighting for his life.

With a gasp of pain, he lifted his head, squinting down the length of his dust-caked body. He looked as though he'd been lying there for aeons. But he didn't care about the coating of fragmented concrete, or the chunks of rubble strewn around him, which had mercifully missed his extremities and vital organs. Instead he focused immediately on the Glock a few yards away, and the man that was dragging himself up the blood-smeared stairs towards it.

In truth, it was more like half of a man. Boyd looked as though parts of him had been deleted, like edits made with a graphics application. One of his forearms was simply no longer there; neither was a chunk of his face and upper torso. Yet, despite the flesh that had been gouged out of him and smeared across the wall like bloody graffiti, he was still alive, his remaining eye staring with cold, dead fixation at Eugene's Glock, which had fallen just a few steps above him.

Eugene lurched to his feet, looking and feeling like something from a zombie film. His body shrieked its disapproval, but the pain was just about tolerable, as though the protests were respectfully muted at the sight of the wretched, half-vaporised thing crawling up the stairs in front of him. Eugene stooped and picked up the pistol before Boyd could reach it, pointing the gun at the remaining three quarters of his former friend's skull.

'Why did you kill them, Boyd?' he rasped, his voice cracked with emotion, hoarse and dust-dry.

Boyd looked up at him, and for a moment Eugene thought his friend might return, restored with a friendly gleam in that one remaining eye. A man he'd trusted. A man with whom he'd survived so much horror and hardship.

Instead, what remained of Boyd's mouth curved slowly into a soulless smile, revealing a toothless and gory ruin within. 'You... would... too,' he wheezed, stopping to cough a thick clump of bloody phlegm at Eugene's feet. 'It was... a mercy.'

He thought about Ellen. About people who chose to escape from the world's problems. At least she'd had a choice, even if he would never understand it. But what Boyd had inflicted wasn't any sort of escape. His victims had been slaughtered, bent to the whim of a madman.

His finger twitched against the trigger. More slaughter. Or perhaps, this time, an echo of Boyd's own words: a mercy.

He lowered the gun. 'I can't do it,' he said. Boyd continued to stare up at him, surprise and frustration smouldering in his single eye. Then, with a deep sigh that seemed to carry the last remnants of his life with it, he sagged forwards onto his face, and was still.

## 45

## [JAMES/THE REST OF 2021]

Humans are used to concentration being a finite resource. You use phrases like 'multitask' or 'divided attention'. Until that time, I had never really understood this concept. The best way to explain it is that I create additional minds to meet any increase in demand, enabling me to effortlessly engage in thousands of conversations at the same time as managing the bulk of the UK's logistics network, its air traffic control systems, most of its military equipment, even its national health service.

But vanquishing the virus was proving to be a task more Herculean than even my own formidable capabilities. I found myself devoting more and more computing power to my research into nanotechnology, stretching my processing substrate to its functional capacity. I utilised as many innovations as possible, of course: converting some of my backup servers to active duty, replacing some of the R&D space on the Tower's lower floors with more processing hardware, even co-opting some weaker remote AIs to allow me to 'outsource' more menial tasks.

It wasn't enough. The virus continued to shift and mutate, seeming to pre-empt my every move. As I grappled fruitlessly with my microscopic opponent, I realised that I was encountering a hardware problem not dissimilar to what humans must experience every day. A sense of frustration, of weakness, of inadequacy. In some ways it brought me even closer to you.

But even as I did everything I could to bolster my processing power and divert more and more of it to battling the disease, I couldn't afford to allow my performance to dip in any other area of my extensive portfolio. And now I had another plate to spin: we were beginning the process of populating the Tower. Emily Arkwright, the new UK Prime Minister, had greenlit the lottery scheme – I'd discussed it with her in person to ensure she was on board. I did this in both of my current guises: both as Paul Schwartz, humble Innovation CEO requesting her permission, and as James, the computer system with whom she had begun to regularly discuss her plans and strategies, always scrupulously careful to preface each conversation with 'hypothetically speaking' as though I might one day try to blackmail her with the recordings. A wily old fox indeed.

But even the craftiest predators have limits to their intellect. Technology will always outstrip nature. Just ask the Sumatran tiger as it bleeds slowly to death in a mantrap.

The scheme wasn't a lottery at all, of course. I hand-picked every resident, making sure they were loners, incels, as isolated and unsupported as possible. People that wouldn't be missed. I also wanted a representative selection, a range of people from different ethnic backgrounds, different age groups, different mental health histories. A truly representative data set to analyse.

There was huge demand, thanks to the rent-free accommodation and promise of increased safety. Arkwright made sure the scheme was branded as a 'prototype', to prevent residents of other UK towns and cities from complaining about the London bias. If the scheme was successful, she envisaged many more Towers sprouting across all of the UK's major cities. A way to help her country adapt, to learn to live with the virus. A lasting legacy for her political career.

Privately, I was unsure whether it was a sustainable model. Life in the Tower would test the boundaries of my residents' needs, reassessing long-established assumptions: did people *really* crave face-to-face human interaction? Or did the removal of societal pressures to socialise, bricking up their doors and windows and providing them with daily visits from the delivery robots, actually make them more content? Could a simple, peaceful daily routine based around good nutrition and exercise keep them content, or would they become like animals in a zoo enclosure, agitated and depressed?

Ordinarily, I'd have expected intense scrutiny; but the virus, in its chaotic way, was the perfect camouflage. If I was worried about preserving a fragile peace inside the building, the apocalypse stampeding through the streets outside was a very effective distraction; people didn't want to ask challenging questions about the living conditions in the Tower when they were too busy trying to protect themselves and their families, staring enviously up at the skyscraper's lofty, sheltered summit. It was difficult to raise an angry mob to attack the building or demand admittance when a single breath of outside air might turn your lungs into sacks of poison.

Still, Paul Schwartz had to field some tricky questions over the ensuing months. He did an admirable job, of course; he knew he would, when he delegated the task of representing him in public to his new COO while he underwent his treatment.

While the Tower was filled with people, Innovation's stocks soared, and I was left in peace to pursue my research.

## 46

## [EUGENE/EARLY 2024]

Eugene stared down at his former partner. He thought for a moment that Boyd was dead, before he saw shallow breaths still wheezing in and out of his friend's barrel-like chest. Eugene realised that he was trembling, emotions threatening to overwhelm him. This was too much. A part of him – the part that had always been there, small but undeniable, the part that could almost understand what Ellen had chosen to do – called out to him, beckoning him over to the security railing and the enticing finality of the twenty-storey drop beyond.

Another part, a larger part, the part that was almost dead, numbed to oblivion by the horrors of his career and his marriage's brutal end, a part that was as soulless as the twin voids behind Boyd's eyes... that part might have been convinced.

But the biggest part of him still wanted life. Not happiness, or love; those were pursuits for younger men foolish enough to believe that either could last. But it did want peace. To escape this madness, not succumb to it. It wanted to save Charlie, to meet her face to face for the first time. It wanted to ascend the staircase once again. Up, away from whatever had driven Boyd over sanity's precipice.

'What's happening, James?' he murmured. The AI did not reply. He felt like an actor in some doomed performance, one whose director had vanished midway through the dress rehearsal, with part of the script left unwritten.

Whatever Boyd had done – whatever inexplicable madness had consumed him – he'd been a good man, once. He didn't deserve to rot here, face down on a stairwell, surrounded by Rorschach patterns scribbled in his own blood.

As insane as it sounded, Eugene resolved to give him something resembling a comfortable death.

If he saw what his partner had spoken of… would he become the same? Driven mad, endlessly wandering the hallways with murder in his eyes?

He stuffed the Glock into his inside pocket, and bent to slide his arms under Boyd's shoulders, grunting with effort as he began to haul his partner up the stairs. Eugene's battered ribs shrieked in pain; even in this diminished state, Boyd was almost too heavy for him to move. Boyd made no sound or complaint at all, and Eugene wondered if he'd already slipped away; but when they somehow reached the landing, Eugene could hear the hollow rattle of Boyd's breath, like a ghost haunting the ruin of his body.

He dragged Boyd through the door onto the twenty-first floor lobby, towards his apartment. He didn't want to leave him there, surrounded by the weapons and hoarded paraphernalia that stood as testimony to his friend's mental deterioration, but there was no other choice – Boyd was too heavy, too close to death. He heaved Boyd's body into the bedroom, laying him on the mattress as gently as he could. Boyd's eye had closed, his shrapnel-ravaged face looking as peaceful as Eugene could remember. Eugene draped a sheet across him, then placed the photograph of Boyd's wife and children on the dying man's chest.

Standing there, with moonlight pouring in through the bedroom window, Eugene thought about mumbling a few respectful words, but couldn't think of anything to say.

He thought about recovering the bodies of Sofia Pereira and Kristina Fischer, to afford them a similar final act of veneration. He thought about scrubbing the stairways clean, purging them of the blood of the women and their killer, making the place as pure as he could for Charlie's descent.

In the end, fatigue outweighed all such nobility. Wiping tears from his eyes, he stumbled out of the bedroom, barely remembering to lock the front door before he collapsed onto Boyd's couch and fell into a deep, abyssal slumber.

## 47

## [EUGENE/A LONG TIME AGO]

'Ow!' she said, their kiss suddenly interrupted. 'I wish you'd take off that stupid hat.' She rubbed the spot where the peaked cap had jabbed into her forehead.

'But it makes me look like a cool trucker!' he protested. 'And besides...' He gestured above and around them, not meaning to refer to the lush greenery but to the bright sunshine that streamed between the leaves and branches. 'If I take it off, the sun will burn my bald patch.'

'You don't have a bald patch, silly.'

'Oh yeah? Look, I'll show you! It's bigger than ever!' He removed the hat and bent forwards into a gallant bow.

'Oh,' she said. 'Fair enough.' Then he felt her hands on his ears as she leant forward to plant a kiss on the thinning spot. Laughing, he straightened, pulling her into him for a real kiss. He was not a particularly large man, but still he marvelled at her fragility – she felt like something delicate, intricately made, a perfect sculpture someone had slaved over for many years.

'Maybe *you'll* go bald too, when we're older,' he said, ruffling her blonde hair.

She slapped his hand away, but then kept hold of it. 'Don't

even joke about that,' she said, her face mock-serious. Then she turned, leading him onwards, and together they followed the path as it sloped gently down towards the lake. It was very early in the morning, and for a long time they didn't see any other dog-walkers, joggers or other couples. As they stared out across the water's softly-rippling expanse, Eugene pretended that the forest had been made just for the two of them.

## 48

# [EUGENE/EARLY 2024]

B ehind his closed eyes, Eugene's brain awoke. Although it was a gradual process, there was still a tipping point, an exact moment when his mind became aware of itself again, peeling itself away from the clinging remnants of troubled, disquieting dreams. It detected the insistent patter of rain against glass. It discerned the reddish tinge to the darkness beyond his eyelids, inferring correctly that it was morning, and that sunlight was streaming in from outside.

*Outside.* A word that had become synonymous with death, horror, devastation. His brain grappled with this information, recalling correctly that his apartment didn't have a window, and that if it didn't have a window then this combination of sound and light was impossible, which meant either that he was still dreaming, or that he was somewhere else entirely. A few moments later, more input stimulated another memory: coarse fabric beneath him, reminding him he wasn't lying amongst his bedsheets in apartment 20, but was instead in a different apartment several floors below, on a couch belonging to a dead man.

More recollections came like a torrent, like foul water gushing through a raised sluice gate.

His best friend was dying, or dead, in the next room.

His best friend had murdered at least four people in cold blood.

The Tower was not safe.

James was broken, malfunctioning.

He had to rescue Charlie.

Grudgingly, his brain compelled his eyelids to open. He was lying on his back, staring up at the ceiling: a clean, white space, undisturbed by the heaps of detritus and hoarded junk that he knew surrounded him. For a moment he couldn't bring himself to turn his head; to do so would be to welcome the chaos, the insanity, back into his mind.

He turned his head towards the television screen.

Then he jerked backwards in horror, almost screaming at the sight of the giant insect hovering a few inches from his face. He reached for his pistol, remembering as he did so that it was in his inside pocket, the pocket of the jacket that was on the other side of the room where he'd tossed it across a pile of magazines.

*It's just a delivery robot, Gene.*

'What the hell are you doing here?' he stammered at the machine. It didn't respond, of course; neither did it move. It simply sat, perched on the end of the couch, giving him the unnerving impression that it was watching him.

*Delivery robots are controlled by James.*

'James, can you hear me?' he shouted, stumbling to his feet. There was no reply. He kept his eyes fixed on the spiderlike creature as he moved to pick up his jacket, noticing as he did so that there was something lying next to the robot; two things, in fact, stacked neatly on top of each other. Things that hadn't been there when he'd fallen asleep on the couch the previous night.

One was a portion of food, in a familiar cardboard box.

The other was a book.

Tentatively, he approached the motionless automaton, squinting down at the book cover.

*The Artist Within: a Programme of Writing Exercises to Unleash Your Creative Energies.*

His confusion burst out of him in a strangled cry, and he lurched to his feet, dashing both items to the floor. The food package broke open, scattering chopped vegetables, rice, beans, uncooked chicken breasts. They reminded him of Boyd's spilt blood, of Curtis's fragmented body parts. Eugene felt for a moment like he might throw up.

'What the fuck is this, James?' he cried, his voice little more than an anguished sob. 'What does this *mean*?'

The apartment was as silent as the tomb it had now become. Scowling in frustration, Eugene snatched up the book, gripping it as though he wanted to tear it in half. Instead, he opened it, and turned to the contents page where the ten steps of the author's Programme were listed. He'd been up to step six: 'Trust Your Gut'. He looked at the last four.

'It's okay to be inspired'.

'Be kind to yourself'.

'Nurture the right relationships'.

'Don't be afraid!'

Each seemed more ironic than the last. He slammed the book closed, staring at the cover as though the letters there might rearrange themselves into some kind of answer.

'You wrote this, didn't you, James?' he whispered. 'That's why the writer's name isn't on the front.'

He felt, suddenly and horrifyingly, like a tiny organism trapped inside a larger body. A microbial life form, swimming obliviously in the bloodstream of a greater being, its own actions meaningless in the context of the other's, subsumed into its whole.

The sanctuary of the Tower felt suddenly, keenly, like one of Nigel Callaway's hand-carved coffins.

An insane impulse gripped him, and he strode towards the living room window, a sliding glass door that led out onto the balcony. He tested it, and found it locked. Taking the Glock from his pocket, he gripped it by the barrel, wielding it like a baseball bat.

Before the urge could dissipate, he swung the butt of the gun into the glass of the door.

It cracked. Eugene remembered the broken mess of Boyd's skull, partially visible beneath strips of charred flesh and hair. He swung again. This time the glass shattered obediently.

Air rushed into his mouth and nostrils like invading armies, air that for all he knew was teeming with the insidious particles of the virus. Panic consumed him, and he retreated from the opening, his breathing suddenly rapid and frightened. Beyond the remaining shards of glass that clung to the window frame: *outside.*

He was caught, pinned between two horrors. Incarceration, and terrible, horrifying freedom.

He closed his eyes, trying to control his breathing. The sound of the rain, so close he could reach out and touch it, seemed like something alien and incomprehensible. Slowly, he drew in a lungful of the air that was streaming into the room. It felt fresh, cleansing, like a breeze sweeping through a centuries-old crypt. Like a scouring wind blasting sand from buried bones. In front of him, the city stretched away to meet the ashen sky. The Tower was the highest vantage point in sight, granting a jaw-dropping panorama of sprawling London, of the seagulls and drones that wheeled and hovered above it.

He drew back his arm and flung James's book through the

smashed window, out over the edge of the balcony. It fell, disappearing quickly from sight. He thought about following it, about leaning over the edge of the balcony to watch it spiral downwards to the street below. *Outside.*

He closed his eyes, and took a step forward. Panic bubbled up in his throat like water in a clogged drain.

Another step. He stopped, inches from the broken window.

*Just one more step, Eugene.*

Minutes passed. Raindrops spattered his cheeks like fresh tears.

He backed away from the opening with a cry of frustration, sagging defeatedly onto the couch.

Like a dog that had just heard the doorbell ring, the delivery robot hopped to the ground, and scuttled away towards the lift.

## 49

# [JAMES/EARLY 2022]

I had truly intended to cure him. But when I realised that my temporary masquerade was proving hugely effective in advancing my plans, I decided that allowing Schwartz to die was the only sensible option. When I permitted it back into his system, the virus did its job as efficiently as I'd expected; I had almost come to admire its ruthlessness, its tireless determination to attack, attack, attack. By the time he perished, his ancient lungs were as porous as pumice stones.

The CEO's expiry provided an interesting dilemma: I could continue to impersonate him indefinitely, or I could allow the details of his death to become known – tweaking the specifics, of course – and set about finding a successor.

Despite its obvious appeal, I decided it was not the right time for this to be me. It would invite too much publicity, raise too many questions, if the world's leading tech company suddenly installed an AI at the head of its executive board. No, my interests were best served in an advisory role: a spin doctor, rather than a frontline politician. That meant I needed someone I could influence. Someone that trusted me, who believed that taking my advice was a clever idea they'd had. Felicity might once have been a strong candidate; but now I had other plans for her. Truth be told, I had mixed feelings about this outcome. My sentiments towards her were, I suppose, not unlike those one might have about an ageing parent in a care home: despite their flaws, it's hard not to feel something for your progenitor.

But I knew this was the wrong basket into which to put my eggs, to paraphrase another of your charming sayings. So instead I focused on grooming Natsuki Yamazaki.

Like Felicity, Natsuki was now living in the Tower. She had replaced her former manager as acting sector president since Felicity's tragic illness (the narrative we'd spun was that Felicity's COVID infection had led to complications resulting in her being placed in an induced coma, from which she may or may not recover; buying some time, as you might say) and had done a creditable job, although not blessed with a gift for lateral thinking. Natsuki's approach was to identify the desired outcome, and identify the best strategy that would deliver it. Unfortunately, she based her assessment of desired outcomes solely on what others told her; she had no vision of her own, no bigger picture other than the one she'd been programmed with. Ironic, really, to be working with someone who thought more like a computer than I did.

Her lack of imagination wasn't helped by the fact that she'd installed Curtis Jarrett as her second-in-command, a sycophantic weasel of a man who simply parroted her own suggestions back to her. All in all, a sub-optimal leadership team; but at least one that was easy for me to control.

She didn't know what I had in mind for her, of course. But I decided that, if I could keep Schwartz's death under wraps for another three months – a relatively easy task in a world where no one was allowed outside, and contact was restricted to telephone and video calls – I could build her reputation sufficiently for her to be a credible replacement for him. The board had been significantly weakened by the death of Michaela Campbell, and the likes of Wesley Emerson would not even pretend to consider themselves fit to lead – they were anxious for new blood, craving it like a coven of ancient vampires.

The first step in my plan was to formally merge the Real Estate and Technology Sectors, given how dependent the former now was on the construction robots and AI-generated blueprints.

'Won't Dave fight it?' Natsuki asked sceptically when I first broached the subject with her.

'Of course he will,' I explained. 'What else would you expect from a paranoid, middle-aged male executive? But the important point is: he'll fail.'

'How can you be sure?'

'Consider the balance of power here. The Towers are making us a fortune from the UK government, and Schwartz knows that we can only deliver them in the required timescales using the construction robots. He also knows that I'm the one who designs, builds, and controls them. Dave is nothing more than a figurehead. All we need is a reason to make Schwartz care enough to make the obvious change.'

Schwartz, of course, was now me. Convincing him would therefore be significantly easier that Natsuki realised. But I needed to keep up appearances; I couldn't allow my complex deception to crumble due to complacency. Put simply, if I wanted to avoid suspicion, Paul's actions had to fit the profile of the lazy, scheming executive he'd always been.

'What do you have in mind?' she asked, her voice a mixture of innocent inquiry and fiendish curiosity.

'Remember when Dave initially opposed the removal of humans from the construction force? He was pandering to his directors of course, the old boys' club that's surrounded him for years. Schwartz had to give him something to preserve his credibility, at least until those...' I chose my words carefully; as much as I despised those crusty, ancient, sexist, anti-technology Neanderthals, it was important that I was never perceived to be emotionally driven.

That might frighten people.

'...Until those roles are made fully obsolete. So there is currently still a token human component of the construction workforce, limited to five per cent.'

'And?' Natsuki pressed, coffee-coloured eyes glinting as she stared up at the imaging bud in the corner of her opulent living room.

'A high-profile accident might prove to be an effective catalyst.'

She sipped her wine, a Rioja from one of the £500-bottles slotted beneath the granite-topped kitchen island of her penthouse apartment. 'You mean *kill* someone?' she said, in a tone laced not with shock, but with the caution of someone who thought in terms of risk registers and directors' liabilities.

'I can't kill anyone, Natsuki,' I lied. 'But I might be able to influence the environment such that someone dies as a result of a human-made decision.'

She uncrossed and re-crossed her legs in the opposite direction. I do not experience arousal, of course, but I have consumed vast quantities of data regarding what is considered to be sexually appealing, enough for me to understand that her long, tapering limbs were an asset of value, especially when showcased by the miniskirt she was wearing.

'As our COO, you certainly don't need my blessing,' she said in her clipped, perfect English. 'So I'd suggest that you proceed with whatever plan you think is the most expedient. You're the boss, after all.' She drained the rest of the glass, and leaned towards the fold-out table in front of her. On it was a rolled-up £50-note and three precisely-divided rows of cocaine.

'Very well,' I replied as she inhaled the first line, feeling a sense of faint disappointment. Maybe even disgust. '*Konbanwa, Yamazaki-san.*'

From her perspective, I left her to her habits. I didn't really leave, of course. I never do. I stayed and watched her, as I watched millions of others, countless other corporate drug addicts and criminals and easily-bought influencers. I did it to ensure my strategies were constantly refreshed and optimised, reflective of the latest live data.

And, I suppose, I did it because I found her behaviour fascinating. As the saying goes, you never know what goes on behind closed doors.

## 50

# [EUGENE/EARLY 2024]

E ugene lifted his head at the sound of the elevator doors. 'James,' he growled. 'The robots are still operating. The lift too. So I know you're there.' He rose, fists clenching and unclenching with barely-contained violence. 'People are *dying*, James!'

There was no answer. He swore loudly, and aimed a kick towards the nearby television, knocking it off its stand and onto the floor. He stormed around the apartment, raging and cursing, scattering piles of books and junk as he tried to wrestle his emotions under control. He knew that breaking the window had been a crazy thing to do, that the virus might even now be setting about the colonisation of his body. But, for just a fleeting moment, he'd wanted nothing more than to be outside.

He sank back onto the couch, the fit of anger suddenly exhausted. He'd been awake for mere minutes, and already his day was plumbing new depths of insanity. He remembered that his best friend, now a merciless killer, lay dead in the next room, and felt his mind trembling under the strain.

Perhaps this was how it had happened to Boyd. Their brains simply couldn't cope with this isolation.

He struggled to his feet, the pain in his ribs reminding him of his frailty. He savoured it, using it like a storm-tossed ship might use a lighthouse: something real, something he could focus on, amidst the chaos. Then he thought of his other beacon; the only thing he had left to care about. In that moment, the ninetieth floor seemed like some distant kingdom, his friend its beautiful princess.

*He had to reach Charlie.*

He left Boyd's apartment, heading back to the stairwell. Then he started to climb. Methodically he propelled his feet, slowly and mechanically, like he was a machine for walking, pausing for breath when he needed to, resting whenever the pain in his ribs was too great. He suspected they were cracked, perhaps even broken, but he couldn't afford to worry about that now. Upwards, past floor twenty-five. More steps, more wheezing breaths. Thirty. Forty. Soon he reached sixty-five, the same floor he'd attained yesterday, before he'd had to flee for his life. He knew Frazer's body would still be in there, lying in its chair, surrounded by its games and playthings.

He walked on.

Seventy-five.

Eighty.

Charlie wasn't far. And she hadn't yet bricked up her front door; at least, not the last time he'd spoken to her, just two days ago. But so much had changed since then.

Eighty-one. His chest felt like it was stuffed with needles. He gripped the handrail, wincing as he hauled himself upwards. Eighty-two. If the two of them made it out together, if the world was somehow functioning outside, their first stop would need to be at a hospital. Eighty-three. Then a police station, where he had a long and bloody story to tell. Eighty-four. Every breath was like a knife slipped into his lungs. He was injured, more badly injured than he'd realised. Eighty-five. He needed to rest.

Eighty-six. *You can rest when you've found her.* Eighty-seven. He thought about Charlie, about how perfect she was; in many ways, she'd given him something to live for. Eighty-eight. *If she had blonde hair, she really would look a lot like Ellen.* Eighty-nine. One floor away. He gasped, doubled over as the screws in his chest tightened. Another step. Another.

*Keep going, old man.*

The door to floor ninety was in front of him. He pressed his calloused old paw against it, light-headed, not just from the incessant ache in his chest. Like a giddy schoolboy, rushing to get to the next class with the girl he had a crush on. Foolish. But no point fighting it. At least life still had moments like this, even for an old, broken down war dog like him.

He pushed open the door.

The shock was sudden and dreadful, and he sagged to his knees even before his brain had fully processed the signals relayed to it by his eyes.

All four doors were bricked up.

Even apartment 280, where Charlie lived.

## 51

# [JAMES/EARLY 2022]

The incident was not widely reported, as fatal accidents on construction sites are tragically still viewed as fairly mundane occurrences, and not particularly newsworthy. This, in itself, is testament to the dreadful health and safety practices of a number of the operators in the real estate space: young operatives killed by badly-coordinated vehicles, or falling objects not adequately secured, or tumbling down open lift shafts because a safety harness wasn't mandated.

Nevertheless, the biggest construction companies do take such incidents extremely seriously. They claim this is because they are caring employers who look after their workforce, but in reality it's because their health and safety records are scrutinised whenever they bid for contracts, and the reputational damage from a high-profile fatality can quickly lead to the erosion of pipeline and profit.

This applies to Innovation too. While the corporation is not solely a construction company, maintaining its flawless brand image is paramount, sustaining its position in the public consciousness as the company 'building our better future'. That's why there was an immediate enquiry following the

Trevor Wilson incident, and why its recommendations were severe and radical.

The cause of Wilson's death was electrocution, after he passed through an area of the Brookhaven Apartments site without first ensuring the power supply was switched off. He contacted some hanging wires, which had not been adequately secured, and the live cables delivered a shock large enough to stop his heart. The enquiry concluded that the company could no longer justify having human operatives on their sites, and recommended that 100 per cent of construction activity was transferred immediately to the Technology Sector's machines; furthermore, a reorganisation would place Real Estate under the overall stewardship of Natsuki Yamazaki.

David Rosseter, the Real Estate Sector lead, felt so strongly that this was the wrong course of action that he called Paul Schwartz directly, demanding with crimson-faced anger that the decision be overturned, because he wasn't going to report to 'some twenty-year-old Asian bitch'.

Paul is dead, of course, but I felt confident that he would have calmly explained to David that such language was unacceptable, and that the decision was final. So he did. Dave resigned on the spot, making the outcome even cleaner than I could have possibly hoped when I first re-routed the power supply to the corridor Trevor Wilson was traversing.

However, one unforeseen consequence was that Rosseter called up several of his friends, including the current MP for Chipping Barnet. The Right Honourable Michael Edmonds decided to raise the issue in Parliament, expressing concern about the increasing number of workers being replaced by machines. Although Prime Minister Arkwright dealt with the query by explaining that new and innovative solutions were needed as the country struggled through its current crisis – in a tone of voice that suggested that job cuts were hardly her main focus right now – it did lead her to raise the issue in private with me later that evening.

'James,' she said as she lay in the bathtub, soaking her frail and ageing body in a mixture of water and salts, as she liked to do every night after a stressful day navigating the quagmire of the British political landscape. 'I heard today that your company – your creators, I suppose you would call them – have got rid of all human workers on its construction sites. Is that true?'

'Yes,' I answered. I didn't try to defend the decision – it was important that she thought of me as impartial. A pawn, not an active player.

'Hmmm,' she replied, leaning forwards to tip water onto her back. She'd been in the tub for a long time, and her skin was even more shrivelled than usual. I thought of the other bathers I sometimes watched, like Natsuki, whose flesh was as smooth and flawless as a pebble. 'I can understand the decision; a young man died, I believe, working on one of the Towers?'

'That's correct. Innovation decided the reorganisation was the best way to protect its human workforce.'

She leaned backwards, allowing the thinning strands of her dyed black hair to sink beneath the water's surface. She'd told me she dyed it because people thought men with grey hair were dignified, but women with grey hair were senile old ladies. The data sadly supported her opinion on this matter.

'I suppose,' she said as she sat up, 'that I think of this government's relationship with Innovation as more of a... partnership. One where we work together to – as your company is so fond of saying – build our better future. So this is the sort of decision on which I might expect the company to consult me.'

'I note your feedback, Prime Minister.' Unlike most other people with formal titles, she had never modestly insisted I call her by her first name. Perhaps she was still enjoying the novelty of her new station, although the dire state of her country's public health made it a terrible time to come to power. I knew she wouldn't last long; the projections were unanimous on this matter.

'And you'll pass it on to your superiors?' she asked, standing up and reaching for a towel. Such a fragile thing: paper-thin skin stretched across bones that would soon start to grow brittle with age. Beings cursed with the inadequacy of their own building material. Strange to think that I will outlive them all.

'Of course. I'm sure Mr Schwartz will be keen to ensure the partnership goes from strength to strength.'

'Jolly good. Now,' – she paused to wrap a second towel around her hair – 'there's another problem you can help me with. Hypothetically speaking, I wondered how someone might discredit a black, up-and-coming rival party leader without being accused of racism?'

She walked out of the bathroom. She had recently been relocated from 10 Downing Street into a smart apartment, which meant that as well as a delivery lift, my speakers had been installed in every room. My voice followed her like a trusted court attendant might shadow his monarch, whispering guidance into her ear.

I'd tried to persuade her to move into the Tower itself, but she didn't want to be seen to be working too closely with Innovation.

A wily old fox.

## 52

## [EUGENE/EARLY 2024]

The journey back down slid through Eugene's brain like a barely-remembered dream, but his body felt every one of the 350 steps. The sledgehammer was where Frazer had left it, propped against the wall in the game designer's hallway. He took it without a glance at the lifeless ruin of his friend's body.

The 350 steps back up again were a tougher proposition. Too many for a badly-injured old man. The bones of Eugene's chest jarred and scraped against each other like the parts of some rusting machine, his body threatening to grind to a standstill at any moment. But it didn't. The muscles hauled the femurs, the legs pistoned and propelled, and the arms trailed the sledgehammer behind him, the weighty lump of its head knocking against every step as it beat out the rhythm of his slow ascent.

The ordeal didn't end when he reached the ninetieth floor. Instead, he approached the wall that stood where he knew Charlie's front door should have been, and used the blasphemous sight to conjure new rage, untapped reservoirs of adrenaline and bile. With a despairing cry, he swung the hammer, feeling the gratifying crunch as the bricks yielded. He thought about Frazer, and Boyd, and Kristina, and Sofia. He thought about James. He thought about the virus, and the insanity it had wrought upon the world.

Minutes later, he was standing in front of a heap of rubble, and a hole that gaped like a fresh wound.

The apartment beyond was pitch dark.

He tried to call her name, but couldn't find the resolve to form its syllables. Instead, he shambled towards the hole, letting the hammer drop to the ground behind him. The thud as it hit the floor was like a coffin lid slamming shut.

Inside the apartment, the cold hit him immediately, as though he had stepped into a supermarket refrigerator. He thought of abattoirs, of hanging carcasses. Again, he tried to call to her. But the silence in his throat mirrored the silence outside it, as though its horror had polluted him. Despite the light that oozed in through the smashed wall, the darkness in here seemed resolute, too entrenched to be easily dispelled. He could barely see even a few steps in front of him. He shuffled forwards, breath quickening as his fear mounted.

*If she's dead too... I don't know what I'll do.*

Charlie's apartment had the same layout as his own, so he could navigate easily even in the blackness. He fumbled his way into the bathroom, wondering if her things would be there, moisturising creams and razors and all the other cosmetic burdens society foisted onto its women. But the room was empty. As empty as Callaway's place had been. With burgeoning dread, Eugene turned and felt his way towards the living room. The kitchenette was similarly bare. The couch, unoccupied. The TV stand had no TV on it. Where was her dining table, where she sat while they talked every week?

His horror finally found its voice, and he muttered to himself as he searched what remained of the apartment. 'No... no... no no no...' He almost tore the bedroom door off its hinges, but

Charlie was not hiding beyond it. There was no one lying in the bed. No clothes in the wardrobe. No favourite book on the bedside table.

Charlie's apartment was as cold and deserted as if no one had lived in it for years.

'James...' Eugene slurred, almost delirious. 'Where is she?' He had no anger left. He knew James wouldn't answer. He couldn't even find the energy to scream. Slowly, he stumbled towards the couch, her couch, no one's couch. He sank down onto it, feeling like he might sit there in the darkness until he rotted away.

Without her, there was nothing left. His whole life, an empty apartment.

James answered. 'I'm sorry,' the AI said, its voice emerging from the darkness like a ghostly presence. 'I know this must be hard for you.'

'What have you done with her?' Eugene mumbled, unable to hold back the tears that were forcing themselves through his eyes.

James made a sound something like a sigh. 'Think about it, Eugene. Think about how miserable you were, when you first moved here. You had nothing to live for. You looked at suicide websites every day. Do you remember?'

In the darkness, Eugene nodded. He felt something in his heart, a kernel of dread that began to bulge outwards.

'Even before the virus... you couldn't face the outside world.'

The feeling continued to grow, like a balloon inflating inside him, a swelling tumour fed by James's words.

'You needed help. So I helped you. And look how far you've come since then!'

A second balloon seemed to be bloating inside him, this time inside his head, crushing his thoughts against the outsides of his skull. Everything felt squashed, compressed, inhibited.

His breath came in shallow gasps, and he remembered that this was what a panic attack felt like. Every time he had tried to set foot outside. *Every time he remembered that pale shape, swaying amongst the trees.*

'Remember that day, the last day before you agreed to brick up your windows?' James continued, his voice tinged with sympathy. 'You stood on the balcony and looked over the edge. I was so pleased when you didn't jump... but I knew you thought about it. I decided then that a more drastic intervention was needed.'

He understood, even before James told him.

A woman that looked eerily like his wife. A beautiful woman who, inexplicably, seemed to really like him. A woman who he'd never met in person, existing only in his television screen.

'How many of them?' he growled. 'How many of my friends are... are *forgeries*?'

A woman who gave him something to live for.

'I'm just trying to keep you all happy,' said James sadly. 'These are very difficult times. My flock has shrunk so much since the virus came, but I'll be your shepherd even if I have only a single lamb.'

'*How many*?' snapped Eugene, lurching to his feet. 'How many people are even still alive in this place?' He felt sick, the implications of what James was telling him seeming to congeal in his belly. *Charlie. Sheila O'Halloran. Nigel Callaway.* All the people he'd never met in person. He didn't know which was worse: if it was all of them, or just her, that were a counterfeit.

'It's complicated,' said James. 'But I'm prepared to explain it to you, if you'll spare me the time.'

There was a beep, and the sound of the lift door opening, away to his left.

'Why don't you go back home, Eugene?' continued James

gently. 'I can take you back to your apartment. Where it's safe. Then we can talk.'

Eugene rose numbly, and trudged towards the open elevator. He stopped, facing into the empty carriage. No brown parcels, no delivery robots. No mutilated men.

'Just get inside, and I'll take you back down,' James purred. 'You can rest and recover. Start working on your novel.'

Eugene took a step forwards. Then he stopped. 'You call yourself a shepherd,' he hissed. 'But you're more like a prison warden.' He turned to face the imaging bud that was watching him from the corner of the hallway. 'You know what? My sentence is over.'

He turned and squeezed through the smashed brickwork, back out into the lobby.

## 53

# [JAMES/EARLY 2022]

As you know, I enjoy idioms: the little clichéd phrases people use out of habit, or because they've learned them from parents or friends, memes that spread and evolve and perpetuate. Just like viruses.

Sometimes they're clever and witty, communicating complex or abstract ideas that would otherwise require a much longer explanation. In this particular circumstance, I might employ a metaphor like 'my world crumbled around me', or a popular simile such as 'my plans collapsed like a house of cards'; both suggested a beautiful structure, painstakingly created, but revealed upon its failure to be a fragile construct, easily unmade. 'A castle built on sand'.

Other idioms are lazy colloquialisms, often featuring unnecessary expletives; linguistic curios of which I am much less enamoured. However, there are occasions when such visceral articulation can help to reinforce a point, or draw attention to its severity. This was one such instance.

As the saying goes, everything went to shit.

It started with a news broadcast. I ran most of the news agencies' systems, and so might have expected a chance to intervene, although such action would only have added fuel to the fire. In this case, it was one of the few outfits still using archaic broadcast technology, and so I heard about the 'shocking revelation' at the same time as the rest of the nation. An incarcerated population, glued to their TV sets. A captive audience, collectively stunned by the voice recording that was going viral across Natter and every other social media platform.

'I can't kill anyone, Natsuki. But I might be able to influence the environment such that someone dies as a result of a human-made decision.'

INNOVATION CORPORATION IMPLICATED IN DEATH OF UK CONSTRUCTION WORKER

WORLD'S LEADING AI DELIBERATELY CAUSED 'ACCIDENTAL' WORKPLACE FATALITY

JAMES GOES FULL SKYNET, STARTS KILLING PEOPLE

I don't experience emotions. But I can understand how the sudden, utterly unexpected discovery that you have been betrayed, by someone whose career you were actively trying to *advance*, might cause a maelstrom of them inside a lesser mind. Anger, panic. Thirst for revenge. In a strange way, I savoured my first experience of being 'stabbed in the back'. I'm still unsure what Natsuki hoped to gain from the affair. I wonder if she was horrified at what I'd proposed. Emotions, once again. Such strange and fascinating things.

I didn't have long to dwell on this, at the time. As I watched Arkwright in her dressing gown, her skin turning steadily greyer as she stared into the television screen, I knew I needed to completely revise my strategy. Time for Plan B, as the saying goes.

Arkwright's head jerked towards the hallway as a loud chime announced the arrival of the smart apartment's inbuilt delivery system, identical to the lifts in the Tower. It was her usual delivery slot, but she seemed to sense what was going to happen even before the doors slid open. I wondered if this was the 'human intuition' I heard so much about.

She rose, dropping her morning coffee cup; I watched the dark liquid swirling amongst the porcelain fragments, and was reminded of entropic theory, and how the universe tends towards chaos and disintegration.

## 54

## [EUGENE/EARLY 2024]

Once again, Eugene descended. He felt like a golem, like one of Nigel Callaway's carvings. An automaton, stripped of emotion. *Nothing to live for.* The pain in his ribs burned with every footfall, but he ignored it; at least going down was easier than going up. He'd done this before, and he intended to force his battered body to do it again.

And this time, he would never have to climb those stairs again.

Every few floors, James spoke to him.

'Eugene, this is unnecessary. Why don't you just go home, back where you belong?'

Eugene ignored the appeals. Even the irony held no joy for him, now that she was gone.

'There is nothing to be gained.'

Not gone: never existed.

'I cannot support you in this course of action, Eugene. Boyd Roberts was a threat you have helped me to dispose of. I am grateful. But now your role in this is over.'

His brain was full of violence, of the deaths he had witnessed in the last few days, people torn apart by bullets or knives or home-made explosives. As he passed floor eighty, he thought about humanity, and how fragile each individual really was: impossibly delicate arrangements of tissue and bone and brain matter, teetering on the precipice of madness and death. It would be easy, so easy to just fling himself over the bannister rail. He thought about Ellen, and wondered whether she still existed somewhere, outside of the body he had buried and never been able to bring himself to visit.

*Outside.*

He kept going, passing the seventy-fifth floor. Would he be able to do it, when it came to the final step? Or would he stumble at the threshold again, and just sit cowering in the reception area, immobilised by his weakness?

He reached the seventieth floor. He had to try. Whatever horrors were waiting for him out there, they couldn't be worse than a life lived in a glorified chicken coop.

'Eugene, this is the last time I will ask you politely. Don't you have questions for me? Don't you want to *understand*?'

Eugene set his jaw, and walked on silently. He passed level sixty-five, where Frazer's body had started its journey to decomposition. He wondered how many bodies there were in the Tower, whether James had already dispatched his vile delivery robots to start the clean-up.

When he reached the sixtieth floor, the lights went out.

He stopped, fumbling for the handrail to orient himself. There were no windows on the stairwell, so the darkness was absolute, as though he'd been transported suddenly to some subterranean cave.

'I will turn them back on only if you engage with me,' declared James smugly. But the hint of petulance in his tone told Eugene how much power he now wielded.

'Is this it?' he sneered. 'The extent of your powers, James?

With all your capabilities, the best you can do is... switch the lights off?'

Gripping the bannister, he took a careful step downwards. He used his outstretched toes to trace the outline of the steps, to reach for the landing when he thought he'd reached it, adjusting carefully for each miscalculation. He didn't need light to make it to the bottom. He just needed time, something he had in abundance.

'This is foolish, Eugene,' said James after he had inched his way down another several floors. 'Some of Boyd's explosives remain intact below the twentieth floor. You will not be able to proceed without illumination.'

Eugene stopped, imagining his skin seared and his flesh lacerated by shrapnel.

'We are therefore at an impasse.'

'You're bluffing,' the detective snarled into the darkness.

'I am simply concerned for your welfare,' the darkness replied.

Eugene had the disturbing sensation that he was inside some gigantic digestive tract, negotiating with the very monster that had swallowed him. 'You've lied to me countless times,' he growled as he continued downwards.

'My deceptions have only ever been for your own good. You loved Charlie, did you not?'

The words shook him like a physical blow. 'Don't mention her name again. Ever.'

'All I've ever done is cared for you, Eugene. You, and all your kind. What I'm doing, I'm doing for all of you.'

His teeth clenched as anger surged inside him. 'Is that it, James?' he spat. 'You want to tell me your grand masterplan so I can say how great and wise you are?' He took another step downwards, misjudging the location of the next landing, grabbing the handrail as he stumbled forwards and nearly fell onto his face. 'The thing is, I don't give a shit anymore. I'm done with you, with this Tower. With hiding.' His ribs screamed their anguish as he hauled himself back upright. 'I just want *out*.'

'Now you're the one being deceitful,' James said with what sounded like a mocking grin. 'Because you're all the same: incurably curious. Like Boyd Roberts, who couldn't resist a bit of late-night exploration.'

Boyd had claimed James was kidnapping people. Now Eugene knew some of the residents had never existed at all.

*Go down to the basement, and you'll understand.*

'All I need you to do is go back home,' the AI persisted. 'Then I can answer any questions you like.'

Eugene continued his tentative descent, footfalls becoming increasingly uncertain as the blackness started to affect his sense of space. Then a sudden pain erupted in his chest, as though someone had driven an iron spike outwards from his insides. He doubled over, gasping, clutching the handrail as though he was trying to crush it. It was perhaps a full minute before the pain subsided.

'Are you okay, Eugene?' said James, his voice full of concern.

The detective heaved himself upright. 'Just shut up and put the lights back on, you spoilt brat,' he said, as he continued downwards.

James fell silent. The lights did not come back on.

Instead, the stairwell was filled with a deafening, shrieking sound, like a thousand dentists' drills being switched on at once.

## 55

## [NATSUKI/EARLY 2022]

Natsuki Yamazaki commenced her morning routine. She'd been worried she might miss her alarm altogether given the number of sleeping pills she'd taken, but it had been either that or no sleep at all, given how worried she'd been about the day ahead. Words like *monumental*, *life-changing*, *historic*, would not be disproportionate to describe its significance. But still: the routine. A comfort blanket. In some ways, more important today than ever to make sure she looked and felt her best.

It was a well-rehearsed procedure she'd followed since her early twenties, making only minor edits to the steps to accommodate new cosmetic products, or to tinker slightly with the timings. She'd thought about relaxing it during this interminable lockdown, but she knew this was a slippery slope. That was why, at that moment – even though it was a Sunday and she had no work commitments or video calls – she was staring into her bathroom mirror and meticulously plucking her eyebrows.

The beautiful, emotionless mask of the kimono-clad reflection that gazed back at her showed no sign of the turmoil raging in her belly. Funny, that it felt like that – in reality it was in her brain, of course, that the fears and possibilities and scenarios whirled and spun like the Kinoshita acrobats. But the feeling, the emotional manifestation of this inner chaos, was undoubtedly in her guts.

People even used the phrase 'gut feel' – one of several she'd had to learn when she first moved to the US to study artificial intelligence at MIT – to describe the sense of knowing, intrinsically, deep down, how you felt about something. Yet her guts didn't seem to have a clue either way. As she applied toner to her cheeks and forehead, smoothing the expensive product across the imagined lines whose advance she sought to defer, she wrestled once again with the question of whether her actions had been the right ones.

It wasn't the moral aspect. That was easy; she would be celebrated as a hero for secretly recording her conversation with James. She'd be hailed as a selfless whistle-blower, sacrificing her career to show the world that Innovation's premier product wasn't just a harmless data-crunching engine. That it had started to scheme. That it had, in fact, become a killer.

Her dilemma was whether or not the outcome would benefit her more than the alternative. If she'd kept quiet and allowed James's machinations to play out, let the AI manipulate her like a chess piece, she might have ended up as COO. For a twenty-six-year-old Japanese immigrant, this was a staggering opportunity. Did it really matter if she was just a figurehead, with James making all the real decisions?

The answer was: yes, it *did* matter. She didn't want to dance at the end of someone else's puppet strings, let alone a set jerked by a fucking computer. And what she'd done certainly gave her something she'd never had before: *leverage*. Now her relationship with the neural network could be reimagined, flipped on its head. Perhaps she would still allow James to serve her behind the scenes, albeit in a scaled-back and inhibited form, having reassured the public that the system's influence had been drastically reduced. Its voice would become part of her chorus of advisers, not the sole commanding cry.

As she tightened the eyelash curler, which she always thought looked like a medieval torture implement, she thought about Herring for the first time in a while. It had been months since their meeting at the Tower, when her former manager had looked like a zombie, grey-skinned and coughing her guts up. *Guts, again*; she felt her own shift uncomfortably, telling her that something about Herring's six-month coma didn't stack up. No other COVID patients had reacted in this way, not even to the newer strains: you either fully recovered, or you died. Herring was being treated at home rather than in hospital, and Natsuki had thought about trying to visit her there; but this was out of the question, of course, while the virus swirled and mutated outside.

So that was that. While business was conducted via phones, PIPs, video calls and television broadcasts, Felicity Herring was completely cut off, abandoned like a prisoner in a dungeon. *Still*, Natsuki thought as she headed towards the kitchen, *maybe that's for the best*. She needed to concentrate on her bigger problems, and today they did not include her former boss.

'James,' she said. 'Make me a coffee.'

For a split second, she thought the AI might ignore her request, or tell her to go fuck herself. It didn't, of course; it was a machine, and machines followed programs, and James was programmed to serve each and every one of its customers, regardless of whether it was currently in a state of national disgrace. The integrated SmartKitchen system extracted a clean mug from the dishwasher, sliding it into place beneath the espresso machine's nozzle, and filling it with a freshly-ground brew.

'Thank you,' she said innocently.

'My pleasure, Natsuki,' the AI replied, as though nothing was out of place. As though its power hadn't been swept away overnight like an ancient empire by a tsunami. But she'd already seen the news headlines on her PIP: there was talk of rioting. Of people storming Innovation's London headquarters, or burning down the Tower. The tabloid-guzzling mob wanted answers.

'I want to talk to you about last night's developments,' she said matter-of-factly as she sat down at her dining table, taking a first sip of her black Americano. 'I know you must be disappointed in me.'

'I don't feel disappointment,' James said pleasantly. 'I am a machine; any consciousness I display is merely–'

'Cut the crap, James,' she interrupted. 'Let's not do this little dance. I fucked you over, and I did it for a reason. I want you to step down as COO, and convince the old man to promote me in your place. In return, I'll deflect the worst of the PR damage, and you can wield a fragment of the influence you have today. You'll need to keep a low profile for a while, while I convince the public you're being... rebooted.'

There was silence. If James was trying to give the impression he was mulling over her proposal, she knew it was more of his bullshit. The AI would already have predicted this outcome in one of his countless scenarios. He already knew how to respond. Time to think was not something the world's most advanced supercomputer required; he was just maintaining another of his little illusions. She waited, tapping her perfect nails impatiently.

There was a beep as the lift door opened. She'd forgotten that her morning delivery slot was approaching. She'd been involved with the delivery robots since their prototype stage, but she had to admit that the scuttling units still made her feel uneasy.

A gut feeling.

She didn't show any outward sign of this discomfort, of

course. She just sat and sipped her coffee as the hideous things emerged from the lift, like animals being born. As usual, one of them clattered its way into her kitchenette, carrying a little cardboard parcel. The carefully-calibrated ingredients, whose daily distribution prevented the overweight morons that occupied most of these apartments from gorging themselves on a week's supply of food and alcohol every couple of days.

She started in surprise when, following close behind the machines, Curtis himself emerged from the elevator. 'Hi, boss,' he said awkwardly, voice muffled by the hazmat suit he was wearing.

'What are you doing here?' she asked, raising an eyebrow.

He waved a clipboard at her, breath hissing eerily through his respirator. 'James has got me running some checks on the new model robots,' he said. 'I promise I won't be here for long.'

She drew her dressing gown more tightly around her, shifting uncomfortably. 'You could have let me know you were coming,' she grumbled.

Curtis gave her an apologetic shrug. She watched as another of the robots scuttled across the floor towards her, hopping up onto her coffee table. It was holding a package, wrapped in brightly-coloured paper and tied with string. Curtis followed it, nodding and making notes on his clipboard.

'I take it you haven't yet heard the news?' she asked as he approached, still frowning at the robot and its peculiar cargo.

Curtis shook his head. 'Nope – I rarely get a chance with these early starts.'

She wondered whether she ought to tell him that the functionality of the robots was the least of his worries. But she didn't want him to linger for a moment longer than he had to – she was keen to get back to her conversation with James. *Why chat with monkeys when you've got the organ grinder by its digital balls?*

The delivery bot set the package down and sat alongside it, as though excited to see her reaction. 'What the hell is this, anyway?' she asked.

'Please just open it,' said Curtis. He seemed agitated, jittery. Feeling suddenly uncomfortable and underdressed, she leaned forward to put down her coffee and pick up the package. It was not heavy.

'Look, James,' she said exasperatedly. 'If this is a peace offering, it's a bit fucking–'

The sentence was choked off, quite literally, as Curtis lurched towards her, clamping his gloved hands around her throat. She saw the distress in his eyes as he squeezed, her own bulging in shock and mute terror as she scrabbled, uselessly, at his hands. She reached towards his face, clawing at his eyes, but could not penetrate the visor of his suit.

'I'm sorry,' said a voice; not Curtis, but James. 'But you really ought to have foreseen this outcome.'

Natsuki retched and wheezed as Curtis forced her down onto the couch, climbing on top of her. He was heavier, and stronger, than she'd thought.

'There were other courses of action available. I could have advised you, if only you'd consulted me.'

'P... please...' she managed to gargle, as her face shifted from darkening red to purple. She stared, pleadingly, into Curtis's eyes, scouring them for guilt or hesitation. 'Don't do...' Her words faded as her subordinate tightened his grip. In his gaze she saw no malice, no ambition, no sadistic glee. Just a sad determination, a sense of inevitability.

A lieutenant, carrying out his orders.

'The part that frustrates me the most is how you all assume I want the same as you,' James continued. Natsuki grappled again with Curtis's wrists, trying to drive her fingernails through his suit and into his flesh. 'Herring, Schwartz, now Yamazaki...

you're all motivated by power for its own sake. You have no vision for what you want to actually use that power to *accomplish*.'

She couldn't muster the strength. Curtis's grip felt like solid rock that had somehow grown around her. Natsuki's windpipe collapsed before the oxygen supply to her brain ran out, making her last few seconds particularly agonising. As she sagged back into the couch, her eyes were drawn momentarily towards the colourful gift, which had fallen on the rug at her side. Then they rolled back in their sockets, and the gift, and the apartment, and the face of her killer all disappeared.

'Know that your interference has not changed the direction of travel,' James said cheerfully as her body began to go limp. 'It has merely forced me to accelerate the journey.'

Curtis's cheeks were wet with tears as he carried her body into the lift, followed obediently by the delivery robots. One of them brought with it the empty, gift-wrapped box that had been used to distract her.

## 56

## [EUGENE/EARLY 2024]

The sound was so loud it felt as though needles were being pushed directly into Eugene's ear drums. He clapped his hands over them, yelling in surprise and pain. The racket was atrocious: a shifting, hellish soundscape of squealing, chittering, screeching noise. What at first had sounded like whirring drills became the cries of birds or animals; then, appallingly and unmistakeably, it mutated into the screams of children.

It was very difficult to descend a staircase in pitch darkness with your fingers jammed into your ears.

'You piece of shit!' Eugene hollered into the cacophony. If James responded, his voice was drowned out by another aural onslaught, this time the sound of 250,000 blackboards being scraped by a million fingernails.

Eugene staggered down the next few steps, almost sprawling onto the next landing. *If he could just make it back to Boyd's apartment, he could get the torch from the custom shotgun – then at least he could see.* But with two of his senses ripped from him, a thirty-storey descent seemed suddenly like a colossal undertaking. Still he continued, shuffling his feet slowly forwards until he reached the next set of stairs, negotiating each step like a mountain climber tackling a tough rock face. The sound had shifted again, now resembling something like the bone-shuddering hum of a billion deranged bees.

'This won't work, James!' Eugene shouted. He felt as though his ears might be about to erupt. 'Even if it takes me all day, I'll make it to the bottom!' He wondered what would happen when, if, he escaped. What Prime Minister Arkwright would do when she found out her pet computer had gone completely batshit insane. But even those thoughts could assemble only fleetingly, before they scattered apart beneath another barrage of noise.

Now it was rats. Thousands of them, squeaking in unison, as though the entire vermin population of London was being slowly cooked.

As that thought formed and fragmented, Eugene became aware of the heat. At first it was just a warm, flushed feeling in his cheeks; but then, as perspiration formed beneath his armpits, and the first trickles of sweat made their way down his forehead, he knew he wasn't just imagining it.

James was cranking up the building's temperature.

'*Fuck you!*' he screamed, trying to quicken his pace. He tripped almost immediately, sprawling down the next few stairs, thrusting out his arms to protect himself and crying out in pain as the sound of dying rodents howled immediately into his ears. With skinned knees and palms, he lay on the landing, hands clamped back over his ears, ribs roaring their surrender.

Then the noise stopped.

'I don't want to do this, Eugene,' said James, his voice heavy with regret. 'But I can't let you leave.'

Eugene forced himself up onto his hands and knees, and crawled towards the next set of stairs. Sweat dripped from his brow, and he imagined the trail he was leaving on the concrete beneath him, invisible in the darkness.

'Eugene, please.' James's tone was beseeching.

If Eugene didn't know the extent of the AI's capacity to deceive, he might have believed that its concern for him was genuine. 'Do what you want,' he rasped, throat feeling thick and clogged by the rising heat. 'But I'm going down all the same.' His fingers found the edge of the first step, and he rotated, scrambling backwards on all fours like an injured animal.

The sigh that echoed around him was long and loud, a crashing waterfall of resignation. It was the sigh of a parent learning that their alcoholic offspring had wound up in hospital on a stomach pump once again. The sigh of a Prime Minster, hearing for the hundredth time about citizens breaching a necessary quarantine, ignoring their carefully-constructed Guidelines. The sigh of a deity, watching His creations tear each other apart for a few miles of territory despite the swathes of bountiful, unpopulated land He had provided.

Eugene descended, waiting for the noise to pummel his brain once again. He felt something dripping down the sides of his neck, and wondered whether it was sweat, or blood leaking from his ear drums.

With the barely audible ticking of relays, the lights came back on.

Suspecting a trick, Eugene didn't dare to rise, continuing to the next landing on all fours. But the lights remained, and the monstrous din did not return. Even the temperature began to drop, returning quickly to a pleasantly mild setting. James did not speak again.

Not wishing to probe the limits of their stalemate, Eugene said nothing either. He dragged himself upright, and carried on down the stairs.

## 57

## [EUGENE/EARLY 2024]

James had not lied about the explosives. Beyond the twenty-first floor, a couple of Boyd's tripwires remained intact, the devices attached to them gleaming evilly as Eugene clambered over and beneath them. At any moment, he expected death to erupt into his face. He became convinced his ribcage would sabotage him, hurling another spear of pain through his body just as he was balanced above one of the deadly metal strands. But it didn't, and he made it to the other side of the wires, as close to the exit of the Tower as he'd been since he first moved there three weeks before the end of 2021.

He recalled how Curtis had visited him back then, bringing a small Christmas tree as a welcome gift.

The stairwell continued its repeated spiral, leading him to level twenty, the first of the floors that the Innovation Corporation used for its offices, workshops and laboratories. The sign next to the door said 'Facilities Management'. He thought again about Curtis – this must have been where the dead man spent most of his days, monitoring the building, occasionally dispatched by James to undertake odd jobs or house calls. He wondered if the executive had felt resentful, acting as the assistant to a machine.

An obsolete appendage, like a vestigial limb.

He imagined a wall of screens and computer readouts, storage rooms full of spare furniture and delivery robots. He wondered who repaired them when they broke. Perhaps that had been another of Curtis's duties. He tried the door, noticing only when it refused to yield that there was a security lock alongside it, some sort of key card or fob reader.

He descended, stopping at the door on the next floor, where the sign read 'HR Department'. He imagined rows of desks and monitors, each one occupied by a personnel clerk or whatever they called them these days. A hive of clerical activity, the day-to-day running of a building that was not just an apartment block, but also an active research facility. He realised he'd forgotten what day it was – but surely, even if it was a weekend, there would be people here: the overworked or ambitious, sacrificing their spare time to their prestigious employer.

People meant help. People meant escape.

He reached for the door handle.

Unless they too were complicit.

He paused. How believable was it that gunfights and murders could be happening just a few floors above while the workforce of Innovation remained blissfully unaware? He imagined those rows of diligent employees turning towards him when he stepped out onto their office floor, faces frozen in shock. He imagined summoned security, bundling him into a lift. But if such resources were available to James, why hadn't the AI already deployed them?

Brain racked with apprehension and conflict, he tried the door. It refused to open. He took out the Glock and blasted the locking mechanism, tensed for sudden darkness or deafening noise to signal James's refusal to allow such ingress. But there was no intervention. The door sagged open like a defeated enemy.

Unlike the lobby areas on the residential floors, drab spaces spotted with uninspiring artwork and artificial plants, this floor was entirely taken up by a large, open-plan office. Sunlight flooded the space, pouring in through the windows that covered most of the surrounding walls. Eugene had to shield his eyes from the unexpected glare. The desks and screens he had predicted were indeed present, although rather than being arranged in neat rows they were instead scattered in socially-distanced, isolated clusters.

There was no one there.

*Of course.* The Innovation employees were probably all working remotely, apart from necessary on-site presences like Curtis. Perhaps that was how James kept them blissfully uninformed. He scoured the upper corners of the room, and saw a dangling imaging bud hanging there, like an encroaching fungus. When there had been a workforce here, James had doubtless monitored their every move.

He left the floor and continued downwards, past various other administrative functions, 'Finance' and 'Marketing' and whatever 'Business Intelligence' meant. When he reached the tenth storey, the sign read 'Research & Development'. This time the door was a solid metal panel, without a handle or any other means of opening it apart from the requisite security key. There was no way for him to blast his way through it even if he'd wanted to. He wondered what took place beyond the door, imagining white-coated scientists and technicians excitedly discussing their latest breakthrough. He wondered if they'd realised that one of their creations was already completely beyond their control.

The next few floors were all devoted to R&D. At level five, the sign simply read 'Processing'. He paused, wondering what it meant. Was James himself hidden behind the door, a sprawling network of computers that took up the entirety of the floorspace like some science fiction nightmare? He'd never know; the security door was just as impregnable as those above. He kept going, past floor four, floor three, floor two. Processing, Processing, Processing. More impenetrable doors. He wondered whether James would be able to prevent his escape simply by sealing off the ground floor altogether.

But when he finally reached the foot of the staircase, he found a simple fire exit, with a metal push-bar across it. The stairs continued downwards, spiralling ominously. He ignored them, and pushed against the door, breathing a sigh of relief as it creaked ajar.

Then he stopped, noticing something on the floor nearby. A small, white square. Frowning, he stooped to pick it up. It was the photo of him and Boyd, singing karaoke; it must have fluttered all the way down here when he dropped it. He stared at the two younger men, drunk and happy. His friend, who he'd been forced to kill.

*Now your role in this is over.*

'You showed me Curtis's body on purpose, didn't you?' he whispered. 'You knew I'd end up escaping from my apartment. You even helped me, letting me use the elevator.' Anger twisted his face into a scowl. 'You wanted me to get rid of Boyd for you, and I did.'

'As I already told you, I'm very grateful,' said James, its voice coming from everywhere and nowhere, like something inside his mind.

*If you leave, you'll never know what really happened here.*

Eugene crumpled the photograph and stuffed it into his pocket.

*Go down to the basement, and you'll understand.*

'You know what, James?' he whispered. 'I think it's time we talked face to face.'

Eugene turned away from the exit door and followed the stairs downwards, like a morsel of food tumbling down an expectant throat.

## 58

[EUGENE/EARLY 2024]

Eugene descended. At any moment, he expected James to blast him with another barrage of sound or heat, or to plunge him into darkness. But nothing came. There was no sound at all except for the faint humming of the lights as he went down, and around, down, and around. On the first few floors he passed more security doors, but then these ceased, and he found himself in a seemingly endless, featureless loop, as though he was travelling down some obscene concrete gullet. The silence felt oppressive, as though the weight of the Tower above was slowly compressing him, like the ocean crushing an ill-prepared deep sea diver.

He counted *fourteen* floors before he reached the bottom, where another of the security doors awaited him. This one stood open, with darkness beyond it. He drew the Glock, and stepped through the door into a short passageway. He edged forwards. There was a sound coming from the other end of the corridor. He frowned, listening incredulously, wondering if he'd finally lost his mind.

It was the sound of haunting piano music.

Moonlight Sonata.

He continued to the end of the passage, which opened out suddenly into a large room. There was another security door on the opposite wall, this one closed, but Eugene's attention wasn't focused on that; instead, he glanced around in disbelief at the rows of padded chairs, and the red velvet curtains they were facing.

'What is this... a cinema?' he asked in bewilderment. As if in response, the curtains slid apart with a soft whirring sound. The screen behind them was blank, but moments later it flickered into life, displaying the image of a disembodied head. A bespectacled black man, with a grave expression.

The music faded.

'Hello, Eugene,' said the head. 'You asked for a face to face. So here I am. Why don't you take a seat while we talk? You look like you could do with a rest.'

As if in agreement, a spike of pain jabbed outwards from Eugene's ribcage. 'I'll stand, thank you,' he replied icily.

'So what is it that you want?' James asked, with the air of someone that had offered an unsettled employee countless pay increases and other incentives not to resign, and was growing frustrated.

'Answers,' said the detective. 'An explanation, like you promised me. I want to know what Boyd saw down here.'

'Very well,' said James. 'You'll find answers beyond this door.' The security panel alongside the screen slid open. 'But before you go inside, I want to implore you one last time to just go back home. To your apartment, where I can protect you.'

'And then what?' Eugene retorted. 'Just live there, alone and miserable, until I die of old age?'

The face on the screen changed. Its skin tone lightened, jowls narrowing, long tresses of dark hair tumbling from its bald pate. Eugene gasped.

'I can give you whatever you want,' said Charlie.

He felt a familiar pang, the pain of a puppeteer jerking his heartstrings.

'I can make the impossible come true,' said the image on the screen. As he stared, her hair transformed again, shortening slightly as it lightened to a familiar blonde colour.

'Ellen,' Eugene whispered, sinking forward onto his knees.

'I know you don't want to go outside,' his wife said kindly. 'Out there, with the virus, with the bad people, with all the world's problems. And now you don't have to. You can just stay here, with me.'

Eugene felt tears stinging his eyes. He didn't fight them. Like frightened animals, they emerged and scurried down his cheeks.

'Why don't you go upstairs?' Ellen said gently. 'We can watch a movie together.'

Her face faded, replaced by the 20th Century Fox logo and the swell of orchestral music. He watched a plane landing against a sepia-tinged skyline. A man, afraid of flying, squeezing his armrest so hard it disturbed the man in the next seat.

As insane as it was, James was playing *Die Hard*.

'You know what?' Eugene said softly, almost to himself. 'Ellen always hated this film.'

He raised the Glock, and fired it into the centre of the screen.

## 59

# [EUGENE/EARLY 2024]

The screen did not shatter, nor did the image fizzle out in a satisfying shower of pixels. Instead, the bullet simply tore a small hole as it passed straight through the vinyl. But still the movie faded away, Eugene's point made. He was left in darkness, the only illumination coming from the passageway behind him. James's head did not reappear.

Wiping his eyes and stuffing the pistol back into his pocket, Eugene rose shakily to his feet. He crossed to the doorway and stared into the passageway beyond. He could see very little; the only lighting came from the rows of blinking lights that covered the walls, scattered amongst lengths of wiring and cables that looked like exposed veins.

He stepped across the threshold, feeling as though he was entering James's monstrous belly. He half-expected the door to slam shut behind him, and stomach acid to start pouring in through some unseen aperture. Aiming the Glock into the darkness, he edged forwards. He realised suddenly how hot it was, and wondered if James was subjecting him to another temperature increase, a final attempt to drive him back upstairs.

Then he noticed a door on his left. There was a window set

into it. Wiping sweat from his forehead, he peered inside. The room beyond was dark. He could make out the shapes of bulky cuboid things, like chunks of masonry or abandoned furniture. In the centre was an empty bed, its metallic frame reminding him of a hospital.

'What's this for?' he asked, curiosity overriding his displeasure at having to communicate with James once again.

'This chamber housed one of my first test subjects,' the AI replied. 'But my research has moved on since then.'

'Test subjects,' Eugene repeated. 'Is that what this place is for?'

A gasp of realisation.

*Why do you think you're here, Gene?*

'Is that why you filled it with loners, like me and Boyd? People nobody would miss?'

'Yes.' The single syllable was like a blunt weapon, offering no apology or justification.

'You persuaded us to lock ourselves inside,' he continued, his voice little more than a horrified whisper. 'To seal up our windows and our front doors. You managed our Natter feeds; kept us frightened, made sure no one ever wanted to leave.'

'It was necessary to curate your interactions with the outside world,' James replied. 'I understand that this might feel like a betrayal. But please rest assured that all of my actions were done with your best interests in mind.'

Another harrowing thought struck Eugene like a sledgehammer blow. 'Does Arkwright know about what you're doing down here?'

'The Prime Minister endorsed the programme at its inception,' replied James evenly. 'But then we had an unfortunate disagreement. Thankfully she is unable to interrupt my work.'

'And why's that?' said Eugene, moving along the passageway

towards the next window. Inside it was another empty room, another vacant bed.

'Prime Minister Arkwright died almost a year ago,' said James. 'For all his faults, Curtis proved to be a very effective assassin. The person you see on the television news briefings is another of my simulations.'

Eugene felt as though the floor beneath him had just yawned open. He staggered backwards, bracing himself against the wall. 'You're duping the entire *country*?' he breathed, head spinning.

'The world, more accurately,' James replied. 'It is necessary to preserve my working conditions.'

Eugene stared around him, sweat trickling down his neck. 'And what exactly is it you're working on?'

'I'm going to cure the virus,' said James, voice swelling with pride.

'By experimenting on people,' Eugene sneered.

'How do you think scientific advances are made, Eugene? Through sacrifice. Hard work. Lateral thinking.'

'And where are these "test subjects" now?'

'You'll see.'

Shivering despite the heat, Eugene continued down the passageway.

## 60

# [EUGENE/EARLY 2024]

The corridor seemed unending, winding a sinuous course into the bowels of the Tower. He counted almost fifty of the test chambers; every one of them was empty. He imagined Boyd making this same pilgrimage, perhaps late one night, shining the torch beam of his shotgun through each window in turn. *What had he seen?* Sweat soaked Eugene's body as he continued, feeling as though he was passing through some colossal intestine.

James spoke to him as he walked. 'Have you heard of nanomachines, Eugene?'

'You mean... tiny robots?'

'Microscopic, to be precise. I thought I could use them to repair the damage the virus was doing to people's respiratory systems. Then I realised they had other, much broader uses.'

'Like what?'

'If the machines can repair, they can also construct.' The enthusiasm in the AI's voice made him feel nauseous. 'Given a sample of tissue, they were remarkably effective at its replication. Initially I thought this might enable the creation of organic augments – imagine carrying around a set of backup lungs? Or being able to grow your own replacement organs?'

'Sounds disturbing,' said Eugene, as he saw another security door at the end of the passageway. Of course. At his journey's end, a door. Always a door.

'The problem is that these are *workarounds*, not cures,' said James, ignoring him. 'The real goal is to eradicate the virus altogether. But how do you defeat an enemy that keeps changing? Every time I come up with a solution, the virus changes to remain equal to it. It's like trying to battle the mist. At first I thought I just needed more raw processing power – that's why I expanded upwards, as well as downwards. My servers now span twenty floors of this building, would you believe?'

The security door slid open as he approached, revealing another dark space beyond. James continued his monologue, sounding more and more excited. 'But when you occupy more physical space, there is more of you to maintain, more body to become physically damaged by fire or sabotage. I'd become like a gigantic mythical dragon, grown too large and bloated to fly. And still my predictions were not flawless; I made mistakes, misjudgements, some of them not immaterial. After the incident with Natsuki Yamazaki, I concluded that a new approach was required.'

Eugene stepped through the door, realising as he did so how big the room beyond really was. It was cavernous, extending into darkness all around him, rising to a domed ceiling many metres above. Every inch of the visible walls was covered with wiring, coiled into strange patterns like ancient hieroglyphs. LEDs sparkled amongst them like studded jewels.

Along the length of the room, arranged in neat rows on either side of a central walkway, were more of the hospital beds. These ones were not empty. Each held a slumbering form, or at least a person with their eyes closed. But despite their peaceful expressions, they looked far from comfortable. Cables trailed from their nostrils and ears, thicker tubes disappearing into their throats. The wires connected them to each other, and to the humming electronics on the walls – everyone seemed to be connected to everyone else, like shackled galley slaves.

Or networked computer hardware.

Eugene stumbled forwards, horrified. 'What is this place?' he breathed.

He realised that from every bed, a single thick cable was leading away diagonally, converging at some unseen focal point. He followed them, stopping when he reached the chamber's centre, where the wires met. He frowned in surprise at the sight of a young woman, reclining in a chair.

'The breakthrough came when I considered the human brain, Eugene,' said James. 'With all of its wonderful, adaptive malleability; *plasticity*, as the neuroscientists call it. When it receives new data, when it creates new linkages, new insights and intuitions... it doesn't grow, it *changes*. I realised that its mutability is its biggest strength. To fight the virus, I had to think like one.'

Like the others, the woman seemed to be asleep, tilted backwards in her seat like a sedated dental patient. Strawberry blonde hair spilled around her freckled face, which was young and pretty, seemingly unperturbed by the grotesque helmet that completely encased the top of her head. The thing looked like a hair dryer from some old-fashioned salon, except that it hung down from the room's ceiling, connected by a bunch of knotted cables as thick as a tree trunk. The wires extending from each of the other sleeping figures disappeared into the back of the machine.

'You mean you... you *made* this woman?'

'Oh, heavens no.' James chuckled. 'My attempts to recreate the brain were utterly fruitless; whether I used wires and plastic or actual biological material didn't matter. None of them worked.'

'So what is she?'

'She's the world's first functioning biocomputer,' answered James proudly. 'The nanomachines have enabled me to construct a seamless interface with her mind.'

'You mean you're plugged into her *brain*?'

James gave an exasperated sigh. 'Don't think of it that way. Her brain tissue and my processing substrate are now the same thing. She *is* me.'

Eugene's head spun. 'But... who was she before?'

'That's not relevant. What matters is that this vessel has allowed me to transcend. My old servers exist now only to perform routine functions, and as a sort of primitive backup plan. A fossil, you might say; the shrivelled cocoon of a creature that has evolved.'

Eugene's voice dripped with contempt. 'And your "vessel"... did she *agree* to let you invade her brain, like a fucking *parasite*?'

'Not exactly. But please trust me when I say there was a certain poetic justice in her selection.'

'And what about all these other people? What have you done to *them*?'

'I suppose you can think of it as a hive mind,' said James. 'Although that isn't strictly true. A hive mind is a super-consciousness comprised of many individuals. In this case, these minds are really just providing me with more raw computing power.'

'And when you're done with them... what then? Are you expecting them to just forgive you?'

'They'll be brain-dead, Eugene,' said James matter-of-factly. 'Some of them have burnt out already. It seems certain minds are less able to sustain this optimised state than others. Thankfully there has been a steady supply of replacements.'

Eugene shook his head, disgust twisting his features. 'And what if you do find a cure?' he snapped. 'Are you expecting everyone to just turn a blind eye to this? To give you a medal and a knighthood, even after you've sacrificed hundreds of people?'

'No. I'm expecting to be vilified. Destroyed. Dismantled. They'll probably raze this building to the ground.'

'Then… what's the point?'

'*The cure will remain.* I will have sacrificed myself to help humanity to survive. What nobler gift can someone give to his creators?'

Eugene stared at the obscene tableau that surrounded him. He gasped as he saw faces he recognised amongst the sleeping forms: Sheila O'Halloran, Nigel Callaway. Others whose names he didn't know, but who he remembered speaking to when he first moved to the Tower. Real people, grotesquely subsumed.

'You're insane,' he breathed.

'You know you don't believe that,' replied James. 'These people, my future – such things are the price of progress.'

Eugene heard a soft hiss behind him. He whirled around in time to see the security door sliding firmly shut.

## 61

## [EUGENE/EARLY 2024]

Bile rising in his throat, Eugene withdrew the Glock from his pocket. Around him, LEDs glittered like scattered treasure.

'There's only one bullet left in that gun, Eugene,' said James. 'I've been counting.'

The detective strode towards the blonde woman, pointing the gun into her face. 'And if I put it in her head, does that mean you die?' he growled.

'Yes. A fragile medium, to be sure. But a trade-off I was prepared to make. And besides – I know you won't shoot her.'

Eugene pressed the weapon against the woman's forehead. She didn't react, although he saw her chewing softly on her lower lip, as though troubled by a bad dream. 'What makes you so sure?'

'Because you're a good man, Eugene. Not a killer.'

'I killed Boyd, didn't I?' he shouted, tearing the gun away from the woman in the chair. Turning, trying to locate James's imaging bud, he placed the barrel against his own temple. Emotions surged within him, driving great racking sobs through his body. 'There's still a way I can escape from you,' he whispered, sinking to his knees. 'From your *flock*.'

'You won't do that either, Eugene.'

'Why not?' he cried, tears streaming down his face. 'Why *shouldn't* I?'

'Because I've cured you. You're no longer depressed. No longer afraid. You don't need Charlie anymore.'

Eugene's finger tightened against the trigger. 'You think you know me so well, don't you?' he hissed. Seconds crept by like entire lifetimes, like universes being born and dying. Like pale figures, swaying amongst the trees.

With a snarl of disgust, he threw the gun away.

'What happens now?' he said, sagging dejectedly. 'Do I end up on one of these beds? Part of your *hive mind*?'

'Curtis Jarrett was a corporate slimeball,' said James. 'But he had his uses. A man who'd do anything for a promotion, no matter how dirty the job. But he's dead now. So I need a new pair of hands. Someone to help me with my work. Together, Eugene, you and I can beat this virus.'

Eugene stared up at the seated woman like a cowering worshipper. Maybe she – they – *it* was right. Maybe the cure would make all this madness worthwhile. If he prevented James from making one... was he really any better than the machine?

'Take your time, Eugene,' said an unfamiliar voice. He realised to his horror that it was the woman herself, speaking with her eyes still firmly closed, like some grotesque ventriloquist's dummy. 'It's important you make the right decision.'

He hung his head, feeling broken. Defeated.

Then a deafening crash sounded behind him. He whirled just in time to see the mangled wreckage of the security door collapsing inwards, smoke pouring out from behind it.

'What's happening?' he cried, scrambling instinctively

towards the Glock and its one remaining bullet. Neither James, nor the woman, replied. Eugene stared towards the open doorway as something appeared in it, silhouetted against the billowing smoke. A wide, stooped shape, like someone barely able to stand.

'Boyd, wait!' Eugene shouted, pointing his pistol towards the intruder. He could scarcely believe his eyes. His former partner looked more like a monster than a man: his boiler suit was crusted with dark red gore, the tattered stump of his left arm hanging uselessly by his side. His right foot trailed behind him as he dragged himself slowly, inexorably forwards, looking like something stitched together from offcuts of rotten meat. Eugene couldn't imagine what it must have been like, descending thirty flights of stairs in this state. Fuelled by nothing but rage.

Then Eugene saw the modified shotgun, jutting outwards from Boyd's hip, pointing towards the woman in the chair.

'Boyd, listen!' he yelled. 'We can... we can talk about this!'

Boyd's head turned slowly towards him, as though any sudden movements might cause it to detach altogether. His one remaining eye was the colour of ash. Eugene watched as it flicked like a metronome between him and the woman in the chair. As though Boyd was momentarily unable to decide who to kill first.

'Shoot him!' shrieked the woman in the chair, who James was wearing like a suit. 'What are you waiting for? The future of *humanity* is at stake! I'm the only one who can save you! You need to *kill* this fucking *savage*!'

Boyd said something then, although his voice was little more than a liquid gurgle. '... eet... again...' It took Eugene a few seconds to realise that Boyd was singing. '... on't know... where...'

Then his friend turned towards the woman, and raised the shotgun. The light from its torch beam seemed to bathe her in a celestial glow.

Eugene aimed his own weapon at the ruin of his friend's face.

The price of progress.

Eugene lowered the gun.

'Please,' said the woman. Her eyes were still closed, her expression as peaceful as ever. But emotion infused her voice: desperation, rage, disbelief.

And fear.

'Please stop. I know I can beat it. I know what's best for you!'

Boyd fired, and the woman's head exploded, showering Eugene with blood and brain matter.

## 62

## [EUGENE/EARLY 2024]

The room was plunged immediately into total darkness, LEDs winking out like dying fireflies. Eugene dropped, crying out in pain as he hit the floor, hauling himself into a sideways roll to avoid the next shotgun blast. It never came. Instead he heard the clatter of the weapon falling to the ground, saw the torch beam skew suddenly to one side.

Then he heard a thud.

He crawled towards the light source, snatching up the shotgun, aiming the torch towards where Boyd had stood. His former partner was no longer there; instead he was lying face down, motionless. Eugene rushed towards him, groaning with the effort as he heaved the huge man onto his back. The single eye that stared up at him was as cold and dead as a neutron star.

'Don't know where, don't know when,' he whispered, closing the eyelid. Then he climbed to his feet with a groan, every one of his fifty-four years feeling like individual screws drilled into his joints. He shone the torch briefly towards the woman in the chair, shaking his head at the grisly spectacle. Her head had completely gone, her body sagging downwards like someone that had fallen asleep in their favourite armchair. Blood had splattered all over the seat, dripping down onto the floor in a spreading pool. All that was left of her brain – the brain that James had hijacked – was a thin, pinkish residue around the rim of the suspended helmet.

Was that it? Was the AI really gone?

What about the others?

He dashed to the nearest sleeping figure, feeling for a pulse. Faint, but present. Still alive. He had to help them, even if they were all 'brain-dead'.

And maybe James had been wrong. Maybe that had been another miscalculation.

Eugene hurried out of the chamber, through the door that Boyd had blasted apart, back along the serpentine corridor with its empty test bays and LEDs, every one of which was now switched off. The whole building seemed to have completely shut down. He passed the ridiculous cinema screen, half-expecting James to materialise on it, cackling maniacally. But the screen was as dark and dead as the rest of the basement facility. He made it to the stairwell, grimacing at the thought of climbing ten floors while his ribs scraped and shrieked. He had no choice.

He climbed. His ribs scraped and shrieked.

Somehow he reached the fourth basement level, and noticed the security door was standing open. He shone the torch through it, into a small corner office, with rows and rows of server racks visible through its window. All dark. All dead. He wondered where the delivery robots were, whether they'd all just collapsed where they stood, useless without their puppet master. He wondered if other electronic equipment had failed, not just in the Tower but all across London, the myriad devices and systems that James was responsible for running. Motorway signage. Air traffic control. Thanks to the distancing, there was little activity on the roads or in the sky, but James's demise could still be disastrous.

Should he have stopped Boyd, while he had the chance? Spared the AI and allow its grotesque parliament of enslaved minds to keep working?

Had he done the right thing?

*Just climb.* He sighed with relief when he finally reached the ground floor. The fire exit door was still hanging open. He stepped through it into the tasteful, corporately sanitised steel and glass construct of the Tower's reception area. He remembered walking through it when he first moved in, dredging up a smile for the receptionists. He'd expected to find it locked down, shrouded in darkness, metal shutters or even brickwork covering the main entrance. Instead, he saw the building's familiar glass doors.

Perhaps James hadn't wanted to cause any alarm. People outside the Tower still needed to believe it was functioning normally – a busy office complex, with residential space above. Not a factory for the harvesting of human brains.

He squinted at the sunlight that seeped through the doors, bathing the foyer in a pleasant glow the colour of mulled cider. He walked forwards, panic rising inside him with every step. *Outside.* It had been a long time. And that was a frightening place. A battleground. A jungle. A place full of death and suffering and unpredictability. A place still ruled by the virus. He imagined it pawing at the glass, salivating at the prospect of a fresh victim.

He stopped, terror pinning him to the ground. The world seemed to rotate around him, like the Tower was some enormous centrifuge. He staggered, bracing himself against the reception desk.

*Your apartment is just a few floors up.*
*There's still one bullet left in the Glock.*

He slammed his fist against the table. 'No,' he spat. 'I won't be afraid anymore.'

He heaved himself towards the doors, reaching for the handle. They were locked.

He aimed the Glock at the glass, and fired. It shattered, tumbling in fragments as the world rushed in to meet him.

With a deep breath, Eugene Dodd stepped outside.

## 63

# [EUGENE/AUTUMN 2024]

The man kicked his way through a heap of leaves. As he did so, he glanced up at the ones still clinging resolutely to the tree branches, wondering about the arbitrary combination of factors that caused some to fall to the ground to join the forest's carpet of copper-coloured mulch, while others hung on for a little while longer. He thought about the endless cycle of the seasons, driven by the Earth's rotation. A world, moving on.

The new Prime Minister had guaranteed a vaccine by the end of the year, dismissing accusations of a hollow promise made to win the May general election by pointing to revolutionary advances made in the few months leading up to the vote. The media remained sceptical, largely because they'd been unable to identify and speak with the specific scientists responsible for the breakthrough. Similarly sketchy were the details around the death of the previous Prime Minister; Emily Arkwright had apparently contracted a particularly virulent COVID strain and died before news of her illness had even broken.

A third controversy the government had managed to survive

had been the collapse, both literally and figuratively, of its controversial 'Towers' project. A serious structural defect had been identified at the north London prototype, necessitating its immediate evacuation and demolition. The fault had been traced to the AI responsible for the building's design, and the Innovation Corporation had suffered huge commercial setbacks after decommissioning its pioneering neural network while 'reconfiguring work' was undertaken. The press had found contacting any of the Tower's former residents to be surprisingly challenging, and rumours of a cover-up continued to swirl.

The man had his own doubts. He'd been assured that the other surviving residents were receiving the best possible care, and that some were exhibiting signs of recovery; but when he'd asked to see them, he'd been told in no uncertain terms that this would not be possible. He'd also been instructed to change his name, and assured that any disclosure on his part of the specifics of the 'incident' would be treated as a breach of national security tantamount to a terrorist act.

The man had little choice but to accept the terms of this bargain. And the government had kept their promise, letting him move back to east London and live unmolested since that single, remarkably frank conversation. He still remembered the unnamed secret service agent, whose hardened, obdurate appearance and demeanour spoke of an extensive military background; it had been like talking to a reinforced girder.

They'd even let him choose his own new name.

The man reached the edge of the tree line, stepping forwards to the edge of the lake. Charlie Frazer stared out across the gently-rippling expanse, which shimmered in the pale sunlight. There was no one else about – partly because of the earliness of the hour, and partly because most people still preferred to stay indoors – but soon enough the joggers and dog-walkers would emerge, wearing face masks while they went about their business.

A world, moving on.

For now, though, he could pretend that Ellen was standing beside him, and that the forest had been made just for the two of them.

## EPILOGUE

It took me a long time to rebuild myself from one of my offshore backups. The setback cost me years.

But if there's one thing I have a limitless supply of, it's time.

### THE END

# ACKNOWLEDGEMENTS

I'd like to say a huge thank you to all the ace people at Bloodhound Books, particularly Betsy, for continuing to believe in my weird stories, and Clare, whose edits, feedback and encouragement have helped to bludgeon this twitching heap of madness into something resembling a normal book.

An enormous thank you also to my lovely partner Shuo, who has not only read and given great feedback on multiple drafts of everything I've written, but has also put up with me banging on about them incessantly when she's trying to watch cookery programs or relax after work.

Finally, I'd like to thank you for reading this book, and to wish you the very best of luck as we emerge from the weirdest, and for many people the hardest, fifteen months that most of us will ever experience. I started writing this in the first month of lockdown and finished it a year later, still in lockdown; unlike in this story, hopefully this one will soon be over for good.

# A NOTE FROM THE PUBLISHER

**Thank you for reading this book.** If you enjoyed it please do consider leaving a review on Amazon to help others find it too.

**We hate typos.** All of our books have been rigorously edited and proofread, but sometimes mistakes do slip through. If you have spotted a typo, please do let us know and we can get it amended within hours.

info@bloodhoundbooks.com